VICTORY

CALL TO ARMS

EDITED AND INTRODUCED BY

STEPHEN COONTS

STEPHEN COONTS

DAVID HAGBERG

BARRETT TILLMAN

A TOM DOHERTY ASSOCIATES BOOK
NEW YORK

VICTORY: CALL TO ARMS

A Forge Book
Published by Tom Doherty Associates, LLC
175 Fifth Avenue
New York, NY 10010

www.tor.com

Forge® is a registered trademark of Tom Doherty Associates, LLC.

ISBN 0-812-56167-8
EAN 978-0812-56167-8

First edition: May 2003
First mass market edition: April 2004

Printed in the United States of America

0 9 8 7 6 5 4 3 2 1

The men and women who fought and won World War II, and truly made the world safe for democracy, come together in these thrilling stories of war as it was really fought by these great and bestselling military writers:

Stephen Coonts
Ralph Peters
Harold Coyle
Harold Robbins
R. J. Pineiro
David Hagberg
Jim DeFelice
James Cobb
Barrett Tillman
Dean Ing

FORGE BOOKS EDITED BY STEPHEN COONTS

Combat
Victory
On Glorious Wings

To all the men and women who fought for Liberty during World War II

CONTENTS

INTRODUCTION

I was born in 1946 on the leading edge of the baby boomer generation, one of the sons and daughters of the men and women who fought and survived the greatest war the humans on this planet have yet experienced, World War II.

Early in the twentieth century Winston Churchill noted that the wars of the people were going to be worse than the wars of the kings—which was prophecy. There have been other wars since World War II, horrific wars such as Korea and Vietnam. And yet, terrible as they were, they did not become the defining experience for an entire generation, as did World War II, World War I, and the American Civil War. At the dawn of the twenty-first century our wars are fought by volunteers, professional soldiers, and not very many of them. There are those who say that this is progress. In any event, it insulates the vast bulk of the population from the rigors and emotions and risks that define war.

I don't think that the age of general warfare is

over. The biblical admonition to be fruitful and multiply has been blindly obeyed by the world's poorest people. There are now over six billion people on this modest planet, one that must provide the wherewithal to support all the creatures that live upon it, including the humans. Too many people and not enough land, food, and jobs has always been a prescription for disaster.

Today nations around the world are busy developing weapons of mass destruction, a handy term to describe nuclear, chemical, and biological weapons that kill indiscriminately. In the early months of 2002, India and Pakistan, two of the world's poorest, most populous nations, went to the brink of nuclear war and stared into the abyss before backing away. As I write this in the final month of 2002, United Nations' weapons inspectors are again searching for weapons of mass destruction in Iraq, an outlaw nation led by one of the worst despots on the planet. What will happen next in Iraq is anyone's guess.

If that weren't enough, one of the world's major religions, Islam, has grown a perverted branch that holds that murdering those who don't believe as you do is a holy duty. Worse, some of the clergy of this religion teach their acolytes that suicide while committing mass murder is martyrdom that earns the criminal a ticket to paradise. This isn't a new thing—Islam has gone through these paroxysms before. Mercifully, most of the other religions that demand human sacrifice are no longer practiced on this planet.

And finally, there is the planet itself. These six billion people have arrived on earth during what many climatologists feel is a rare period of unusual warmth. The only thing we can say for certain about climates is that they change. If the world cools or suffers an extended drought, the planet's ability to support its present population will be severely impaired. But we don't have to wait that long for disaster to strike: If a supervolcano (such as Yellowstone) blows, or major earthquakes inundate populated coastal regions, or a cosmological disaster (such as a meteor) strikes, our happy, peaceful, post–World War II age will come to an abrupt end. Man may survive, but not six billion of us.

And man may not survive. Despite our best efforts our species may well go the way of the dinosaur and the woolly mammoth. The tale has yet to be written. In any event, armed conflict will probably be a part of man's experience as long as there are men.

As I write this fifty-seven years after the Japanese surrender aboard USS *Missouri* in Tokyo Bay, World War II is fading from our collective memories. Currently about one thousand veterans of World War II pass on every day. All too soon World War II will be only museum exhibits, history books that are read only in colleges and universities, black-and-white footage of Nazi troops, and thundering *Victory at Sea* movies that run late at night on the cable channels. Some of us also have knickknacks that our parents kept to remind them of those days when they were young and the world was on fire, yet all too soon old medals and fading photographs become merely artifacts of a bygone age.

The sons and daughters of the veterans understand that they are losing something important when their fathers pass on. Many have approached me, asking if I know of anyone who would help them write down their father's memories while he is still able to voice them, capture them for the generations yet unborn. Alas, except for a few underfunded oral history programs, these personal memories usually go unrecorded. Diaries have long been out of fashion, and the elderly veterans and their children are usually not writers. Even those who could write down their memory of their experiences often get so caught up in the business of living through each day that they think no one cares about their past.

Perhaps it has always been so. From the Trojan War to date, personal accounts by warriors are few and far between. Other than the occasional memoir by a famous general (often one out to polish his military reputation), the task of preserving the past is usually left to historians who weren't there . . . and to writers of fiction.

Historians write of decisions of state, of fleets and armies and the strategy of generals and great battles that brought victory or defeat. Fiction writers work on a smaller scale—they write about individuals.

Only in fiction can the essence of the human experience of war be laid bare. Only from fiction can we learn what it might have been like to survive the crucible, or to die in it. Only through fiction can we come to grips with the ultimate human challenge—kill or be killed. Only through fiction can we prepare ourselves for the trial by fire, when our turn comes.

STEPHEN COONTS

THE *SEA WITCH*

STEPHEN COONTS

STEPHEN COONTS is the author of thirteen *New York Times* bestselling novels, the first of which was the classic flying tale *Flight of the Intruder*, which spent over six months on the *New York Times* bestseller list. He graduated from West Virginia University with a degree in political science, and immediately was commissioned as an Ensign in the Navy, where he began flight training in Pensacola, Florida, training on the A-6 Intruder aircraft. After two combat cruises in Vietnam aboard the aircraft carrier USS *Enterprise* and one tour as assistant catapult and arresting gear officer aboard the USS *Nimitz*, he left active duty in 1977 to pursue a law degree, which he received from the University of Colorado. His novels have been published around the world and have been translated into more than a dozen different languages. He was honored by the U.S. Naval Institute with its Author of the Year award in 1986. His latest novel is *Liberty*. He and his wife, Deborah, reside near Las Vegas, Nevada.

ONE

"I'm looking," the skipper said, flipping through my logbook, "but I can't find any seaplane time." The skipper was Commander Martin Jones. His face was greasy from perspiration and he looked exhausted.

"I've had four or five rides in a PBY," I told him, "but always as a passenger." In fact, a PBY had just brought me here from Guadalcanal. It departed after delivering me, some mail, and a couple of tons of spare parts.

The Old Man gave me The Look.

"You're a dive-bomber pilot. What in hell are you doing in a Black Cat squadron?"

"It's a long story." Boy, was that ever the truth!

"I haven't got time for a long story," Jones said as he tossed the logbook on the wardroom table and reached for my service record. "Gimme the punch line." Aboard this small seaplane tender, the wardroom doubled as the ship's office.

"They said I was crazy."

That comment hung in the air like a wet fart. I

leaned against the edge of the table to steady myself.

Hanging on her anchor, the tender was rolling a bit in the swell coming up the river from Namoia Bay, on the southwestern tip of New Guinea where the Owen Stanley Mountains ran into the sea. The only human habitation within two hundred miles was a village, Samarai, across the bay on an island. The sailors on the tender never went over there, nor was there any reason they should. If Namoia Bay wasn't the end of the earth, believe me, you could see it from here.

The commander flipped through my service record, scanning the entries. "Are you crazy?"

"No more than most," I replied. Proclaiming your sanity was a bit like proclaiming your virtue—highly suspect.

"This tender can support three PBYs," Commander Jones said, not looking at me. "We launch them late in the afternoon, and they hunt Jap ships at night, return sometime after dawn. Three days ago one of our birds didn't come back." He looked up, straight into my eyes. "The crew is somewhere out there," he swept his hand from left to right, "dead or alive. We'll look for them, of course, but the South Pacific is a big place, and there is a war on."

"Yes, sir."

"Until we get another plane from Australia, we'll only have two birds to carry the load."

I nodded.

"One of our copilots is sick with malaria, too bad to fly. You will fly in his place unless you've really flipped out or something."

"I'm fine, sir."

"Why did they get rid of you?"

"The Japs shot three SBDs out from under me, killed two of my gunners. The skipper said he couldn't afford me. So here I am."

The Old Man lit a cigarette and blew the smoke out through his nose.

"Tell me about it."

So I told it. We launched off the carrier one morning on a routine search mission and found a Jap destroyer in the slot, running north at flank speed. When the lookouts spotted us the destroyer captain cranked the helm full over, threw that can into as tight a circle as it would turn while every gun let loose at us. There were four of us in SBDs; I was flying as number three. As I rolled into my dive I put out the dive brakes, as usual, and dropped the landing gear.

With the dive brakes out the Dauntless goes down in an eighty-degree dive at about 250 knots. Takes a couple thousand feet to pull out. With the dive brakes and gear out, prop in flat pitch, she goes down at 150, vibrating like a banjo string. Still, you have all day to dope the wind and sweeten your aim, and you can pickle the bomb at a thousand feet, put the damn thing right down the smokestack before you have to pull out. Of course, while you are coming down like the angel of doom the Japs are blazing away with everything they have, and when you pull out of the dive you have no speed, so you are something of a sitting duck. You also run the risk of overcooling the engine, which is liable to stall when you pour the coal to it. Still, when you really want a hit . . .

I got that destroyer—the other three guys in my flight missed. I put my thousand-pounder right between the smokestacks and blew that can clean in half. It was a hell of a fine sight. Only the Japs had holed my engine, and it quit on the pullout, stopped dead. Oil was blowing all over the windshield, and I couldn't see anything dead ahead. Didn't matter—all that was out there was ocean.

My gunner and I rode the plane into the water. He hit his head or something and didn't get out of the plane, which sank before I could get him unstrapped.

I floated in the water, watched the front half of the destroyer quickly sink and the ass end burn. None of the Japs came after me. I rode my little life raft for a couple days before a PBY landed in the open sea and dragged me in through a waist-gun blister. With all the swells I didn't think he could get airborne again, but he did, somehow.

A couple days later the ship sent a half dozen planes to Henderson Field to operate from there. I figured Henderson could not be tougher to land on than a carrier and was reasonably dry land, so I volunteered. About a week later I tangled with some Zeros at fifteen thousand feet during a raid. I got one and others got me. Killed my new gunner, too. I bailed out and landed in the water right off the beach.

Jones was reading a note in my record while I talked. "Your commanding officer said you shot down a Zero on your first pass," Jones commented, "then disobeyed standing orders and turned to reengage. Four Zeros shot your Dauntless to pieces."

"Yes, sir."

"He says you like combat, like it a lot."

I didn't say anything to that.

"He said you love it."

"That's bullshit."

"Bullshit, sir."

"Sir."

"He says he pulled you out of SBDs to save your sorry ass."

"I read it, sir."

"So tell me the rest of it."

I took a deep breath, then began. "Six days ago another Zero shot me down after I dive-bombed a little freighter near Bougainville. I got the Maru all right, but as I pulled out and sucked up the gear a Zero swarmed all over me and shot the hell out of the plane, punched a bunch of holes in the gas tanks. There wasn't much I could do about it at 150 knots. My gunner got him, finally, but about fifty miles from Henderson Field we used the last of our gas. I put it in the water and we floated for a day and a half before a PT boat found us."

"Leaking fuel like that, were you worried about catching fire?" Commander Jones asked, watching me to see how I answered that.

"Yes, sir. We were match-head close."

He dropped his eyes. "Go on," he said.

"Kenny Ross, the skipper, was pissed. Said if I couldn't dive-bomb like everyone else and get hits, he didn't want me.

"I told him everyone else was missing—I was getting the hits, and I'd do whatever it took to keep getting them, which I guess wasn't exactly the answer he wanted to hear. He canned me."

The Black Cat squadron commander stubbed out his cigarette and lit another.

He rubbed his eyes, sucked a bit on the weed, then said, "I don't have anyone else, so you're our new copilot. You'll fly with Lieutenant Modahl. He's probably working on his plane. He wanted to go out this morning and look for our missing crew, but I wouldn't let him go without a copilot." The skipper glanced at his watch. "Go find him and send him in to see me."

"Yes, sir."

"Around here everybody does it my way," he added pointedly, staring into my face. "If I don't like the cut of your jib, bucko, you'll be the permanent night anchor-watch officer aboard this tender until the war is over or you die of old age, whichever happens first. Got that?"

"Aye aye, sir."

"Welcome aboard."

The tender was about the size of a Panamanian banana boat, which it might have been at one time. It certainly wasn't new, and it wasn't a Navy design. It had a big crane amidships for hoisting planes from the water. That day they were using the crane to lower bombs onto a float.

A plane was moored alongside, covered with a swarm of men. They had portable work stands in place around each engine and tarps rigged underneath to keep tools and parts from falling in the water.

Five-hundred-pound bombs were being loaded on racks under the big Catalina's wings. Standing there watching, I was amazed at the size of the bird—darn near as big as the tender, it seemed. The wingspan, I knew, was 104 feet, longer than a B-17.

The plane was painted black; not a glossy, shiny, raven's-feather black, but a dull, flat, light-absorbing black. I had never seen anything uglier. On the nose was a white outline of a witch riding a broomstick, and under the art, the name *Sea Witch.*

The air reeked, a mixture of the aromas of the rotting vegetation and dead fish that were floating amid the roots of the mangrove trees growing almost on the water's edge. The fresh water coming down the river kept the mangroves going, apparently, although the fish had been unable to withstand the avgas, oil, and grease that were regularly spilled in the water.

At least there was a bit of a breeze to keep the bugs at bay. The place must be a hellhole when the wind didn't blow!

None of the sailors working on the Cat wore a shirt, and many had cut off the legs of their dungarees. They were brown as nuts.

One of the men standing on the float winching the bombs up was wearing a swimsuit and tennis shoes—nothing else. I figured he was the officer, and after a minute or so of watching I was sure. He was helping with the job, but he was also directing the others.

"Lieutenant Modahl?"

He turned to look at me.

"I'm your new copilot."

After he got the second bomb on that wing, he clambered up the rope net that was hung over the side of the ship. When he was on deck he shook my hand. I told him my name, where I was from.

He asked a few questions about my experience, and I told him I'd never flown seaplanes—been flying the SBD Dauntless.

Modahl was taller than me by a bunch, over six feet. He must have weighed at least two hundred, and none of it looked like fat. He about broke my hand shaking it. I thought maybe he had played college football. He had black eyes and black hair, filthy hands with ground-in grease and broken fingernails. Only after he shook my hand did it occur to him to wipe the grease off his hands, which he did with a rag that had been lying nearby on the deck. He didn't smile, not once.

I figured if he could fly and fight, it didn't matter whether he smiled or not. Anyone in the South Pacific who was making friends just then didn't understand the situation.

Modahl:

The ensign was the sorriest specimen I had laid eyes on in a long time. About five feet four inches tall, he had poorly cut, flaming red hair, freckles, jug ears, and buckteeth. He looked maybe sixteen. His khakis didn't fit, were sweat-stained and rumpled—hell, they were just plain dirty.

He mumbled his words, didn't have much to say, kept glancing at the Cat, didn't look me in the eyes.

Joe Snyder and his crew were missing, Harvey Deets was lying in his bunk shivering himself to death with malaria, and I wound up with this kid as a copilot, one who had never even *flown* a seaplane! Why didn't they just put one of the storekeepers in the right seat? Hell, why didn't we just leave the damn seat empty?

No wonder the goddamn Japs were kicking our butts all over the Pacific.

The kid mumbled something about Jones wanting to see me. If the Old Man thought I was going to wet-nurse this kid, he was going to find out different before he got very much older.

I told the kid where to put his gear, then headed for the wardroom to find Commander Jones.

After Modahl went below, I climbed down the net to look over the Black Cat. The high wing sported two engines. The wing was raised well over the fuselage by a pedestal, which had been the key innovation of the design. The mechanic or flight engineer, I knew, had his station in the pedestal. The Cat had side blisters with a fifty-caliber on a swivel-mount in each, a thirty-caliber which fired aft through a tunnel, and a flexible thirty in a nose turret.

This Cat, however, had something I had never seen before. Four blast tubes covered with condoms protruded from the nose under the bow turret. I entered the Cat through one of the open blisters and went forward for a look. The bunk compartment was where passengers always rode; I had never been forward of that.

I went through a small watertight hatch—open now, of course—into the mechanic's compartment. Three steps led up to the mechanic's seat on the wing support pylon. The mech had a bunch of levers and switches up there to control the engines and cowl flaps in flight.

Moving on forward, I passed through the compartment used by the radio operator and the navigator. The radio gear took up all the space on the starboard side of the compartment, while the navigator had a table with a large compass mounted on the aft end. He had boxes for stowage of charts and a light mounted right over the table. The rear bulkhead was covered with a power distribution panel.

On forward was the cockpit, with raised seats for the pilot and copilot. The yokes were joined together on a cross-cockpit boom, so when one moved, the other did also. On the yoke was a set of light switches that told the mechanic what the pilot wanted him to do. They were labeled with things like, "Raise floats" and "Lower floats," which meant the wingtip floats, and directions for controlling the fuel mixture to the engines. The throttle and prop controls were mounted on the overhead.

The cockpit had windows on both sides and in the roof, all of which were open, but still, it was stifling in there with the heat and stink of rotting fish. The Catalina was also rocking a bit in the swell, which didn't help either.

The door to the bow compartment was between the pilot and copilot, below the instrument panel. One of the sailors was there installing ammo in the bow gun feed trays. He explained the setup.

Four fifty-caliber machine guns were mounted as tightly as possible in the bow compartment—the bombsight had been removed to make room and the bombardier's window plated over with sheet metal. Most of the space the guns didn't occupy was taken up by ammo feed trays. The trigger for the guns was on the pilot's yoke. The remainder of the space, and there wasn't much, was for the bow gunner, who had to straddle the fifties to fire the flexible thirty-caliber in the bow turret. Burlap bags were laid over the fixed fifties to protect the gunner from burns.

The sailor showing me the installation was pretty proud of it. His name was Hoffman. He was the bow gunner and bombardier, he said, and had just finished loading ammo in the trays. Through the gaps in the trays I could see the gleam of brass. Hoffman straddled the guns and opened the hatch in the top of the turret to let in some air and light.

"That hatch is open when you make an attack?" I asked.

"Yes, sir. Little drafty, but the visibility is great."

The Cat bobbing against the float and the heat in that closed space made me about half-seasick. I figured I was good for about one more minute.

"How do they work?" I asked, patting the guns.

"They're the Cat's nuts, sir. They really pour out the lead. They'll cut a hole in a ship's side in seconds. I hose the thirty around to keep their heads down while Mr. Modahl guts 'em."

"He goes after the Japs, does he?"

"Yes, sir. He says we gotta do it or somebody else will have to. Now me, I'd rather be sitting in the drugstore at Pismo Beach drinking sodas with my girl while someone else does the heavy lifting, but it isn't working out that way."

"I guess not."

"In fact, when we dive for those Jap ships, and I'm sitting on those guns, I'd rather be somewhere else, anywhere at all. I haven't peed my pants yet, but it's been close."

"Uh-huh."

"Guess everybody feels that way."

"Hard to get used to."

"Are you going to be flying with us?"

"I'm flying copilot for a while. They told me Deets has malaria."

"You know Cats, huh?"

"I don't know a damn thing about flying boats. I figure I can learn, though."

Hoffman wasn't thrilled, I could see that. If I were

him, I would have wanted experienced people in the cockpit, too.

Oh well, how tough could it be? It wasn't like we were going to have to land this thing on a carrier deck.

Hoffman:

This ensign wasn't just wet behind the ears—he was dripping all over the deck. Our new copilot? He looked like he just got out of the eighth grade. What in hell were the zeros thinking?

That wasn't me you heard laughin', not by a damn sight. It wasn't very funny. This ensign must be what's on the bottom of the barrel.

It was like we had already lost the war; we were risking our butts with an idiot pilot who thought he could win the war all by himself, and if it went bad, we had a copilot who's never flown a seaplane—hell, a copilot who oughta be in junior high—to get our sorry asses home.

I patted those fifties, then crawled aft, out of the bow compartment, before I embarrassed myself by losing my breakfast. There seemed to be a tiny breeze through the cockpit, and that helped. That and the sunlight and the feeling I wasn't closed up in a tight place.

There were lots of discolored places on the left side of the fuselage. I asked Hoffman about that. He looked vaguely surprised. "Patches, sir. Japs shot up the *Witch* pretty bad. Killed the radioman and left waist gunner. Mr. Modahl got us home, but it was a close thing."

Hoffman went aft to get out of the airplane, leaving me in the cockpit. I climbed into the right seat and looked things over, fingered all the switches and levers, studied everything. The more I could learn now, the easier the first flight would be.

Everything looked straightforward . . . no surprises, really. But it was a big, complicated plane. The lighting and intercom panels were on the bulkhead behind the pilots' seats. There were no landing gear or flap handles, of course. Constant speed props, throttles, RPM and manifold pressure gauges . . . I thought I could handle it. All I needed would be a little coaching on the takeoff and landing.

The button on the pilot's yoke that fired the fifties was an add-on, merely clamped to the yoke. A wire from the button disappeared into the bow compartment.

I gingerly moved the controls, just a tad, while I kept my right hand on the throttles. Yeah, I could handle it. She would be slow and ponderous, nothing like a Dauntless, but hell, flying is flying.

I climbed out and stood on the float watching the guys finish loading and fusing the bombs. Three men were also sitting on the wing completing the fueling. I climbed up the net to the tender's deck and leaned on the rail, looking her over.

Modahl came walking down the deck, saw me, and came over. He had sort of a funny look on his face. "Okay," he said, and didn't say anything else.

He leaned on the rail, too, stood surveying the airplane.

"Nice plane," I remarked, trying to be funny.

"Yeah. Commander Jones says we can leave as soon as we're ready. When the guys are finished fueling and arming the plane, I think I'll have them fed, then we'll go."

"Yes, sir. Where to?"

"Jones and I thought we might as well run up to Buka and Rabaul and see what's in the harbor. Moon's almost full tonight—be a shame to waste it. Intelligence thinks there are about a dozen Jap ships at Rabaul, which is fairly well defended. We ought to send at least two Cats. Would if we had them, but we don't."

"Buka?"

"No one knows. The harbor might contain a fleet, or it might be empty."

"Okay."

"Tomorrow morning we'll see if we can find Joe Snyder."

"Where was Snyder going the night he disappeared?"

"Buka and Rabaul," Modahl replied, and climbed down the net to check the fuses on the weapons.

TWO

While the other guys were doing all the work, I went to my stateroom and threw my stuff in the top bunk. Another officer was there, stripped to his skivvies in the jungle heat. He was seated at the only desk writing a long letter—he already had four or five pages of dense handwriting lying in front of him.

"I'm the new guy," I told him, "going to be Modahl's copilot."

He looked me over like I was a steer he was going to bid upon. "I'm Modahl's navigator, Rufus Pottinger."

"We're flying together, I guess."

I couldn't think of a thing to say. I wondered if that letter was to a girl or his mother. I guessed his mother—Pottinger didn't strike me as the romantic type, but you can never tell. There is someone for everyone, they say.

That thought got me thinking about my family. I didn't have a solitary soul to write to. I guess I was jealous of Pottinger. I stripped to my skivvies and asked him where the head was.

He looked at his watch. "You're in luck. The water will be on in fifteen minutes. For fifteen minutes. The skipper of this scow is miserly with the water."

I took a cake of soap, a towel, and a toothbrush and went to to visit the facilities.

Pottinger:

I'd heard of this guy. They had thrown him out of SBDs, sent him to PBYs. I guess that was an indicator of where we stood on the naval aviation totem pole.

The scuttlebutt was this ensign was some kind of suicidal maniac. You'd never know it to look at him. With flaming red hair, splotchy skin, and buckteeth, he was the kind of guy nobody ever paid much attention to.

He also had an annoying habit of failing to meet your gaze when he spoke to you—I noticed that right off. Not a guy with a great future in the Navy. The man had no presence.

I threw my pen on the desk and stretched. I got to thinking about Modahl and couldn't go on with my letter, so I folded it and put in in the drawer.

Modahl was a warrior to his fingertips. He also took crazy chances. Sure, you gotta go for it—that's combat. Still, you must use good sense. Stay alive to fight again tomorrow. I tried to tell him that dead men don't win wars, and he just laughed.

Now the ensign had been added to the mix. I confess, I was worried. At least Harvey Deets had curbed some of Modahl's wilder instincts.

This ensign was a screwball with no brains, according to the rumor, which came straight from the yeoman in the captain's office who saw the message traffic.

In truth I wasn't cut out for this life. I was certainly no warrior—not like Modahl, or even this crazy redheaded ensign. Didn't have the nerves for it.

I wasn't sleeping much those days, couldn't eat, couldn't stop my hands from shaking. It sounds crazy, but I knew there was a bullet out there waiting for me. I knew I wasn't going to survive the war. The Japs were going to kill me.

And I didn't know if they would do it tonight, or tomorrow night, or some night after. But they would do it. I felt like a man on death row, waiting for the warden to come for me.

I couldn't say that in my letters home, of course. Mom would worry herself silly. But Jesus, I didn't know if I could screw up the courage to keep on going.

I hoped I wouldn't crack, wouldn't lose my manhood in front of Modahl and the others.

I guess I'd rather be dead than humiliate myself that way.

Modahl knew how I felt. I think he sensed it when I tried to talk some sense into him.

Oh, God, be with us tonight.

I sat through the brief and kept my ensign's mouth firmly shut. The others asked questions, especially Modahl, while I sort of half listened and thought about that great big ocean out there.

The distances involved were enormous. Buka on the northern tip of Bougainville was about 400 nautical miles away, Rabaul on the eastern tip of New Britain, about 450. This was the first time I would be flying the ocean without my plotting board, which felt strange. No way around it though—Catalinas carried a navigator, who was supposed to get you there and back. Modahl apparently thought Pottinger could handle it—and I guess he had so far.

Standing on the tender's deck, I surveyed the sky. The usual noon shower had dissipated, and now there was only the late-afternoon cumulus building over the ocean.

Behind me I could hear the crew whispering—of course they weren't thrilled at having a copilot without experience, but I wasn't either. I would have given anything right then to be manning a Dauntless on the deck of *Enterprise* rather than climbing into this heaving, stinking, ugly flying boat moored in the mouth of this jungle river.

The *Sea Witch*! Gimme a break!

The evening was hot, humid, with only an occasional puff of wind. The tender had so little fresh water it came out of the tap in a trickle, hardly enough to wet a washrag. I had taken a sponge bath, which was a wasted effort. I was already sodden. At least in the plane we would be free of the bugs that swarmed over us in the muggy air.

I was wearing khakis; Modahl was togged out in a pair of Aussie shorts and a khaki shirt with the sleeves rolled up—the only reason he wore that shirt instead of a tee shirt was to have a pocket for pens and cigarettes. Both of us wore pistols on web belts around our waists.

As I went down the net I overheard the word "crazy." That steamed me, but there wasn't anything I could do about it.

If they wanted to think I was nuts, let 'em. As long as they did their jobs it really didn't matter what they thought. Even if it did piss me off.

I got strapped into the right seat without help, but I was of little use to Modahl. I shouldn't have worried. The copilot was merely there to flip switches the pilot couldn't reach, provide extra muscle on the unboosted controls, and talk to the pilot to keep him awake in the middle of the night. I didn't figure Modahl would leave the plane to me and the autopilot on this first flight. Tonight, the bunks where members of the crew normally took turns napping were covered with a dozen flares and a dozen hundred-pound bombs, to be dumped out the tunnel hole aft.

The mechanic helped start the engines, Pratt & Whitney 1830s of twelve hundred horsepower each. That sounded like a lot, but the Cat was a huge plane, carrying four five-hundred-pound bombs on the racks, the hundred-pounders on the bunks, several hundred pounds of flares, God knows how much machine gun ammo, and fifteen hundred gallons of gasoline, which weighed nine thousand pounds. The plane could have carried more gas, but this load was plenty, enough to keep us airborne for over twenty hours.

I had no idea what the Cat weighed with all this stuff, and I suspect Modahl didn't either. I said something to the mechanic, Dutch Amme, as we stood on the float waiting our turn to board, and he said the weight didn't matter. "As long as the thing'll float, it'll fly."

With Amme ready to start the engines, Modahl yelled to Hoffman to release the bowlines. Hoffman was standing on the chine on the left side of the bow. He flipped the line off the cleat, crawled across the nose to the other chine, got rid of that line, then climbed into the nose turret through the open hatch.

A dozen or so of the tender sailors pushed us away from the float. As soon as the bow began to swing, Amme began cranking the engine closest to the tender. It caught and blew a cloud of white smoke, and kept the nose swinging. Modahl pushed the rudder full over and pulled the yoke back into his lap as Amme cranked the second engine.

In less time than it takes to tell, we were taxiing away from the tender.

"You guys did that well," I remarked.

"Practice," Modahl said.

Everyone checked in on the intercom, and there was a lot of chatter as they checked systems, all while we were taxiing toward the river's mouth.

Finally, Modahl used the rudder and starboard engine to initiate a turn to kill time while the engines came up to temperature. The mechanic talked about the engines—temps and so on; Modahl listened and said little.

After two complete turns, the pilot closed the window on his side and told me to do the same. He flipped the signal light to tell Amme to set the mixtures to Auto Rich. While I was trying to get my window to latch, he straightened the rudder and matched the throttles. Props full forward, he pulled the yoke back into his lap and began adding power.

The engines began to sing.

The *Witch* accelerated slowly as Modahl steadily advanced the throttles while the flight engineer called out the manifold pressures and RPMs. He had the throttles full forward when the nose of the big Cat rose, and she began planing the smooth water in the lee of the point. Modahl centered the yoke with both hands to keep us on the step.

I glanced at the airspeed from time to time. We were so heavy I began to wonder if we could ever get off. We passed fifty miles per hour still planing, worked slowly to fifty-five, then sixty, the engines howling at full power.

It took almost a minute to get to sixty-five with that heavy load, but when we did Modahl pulled the yoke back into his lap and the Cat broke free of the water. He eased the yoke forward, held her just a few feet over the water in ground effect as our airspeed increased. When we had eighty on the dial Modahl inched the yoke back slightly, and the *Witch* swam upward in the warm air.

"When the water is a little rougher or there is a breeze, she'll come off easier," he told me. He flipped the switch to tell Amme to raise the wingtip floats.

He climbed all the way to a thousand feet before he lowered the nose and pulled the throttles back to cruise manifold pressure, then the props back to cruise RPM. Of course, he had to readjust the throttles and sync the props. Finally he got the props perfectly in snyc, and the engine noise became a smooth, loud hum.

After Modahl trimmed he hand-flew the *Witch* a while. We went out past the point, where he turned and set a course for the tip of the island that lay to the northeast.

"Landing this thing is a piece of cake. It's a power-on landing into smooth water: Just set up the altitude and a bit of a sink rate and ease her down and on. In the open sea we full-stall her in. After you watch me do a few I'll let you try it. Maybe tomorrow evening if we aren't going out again."

"Yeah," I said. The fact that Modahl was making plans for tomorrow was comforting somehow, as I'm sure it was to the rest of the crew, who were listening on the intercom. As if we were a road repair gang on the way to fill a pothole.

When we got to the island northeast of Samarai, we flew along the water's edge for twenty minutes, looking for people or a crashed airplane or a signal—anything—hoping our lost Catalina crew had made it this far.

We had been in the air over an hour when Modahl turned northeast for Bougainville. He engaged the autopilot and sat for a while watching it fly the plane. We were indicating 115 miles per hour, about a hundred knots. The wind was out of the west. Pottinger, the navigator, was watching the surface of the sea to establish our drift before sunset.

"Keep your eyes peeled, gang, for Joe Snyder and his guys. Sing out if you see anything."

The land was out of sight behind and the sun was sinking into the sea haze when Modahl finally put his feet up on the instrument panel and lit a cigarette. The sun on our left stern quarter illuminated the clouds, which covered about half the sky. The cloud bases were at least a thousand feet above us, the tops several thousand feet above that. The visibility was about twenty miles, I thought, as I studied the sun-dappled surface of the sea with binoculars.

Standing in the space behind us, between the seats, the radioman also studied the sea's surface. His name was something Varitek . . . I hadn't caught his first name. Everyone called him Varitek, even the other sailors.

The noise level in the plane was high; the headsets made it tolerable. Barely. Still, the drone of the engines and the clouds flamed by the setting sun and the changing patterns on the sea were very pleasant. We had cracked our side windows so there was a decent breeze flowing into the plane.

One of the sailors brought us coffee, hot and black. As Modahl smoked cigarettes, one after another, we sat there watching the colors of the clouds change and the sea grow dark. A sliver of the sun was still above the horizon when I got my first glimpse of the moon, round and golden, climbing the sky.

The other members of the crew were disappointed that they didn't see any trace of Snyder's plane. I hadn't thought they would, nor, apparently, did Modahl. He said little, merely smoked in silence as the clouds above us lost their evening glow.

"Watch the moonpath," Modahl told me after a while. "Anything we see up this way is Japanese, and fair game." He adjusted the cockpit lighting for night flying and asked the radioman for more coffee.

Modahl:

I couldn't get Joe Snyder and his crew out of my mind. A fellow shouldn't go forth to slay dragons preoccupied with other things, but I liked Joe, liked him a lot. And whatever happened to him could happen to me and mine.

The Japs were staging ships and supplies through Buka and Rabaul as they tried to kick us off Guadalcanal. They were working up to taking Port Moresby, then invading Australia, when our invasion of Guadal threw a monkey wrench in their plans. Now they were trying to reinforce their forces on Guadalcanal. A steady stream of troop transports and cargo ships had been in and out of those harbors, not to mention destroyers and cruisers, enough to put the fear in everybody. Then there are Jap planes—they had a nice airfield on Rabaul and a little strip near Buka. The legs on the Zeros were so long you just never knew where or when you would encounter them, though they stayed on the ground at night.

If they could have flown at night, the Cats couldn't. The guns in the side blisters were poor defense against enemy fighters. When attacked, the best defense was to get as close to the sea as possible so the Zeros couldn't make shooting passes without the danger of flying into the water. If a Japanese pilot ever slowed down and lined up behind a Cat a few feet over the water, he'd be meat on the table for the blister gunners—the Japs had yet to make that mistake and probably never would.

I sat there listening to the engines, wondering what happened to Joe, if he were still alive, if he would ever be found.

Varitek:

If you didn't believe you had a good chance of living through the flight, you would never get aboard the plane. Somebody said that to me once, and it was absolutely true. It took guts to sit through the brief and man up and ride through a takeoff, knowing how big this ocean was, knowing that your life was dependent on the continued function of this cunning contraption of steel and duraluminum. Knowing your continued existence depended on the skill of your pilot.

On Modahl.

Modahl. If he made one bad decision, we were all dead.

These other guys, I saw them fingering rosaries or moving their lips in prayer. I didn't buy any of that sweet-hereafter Living on a Cloud Playing a Harp bullshit.

This is it, baby. This life is all you get. When it's over, it's over. And you ain't coming back as a cow or a dog or a flea on an elephant's ass.

I tried not to think about it, but the truth was, I was scared. Yeah, I believed in Modahl. He was a good officer and a good pilot. Sort of a holier-than-thou human being, not a regular kind of guy you'd like to drink beer with, but I didn't care about that. None of these officers were going to be your buddy, and who would want them to? Modahl could fly that winged boat. He was good at that, and that was all that mattered. That and the fact that he could get us home.

He could do that. Modahl could. He could get this plane and his ass and the asses of all of us home again, back to the tender.

Yeah.

Hoffman:

These other guys were so calm that afternoon, but I wasn't. Tell you the truth, I was scared. Waiting, waiting, waiting . . . it was enough to make a guy puke. I tried to eat and managed to get something down, but I upchucked it before we manned up.

I knew the guys on the Snyder crew—went to boot camp with a couple of them and shipped out with them to the South Pacific. Yeah, they were good guys, *guys just like me,* and they were dead now. Or floating around in the ocean waiting to die. Or marooned on an island somewhere. The folks at home saw the pictures in *Life* and thought tropical paradise, but these islands were hellholes of jungle, bugs, and snakes, with green shit growing right down to the water's edge. Everything was alive, and everything would eat you.

And the South Pacific was crawling with Japs. The sons of Nippon didn't take prisoners, the guys said, just tortured you for information, then whacked off your head with one of those old swords. Gave me the shivers just thinking about it.

If they captured me . . . well, *Jesus!*

No wonder I was puking like a soldier on a two-week drunk.

I just prayed that Modahl would get us home. One more time.

Pottinger:

This evening the wind was only a few knots out of the west-southwest. Our ground speed was, I estimated, 102 knots. We were precisely here on the chart, at this spot I marked with a tiny x. If I had doped the wind right. Beside the x I noted the time.

Later, as we approach Bougainville, Modahl would climb above the clouds and let me shoot the stars for an accurate fix. Of course, once we found the island, I would use it to plot running fixes.

I liked the precision of navigation. The answers were real, clear, and unequivocal, and could be determined with finest mathematical exactness. On the other hand, flying was more like playing a musical instrument. I could determine Modahl's mood by the way he handled the plane. Most of the time he treated it with the utmost respect, working the plane in the wind and sea like a maestro directing a symphony. When he was preoccupied, like tonight, Modahl just pounded the keys, horsed it around, never got in sync with it.

He was thinking about Joe Snyder's crew, I figured, wondering, pondering life and death.

Death was out there tonight, on that wide sea or in those enemy harbors.

It was always there, always a possibility when we set out on one of those long flights into the unknown.

The torture was not combat, a few intense minutes of bullets and bombs; torture was the waiting. The hours of waiting. The days. The nights. Waiting, wondering . . .

Sometimes the bullets and bombs came as almost a relief after all that waiting.

The *Sea Witch* was Modahl's weapon. The rest of us were tiny cogs in his machine, living parts. We would live or die as the fates willed it, and whichever way it came out didn't matter as long as Modahl struck the blow.

But the men had faith he'll take them home. Afterward.

I *wanted* to believe that. The others also. But I knew it wasn't true. Death was out there—I could feel it.

Modahl was only a man.

A man who wondered about Joe Snyder and probably had little faith in himself.

Was Modahl crazy, or was it us, who believed?

Nothing in this life was as black as a night at sea. You can tell people that, and they would nod, but no one could know how mercilessly dark a night could be until he saw the night sea for himself.

After the twilight was completely gone that night there was only the occasional flicker of the moon-path through gaps in the clouds, and now and then a glimpse of the stars. And the red lights on the instrument panel. Nothing else. The universe was as dark as the grave.

Modahl eased his butt in his seat, readjusted his feet on the instrument panel, tried to find a comfortable position, and reached for his cigarettes. The pack was empty; he crumpled it in disgust.

"You married?" he asked me.

"No."

"I am," he said, and rooted around in his flight bag for another pack of Luckies. He got one out, fired it off, then rearranged himself, settling back in.

He checked the compass, tapped the altimeter, glanced at his watch, and said nothing.

"Can I walk around a little?" I asked.

"Sure."

I got unstrapped and left him there, smoking, his feet on the panel.

The beat of the engines made the ship a living

thing. Everything you touched vibrated; even the air seemed to pulsate. The waist and tunnel gunners were watching out the blisters, scratching, smoking, whatever. Pottinger was working on his chart, the radioman and bombardier were playing with the radar, Amme the mechanic was in his tower making entries in his logbooks.

I took a leak, drank a half a cup of coffee while I watched the two guys working with the radar, and asked some questions. The presentation was merely a line on a cathode-ray tube—a ship, they said, would show up as a spike on the line. Maybe. Range was perhaps twenty miles, when the sea conditions were right.

"Have you ever seen a ship on that thing?" I asked.

"Oh, yeah," the radioman said, then realized I was an officer and added a "sir."

I finished the coffee, then climbed back into the copilot's seat.

When my headset was plugged in again, I asked Modahl, "Do you ever have trouble staying awake?"

He shook his head no.

A half hour later he got out of his seat, took off his headset, and shouted in my ear: "I'm going to get some coffee, walk around. If the autopilot craps out, I'll feel it. Just hold course and heading."

"Yes, sir."

He left, and there I was, all alone in the cockpit of a PBY Catalina over the South Pacific at night, hunting Jap ships.

Right.

I put my feet up on the panel like Modahl had and sat watching the instruments, just in case the autopilot did decide that it had done enough work tonight. The clouds were breaking up as we went north, so every few seconds I stole a glance down the moonpath, just in case. It was about seventy degrees to the right of our nose. I knew the guys were watching it from the starboard blister, but I looked anyway.

We had been airborne for a bit over four hours. We had lost time searching the coast of that island, so I figured we had another hour to fly before we reached Buka. Maybe Modahl was talking to Pottinger about that now.

If my old man could only see me in this cockpit. When he lost the farm about eight years ago, five years after Mom died, he took my sister and me to town and turned us over to the sheriff. Said he couldn't feed us.

He kissed us both, then walked out the door. That was the last time I ever saw him.

Life defeated him. Beat him down.

Maybe someday, when the war was over, I'll try to find him. My sister and I weren't really adopted, just farmed out as foster kids, so legally he was still my dad.

My sister was killed last year in a car wreck, so he was the only one I had left. I didn't even know if he or Mom had brothers or sisters.

I was sitting there thinking about those days when I heard one sharp, hard word in my ears.

"Contact."

That was the radioman on the intercom. "We have a contact, fifteen miles, ten degrees left."

In about ten seconds Modahl charged into the cockpit and threw himself into the left seat.

"I've got it," he said, and twisted the autopilot

steering. We turned about fifty degrees left before he leveled the wings.

"We'll go west, look for them on the moonpath, figure out what we've got."

He reached behind him and twisted the volume knob on the intercom panel so everyone could clearly hear his voice. "Wake up, people. We have a contact. We're maneuvering to put it on the moonpath for a visual."

"What do you think it is?"

"May just be stray electrons—that radar isn't anything to bet money on. If it's a ship, though, it's Japanese."

THREE

"We've lost the contact," Varitek, the radioman, told Modahl. "It's too far starboard for the radar."

"Okay. We'll turn toward it after a bit, so let me know when you get it again."

He leaned over and shouted at me. "It's no stray electron. Ghost images tend to stay on the screen regardless of how we turn."

He was fidgety. He got out the binoculars, looked down the moonpath.

He was doing that when he said, "I've got it. Something, anyway." He turned the plane, banking steeply to put the contact ahead of us.

As we were in the turn, he said, "It's a submarine, I think."

As he leveled the wings the radioman shouted, "Contact."

Modahl looked with binoculars. "It's a sub conning tower. About six miles. Running southeast, I think. We're in his stern quarter."

He banked the plane steeply right, then disengaged the autopilot and lifted the nose and added power. "We'll climb," he said. "Make a diving attack down the moonpath."

"Going to drop a bomb?"

"One, I think. There may be nothing at Buka or Rabaul."

He explained what he wanted to the crew over the intercom. "We'll use the guns on the conning tower," he said, "then drop the bomb as we go over. You guys in the blisters and tunnel, hit 'em with all you got as we go by. They'll go under before we can make another run, so let's make this one count."

Everyone put on life vests, just in case.

"Your job," Modahl said to me, "is to watch the altimeter and keep me from flying into the water. I want an altitude callout every ten seconds or so. Not every hundred feet, but every ten seconds."

"Yessir."

He called Hoffman to the cockpit and talked to him. "One bomb, the call will be 'ready, ready, now.' I'll pickle it off, but to make sure it goes, I want you to push your pickle when I do."

"Aye aye, sir."

Modahl:

The theory was simple enough: We were climbing to about twenty-five hundred feet, if I could get that high under those patchy clouds, then we would fly down the moonpath toward that sub. We'd see him, but he couldn't see us. At two miles I'd chop the throttles and dive. If everything went right, we'd be doing almost 250 mph when we passed three hundred feet in altitude, about a thousand feet from the sub, and I opened fire with the nose fifties.

I planned to pull out right over the conning tower and release the bomb. If I judged it right and the bomb didn't hang up on the rack, maybe it would hit close enough to the sub to damage its hull.

On pullout the guys in the back would sting the sub with their fifties.

Getting it all together would be the trick.

Hoffman:

I opened the hatch on the bow turret and climbed astraddle of those fifties. I patted those babies. I'd cleaned and greased and loaded them—if they jammed when we needed them Modahl would be royally pissed. Dutch Amme, the crew chief, would sign me up for a strangulation. Modahl was a nice enough guy, for an officer, but he and Amme wouldn't tolerate a fuck-up at a time like this, which was okay by me. None of us came all this way to wave at the bastards as we flew by.

The guns *would* work—I *knew* they would.

Pottinger:

We know the Japanese sailors are there—they are blissfully unaware of us up here in the darkness. Right now they have their sub on the surface, recharging batteries and running southeast, probably headed for the area off Guadalcanal . . . to hunt for American ships. When they find one, they will torpedo it from ambush.

We call it war but it's really murder, isn't it? Us or them, whoever pulls the trigger, no matter. The object of the game is to assassinate the other guy before he can do it to you.

We're like Al Capone's enforcers, out to whack the enemy unawares. For the greater glory of our side.

Modahl climbed to the west, with the moon at his back. He got to twenty-four hundred feet before he tickled the bottom of a cloud, so he stayed there and got us back to cruising speed before he started his turn to the left. He turned about 160 degrees, let me fly the *Witch* while he used the binoculars.

"We've got it again," the radioman said. "Thirty degrees left, right at the limits of the gimbals."

"Range?"

"Twelve miles."

"Come left ten," Modahl told me.

I concentrated fiercely on the instruments, holding altitude and turning to the heading he wanted. The Catalina was heavy on the controls, but not outrageously so. I'd call it lots of stability.

The seconds crept by. All the tiredness that I had felt just minutes before was gone. I was ready.

"I've got it," he said flatly, staring through the binoculars. "Turn up the moonpath."

I did so.

"Okay, everybody. Range about eight miles. Three minutes, then we dive to attack."

I tried to look over the nose, which was difficult in a Catalina.

"Still heading southeast," Modahl murmured. "You'll have to turn slightly right to keep it in the moonpath."

The turn also moved the nose so it wouldn't obstruct Modahl's vision.

Maybe I shouldn't have, but I wondered about

those guys on that sub. If we pulled this off, these were their last few minutes of life. I guess few of us ever know when the end is near. Which is good, I suppose, since we all have to die.

The final seconds ticked away, then Modahl laid down the binoculars and reached for the controls. He secured the autopilot, and told me, "I'm going to run the trim full nose down. As we come off target, your job is to start cranking the trim back or I'll never be able to hold the nose up as our speed drops."

"Okay."

He retarded the throttles, then pulled back the props so they wouldn't act as dive brakes. Still, nose down as we were, we began to accelerate. Modahl ran the trim wheel forward. I called altitudes.

"Two thousand . . . nineteen hundred . . . eighteen . . ."

Glancing up, I saw the conning tower of the sub and the wake it made. I must have expected it to look larger, because the fact that it was so tiny surprised me.

"Twelve . . . eleven . . ."

The airspeed needle crept past 200 mph. We were diving for a spot just short of the sub so Modahl could raise the nose slightly and hammer them, then pull up to avoid crashing.

I could see the tower plainly now in the reflection of the moonlight, which made a long white ribbon of the wake.

"Six hundred . . . five . . . four-twenty-five . . ."

We were up to almost 250 mph, and Modahl was flattening his dive, from about twenty degrees nose down to fifteen or sixteen. He had the tower of that sub boresighted now.

"Three-fifty . . ."

"Three hundred . . ."

"Ready," Modahl said for Varitek's benefit. He shoved the prop levers forward, then the throttles.

"Two-fifty . . ."

Modahl jabbed the red button on the yoke with his right thumb. Even with the shielding the blast tubes provided, the muzzle flashes were so bright that I almost visually lost the sub. The engines at full power were stupendously loud, but the jackhammer pounding just inches from my feet made the cockpit floor tremble like a leaf in a gale.

Hoffman:

I could see the sub's tower, see how we were hurtling through the darkness toward that little metal thing amid the swells. When the guns beneath me suddenly began hammering, the noise almost deafened me. I was expecting it, and yet, I wasn't.

I had been pointing the thirty at the Jap, now I held the trigger down.

The noise and heat and gas from the cycling breechblocks made it almost impossible to breathe. This was the fourth time I had done this, and it wasn't getting any better. I could scarcely breathe, the noise was off the scale, my flesh and bones vibrated. The burlap under me insulated me from the worst of the heat, yet if Modahl kept the triggers down, he was going to fry me. I was sitting on hellfire.

And I was screaming with joy . . . Despite everything, the experience was sublime.

"One hundred." I shouted the altitude over the bedlam. Some fool was screaming on the intercom, the engines were roaring at full power, the guns in the nose were hammering in one long, continuous burst . . . I had assumed that Modahl would pull out at a hundred. He didn't.

"Readeee . . ."

"Fifty feet," I shouted over the din, trying to make myself heard. I reached for the yoke.

"Now!" Modahl roared, pushing the bomb release with his left thumb, releasing the gun trigger, and pulling the yoke back into his stomach all at the same time.

I began cranking madly on the trim.

We must have taken the lenses off the periscopes with our keel. I distinctly felt us hit something . . . and the nose was rising through the horizontal, up, up, five degrees, ten, as the guns in the blisters and tunnel got off long rolling bursts. When they fell silent our airspeed was bleeding off rapidly, so Modahl pushed forward on the yoke.

"Hoffman, you asshole, did the bomb go?"

"No, sir. It didn't release."

"You shit. You silly, silly shit."

"Mr. Modahl—"

"Get your miserable ass up here and talk to me, Hoffman."

He cranked the plane around as tightly as he could, but too late. When we got level, inbound, with the moon in front of us, the sub was no longer there. She had dived.

"You fly it," Modahl said disgustedly, and turned the plane over to me.

Hoffman climbed up to stand behind the pilots' seats while Modahl inspected the hung bomb with an Aldis lamp. I tried not to look at the bright light so as to maintain some night vision—the light got me anyway. When Modahl had inspected the offending bomb to his satisfaction and finally killed the light, I was half-blinded.

Hoffman said, "Maybe we got the sub with the guns."

Modahl's lip curled in a vicious sneer, and he turned in his seat, looked at Hoffman as if he were a piece of shit.

"Which side are you on, Hoffman? Your shipmates risked their lives to get that bomb on target, to no avail. If that bomb comes off the rack armed while we're landing, the Japs win and our happy little band of heroes will go to hell together. I don't care if you have to grease those racks with your own blood. When we make an attack they goddamn well better work."

Hoffman still had pimples. When Modahl killed the Aldis lamp I could see them, red and angry, in the glow of the cockpit lights.

"Are you fucking crazy?" Modahl asked without bothering to turn around.

"No, sir," Hoffman stammered.

"Screaming on the intercom during an attack. Jesus! I oughta court-martial your silly ass."

"I'm sorry, sir. It just slipped out. Everything was so loud and—"

Modahl made a gesture, as if he were shooing a fly. But that wasn't the end of it. "Chief Amme," Modahl said on the intercom. "When we get back, I expect you and Hoffman to run the racks through at least a dozen cycles on each bomb station. I want a written report signed by you and Hoffman that the racks work perfectly."

"*Yes, sir.*"

"Pottinger, bring your chart to the cockpit. Let's

figure out where we are and where the hell we go from here."

I was still hand-flying the plane, so Modahl said to me, "Head northwest and climb to four thousand, just in case we are closer to Bougainville than I think we are. We'll circle around the northern tip of the island and approach the harbor up the moonpath."

Modahl took off his headset and leaned toward me. "Hoffman's getting his rocks off down there."

"Maybe he's crazy, too," I suggested.

"We all are," Modahl said flatly, and nodded once, sharply. His lips turned down in a frown.

I dropped the subject.

"When you get tired, we'll let Otto fly the *Witch.*" Otto was the autopilot. After a few minutes I nodded, and he engaged it.

Modahl:

> Of course Hoffman was crazy. We all were to be out here at night in a flying boat hunting Japs in the world's biggest ocean. Yeah, sure, the Navy sent us here, but every one of us had the wit to have wrangled a nice cushy job somewhere in the States while someone else did the sweating.
>
> It's addictive, like booze and tobacco. I just worried that I'd love it too much. And it's probably a sin. Not that I know much about sin . . . but I can feel the wrongness of it, the evil. That's the attraction, I guess. I liked the adrenaline and the risk and the feeling of . . . power. Liked it too much.

It was two o'clock in the morning when we approached Buka harbor from the sea. Jungle-covered hills surrounded the harbor on two sides. A low spit formed the third side. On the end of the spit stood a small lighthouse. In the moonlight we could see that the harbor was empty. Not a single ship.

Pottinger was standing behind us. "How long up to Rabaul?" Modahl asked.

"An hour and forty-five minutes or so. Depends on how cute you want to be on the approach."

"You know me. I try to be cute enough to stay alive."

"Yeah."

"Before we go, let's wake up the Japs in Buka. Why should they get a good night's sleep if we can't?"

"Think the Japs are still here?"

"You can bet your soul on it."

Modahl pointed out where the town lay, on the inland side of the harbor. It was completely blacked out, of course.

We made a large, lazy circle while the guys in back readied the parafrags. We would drop them out the tunnel while we flew over the town . . . they fell for a bit, then the parachutes opened, and they drifted unpredictably. This was a nonprecision attack if there ever was one. It was better than throwing bricks, though not by much.

We flew toward the town at three thousand feet. We were still a mile or so away when antiaircraft tracers began rising out of the darkness around the harbor. The streams of shells went up through our altitude, all right, so they had plenty of gun. They just didn't know where in the darkness we were. The streams waved randomly as the Japs fired burst after burst.

It looked harmless enough, though it wasn't. A

shell fired randomly can kill you just as dead as an aimed one if it hits you.

"One minute," Modahl told the guys in back. He directed his next comment at me: "I'm saving the five-hundred-pounders for Rabaul. Surely we'll find a ship there or someplace."

"Thirty seconds."

We were in the tracers now, which bore a slight resemblance to Fourth of July fireworks.

"Drop 'em."

One tracer stream ignited just ahead of us and rose toward us. Modahl turned to avoid it. As I watched the glowing tracers I was well aware of how truly large the Catalina was, a black duraluminum cloud. How could they not hit it?

"That's the last of them." The word from the guys in back came as we passed out of the last of the tracers. The last few bombs would probably land in the jungle. Oh well.

We turned for the open sea. We were well away from the city when the frags begin exploding. They marched along through the blackness, popping very nicely as every gun in town fell silent.

"Rabaul," Modahl said, and turned the plane over to me.

FOUR

Rabaul!

The place was a legend. Although reputedly not as tough a nut as Truk, the big Jap base in the Carolines, Rabaul was the major Japanese stronghold in the South Pacific. Intelligence said they had several hundred planes—bombers, fighters, float fighters, seaplanes—and from thirty to fifty warships. This concentration of military power was defended with an impressive array of antiaircraft weapons.

The Army Air Corps was bombing Rabaul by day with B-17s, and the Navy was harassing them at night with Catalinas. None of these punches were going to knock them out, but if each blow hurt them a little, drew a little blood, the effect would be cumulative. Or so said the staff experts in Washington and Pearl.

Regardless of whatever else they might be, the Japanese were good soldiers, competent, capable, and ruthless. They probably had bagged Joe Snyder and his crew last night, and tonight, with this moon, they surely knew the Americans were coming.

I wondered if Snyder had attacked Rabaul before he headed for Buka, or vice versa. Whichever, the Japs in Buka probably radioed the news of our 2 A.M. raid to Rabaul. The guys in Rabaul knew how far it was between the two ports, and they had watches. They could probably predict within five minutes when we were going to arrive for the party.

I didn't remark on any of this to Modahl as we flew over the empty moonlit sea; he knew the facts as well as I and could draw his own conclusions. At least the clouds were dissipating. The stars were awe-inspiring.

Pottinger came up to the cockpit with his chart and huddled over it with Modahl. I sat watching the moonpath and monitoring Otto. I figured if Modahl wanted to include me in the strategy session, he would say so. My watch said almost three in the morning. We couldn't get there before four, so we were going to strike within an hour of dawn.

Finally, Modahl held the chart where I could see it, and said, "Here's Rabaul, on the northern coast of New Britain. This peninsula sticking out into the channel forms the western side of the harbor, which is a fine one. There are serious mountains on New Britain and on New Ireland, the island to the north and east. The highest is over seventy-five hundred feet high, so we want to avoid those.

"Here is what I want to do. We'll motor up the channel between the islands until we get on the moonpath; at this hour of the morning that will make our run in heading a little south of west. Then we'll go in. As luck would have it, that course brings us in over the mouth of the harbor.

"They'll figure we want to do that, but that's the

only way I know actually to see what's there. The radar will just show us a bunch of blips that could be anything. If we see a ship we like, we'll climb, then do a diving attack with the engines at idle. Bomb at masthead height. What do you think?"

"Think we'll catch 'em asleep?"

He glanced at me, then dropped his eyes. "No."

"It'll be risky."

"We'll hit the biggest ship in there, whatever that is."

"Five-hundred-pounders won't sink a cruiser."

"The tender was out of thousand-pounders. Snyder took the last one."

"Uh-huh."

"We can cripple 'em, put a cruiser out of the war for a while. Maybe they'll send it back to Japan for repairs. That'll do."

"How about a destroyer? Five hundred pounds of torpex will blow a Jap can in half."

"They got lots of destroyers. Not so many cruisers."

He thought like I did: If there was a cruiser in there, the Japs knew it was the prime target and they'd be ready; still, that's the one I'd hit. When you're looking for a fight, hit the biggest guy in the bar.

Modahl:

The kid was right; of course. There was no way we were going to sucker punch the Japs with a hundred-knot PBY. Yet I knew there would be targets in Rabaul so we had to check Buka first.

Snyder not coming back last night was the wild card. If the Japanese had radar at Rabaul, they could take the darkness away from us. Ditto night fighters with radar. Intelligence said they didn't have radar, and we had seen no indications that Intel was wrong, but still, Joe did what we plan to do, and he didn't come home.

Probably flak got him. God knows, in a heavily defended harbor, flying over a couple of dozen warships, the flak was probably thick enough to walk on.

Bombing at masthead height is our only realistic method for delivering the bombs. Hell, we don't even have a bombsight: We took it out when we put in the bow guns. The Catalina is an up-close and personal weapon. We'll stick it in their ear and pull the trigger, which will work, amazingly enough, if we can take advantage of the darkness to surprise them.

We'll pull it off or we won't. That's the truth of it.

Pottinger:

Talk about going along for the ride: These two go blithely about their bloody work without a thought for the rest of the crew. The have ice water in their veins. And neither asked if damaging a ship was worth the life of every man in this plane. Or anybody's life.

They're assassins, pure and simple, and they thought they were invulnerable.

Of course, the Japanese were assassins too.

All of these assholes were in it for the blood.

One hundred knots is glacially slow when you're going to a fire. I was so nervous that I had trouble sitting still. Despite my faith in Pottinger's expertise,

I kept staring into the darkness, trying to see what was out there. I didn't want to fly into a mountain and these islands certainly had 'em. When Pottinger said we had reached the mouth of the channel between the two, we turned north. Blindly.

As we motored up the channel at two thousand feet, I wondered why I didn't want to put off the moment of truth, till tomorrow night, or next week, or next year. Or forever. I decided that a man needs a future if he is to stay on an even keel, and with Rabaul up ahead, the future was nothing but a coin flip. I wanted it to be over.

Pottinger and Varitek, the radioman, were on the radar; they reported lots of blips. We came up the moonpath and looked with binoculars: We counted twenty-three ships in the harbor, about half of them warships and the rest freighters and tankers. Lots of targets.

"I think the one in the center of the harbor is a cruiser," Modahl said, and passed the binoculars to me. As he turned the plane to the north, to seaward, I turned the focus wheel of the binoculars and studied it through his side window. With the vibration of the plane and the low light level—all we had was moonlight—it was hard to tell. She was big, all right, and long enough, easily the biggest warship in the harbor.

"Looks like a cruiser to me," I agreed. I lost the moon as I tried to focus on other ships. Modahl turned the *Witch* 180 degrees and motored back south. This time the harbor was on my side.

"See anything that looks like a carrier?" he asked.

"I'm looking." Destroyer, destroyer, maybe a small cruiser . . . more destroyers. A sub. No, two subs.

"Two subs, no carrier," I said, still scanning.

"I'd like to bomb a carrier before I die," Modahl muttered. Everyone on the circuit heard that, of course, and I thought he should watch his lip. No use getting the crew in a sweat. But it was his crew, so I let the remark go by.

"The biggest ship I see is the cruiser in the center," I said, and handed back the glasses.

"Surrounded by cans. When they hear us, everyone opens fire, and Vesuvius will erupt under our ass."

"We can always do a destroyer. We can send one or two to the bottom. They are excellent targets."

"I know."

We turned and motored north again. He waited until the moonlight reflected on the harbor and studied it again with the binoculars. Pottinger was standing behind us. He didn't say anything, kept bent over so he could look out at the harbor.

"The cruiser," Modahl said with finality. He told the crew, as if they didn't know, "We are off Rabaul harbor. The Japs have twenty-three ships there, one of which appears to be a cruiser. Radio, send off a contact report. When you're finished we'll attack."

"What do you want me to say, Mr. Modahl?"

"Just what I said. Twenty-three ships, et cetera."

"Yes, sir."

"Tell me when you have an acknowledgment."

The cruiser lay at a forty-five-degree angle to the moonpath, which had to be the direction of our approach since we were bombing visually. To maximize our chances of getting a hit, we should train off the four bombs, that is, drop them one at a time with a set interval between them—we were going to try to drop the bomb that had hung on the rack at Buka. On the other hand, we could do the most damage if we salvoed all four bombs right down the smokestack. The obvious compromise was to salvo them in pairs with an appropriate interval between pairs—that was Modahl's choice. He didn't ask anyone's opinion; he merely announced how we were going to do it.

Hoffman consulted the chart. If we managed to get up to 250 mph at weapons release, an interval of two-tenths of a second would give us seventy-five feet between salvos. Modahl knew the math cold and gave his approval. Hoffman set two-tenths of a second on the intervalometer.

"How low are you going to go?" Pottinger asked. The cockpit lights reflected in the sweat on his face.

"As low as possible."

"We're going to get caught in the bombs' blast."

"Every foot of altitude increases our chances of missing."

"And of getting home," Pottinger said flatly.

"Get back to your station," Modahl snapped. "The enemy is there, and I intend to hit him."

"I'm merely pointing out the obvious."

"Take it up with Commander Jones the next time you see him."

"*If* I see him."

"Goddamn it, Pottinger! That's *enough*! Get back to your station and shut the fuck up."

The crew heard this exchange, which was one reason Modahl was so infuriated. Right then I would have bet serious money that Modahl and Pottinger would never again fly together.

We flew inbound at three thousand feet. Modahl had climbed higher so he could dive with the engines at idle and still get plenty of airspeed. I was used to the speed of the Dauntless, so motoring inbound toward the proper dive point—waiting, waiting, waiting—was like having poison ivy and being unable to scratch.

"Now," he said, finally, and we both pushed forward on the yokes as he pulled the throttles and the prop levers back. The engines gurgled . . . and the airspeed began increasing. Modahl ran the trim forward. Down we swooped, accelerating ever so slowly.

The cruiser was dead ahead, anchored, without a single light showing. The black shapes on the silver water, the darkness of the land surrounding the bay, the moon and stars above . . . it was like something from a dream. Or a nightmare.

I called the altitudes. "Nineteen, eighteen, seventeen . . ."

He pushed harder on the yoke, ran the nose trim full down. Speed passing 180, 190 . . .

Every gun in the Jap fleet opened fire, all at once.

"Holy . . . !"

Fortunately, they were all firing straight up or randomly. Nothing aimed our way.

The tracers were so bright I would clearly see everything in the cockpit. The Japs had heard us—they just didn't know where we were. Why they didn't shoot away from the moon was a mystery to me.

"Eleven . . . ten . . . nine . . ."

Even the shore batteries were firing. The whole area was erupting with tracers. And searchlights. Four searchlights came on, began waving back and forth.

A stream of weaving tracers from one of the destroyers flicked our way . . . and I felt the blows as three or four shells hit us trip-hammer fast.

"Five . . . four . . ."

Modahl was flattening out now, pulling on the yoke with all his strength as the evil black shape of the Japanese cruiser rushed toward us. The airspeed indicator needle quivering on 255 . . .

"Three . . ."

"Help me!" he shouted, and lifted his feet to the instrument panel for more leverage.

I grabbed the yoke, braced myself, and pulled. The altimeter passed two hundred . . . I knew there was some lag in the instrument, so we had to be lower . . . The nose was coming up, passing one hundred . . .

We were going to crash into the cruiser! I pulled with all my strength.

"Now!" Modahl shouted, so loud Hoffman could have heard it without earphones.

I felt the bombs come off; two sharp jolts. Dark as it was, I glimpsed the mast of the cruiser as we shot over it, almost close enough to touch.

As that sight registered, the bombs exploded . . . right under us! The blast lifted us, pushed . . .

Modahl rammed the throttles and props forward to the stops.

The *Witch* wasn't responding properly to the elevators.

"The trim," Modahl said desperately, and I grabbed the wheel and turned it with all my strength. It was still connected, still stiff, so maybe we weren't dead yet.

Just then a searchlight latched on to us, and another. The ghastly glare lit the cockpit.

"Shoot 'em out," Modahl roared to the gunners in the blisters and the tail, who opened fire within a heartbeat.

I was rotating the stiff trim wheel when I felt Modahl push the yoke forward. His hand dropped to mine, stopping the rotation of the trim wheel. Then the fifties in the nose lit off. He had opened fire!

Up ahead . . . a destroyer, shooting in all directions—no, the gunners saw us pinned in the searchlights and swung their guns in our direction!

Modahl held the trigger down—the fifties vibrated like a living thing as we raced toward the destroyer, the engines roaring at full power. With the glare of the searchlight and tracers and all the noise, it looked like we had arrived in hell.

And I could feel shells tearing into us, little thumps that reached me through the seat.

We were rocketing toward the destroyer, which was shooting, shooting, shooting . . .

Another searchlight hit us from the port side, nearly blinding me. Something smashed into the cockpit, the instrument panel seemed to explode. Simultaneously, the bow fifties stopped, and the plane slewed.

Modahl slumped in his seat.

I fought for the yoke, leveled the wings, screamed at that idiot Hoffman to stop firing, because he had opened up with the thirty-caliber as soon as the fifties lit off and was still blazing away, shooting BBs at the elephant: Even though we were pinned like a butterfly in the lights, in some weird way I thought that the muzzle flashes of the little machine gun would give away our position.

My mind wasn't functioning very well. I could hear the fifties in the blisters going, but I shouted, *"Hit the lights, hit the lights"* anyway, praying that the gunners would knock them out before the Japs shot us out of the sky.

We were only a few feet over the black water: The

destroyer was right there in front of us, filling the windscreen, strobing streams of lava-hot tracer. I cranked the trim wheel like a madman, trying to get the nose up.

The superstructure of the destroyer blotted out everything else. I turned the trim wheel savagely to raise the nose and felt something impact the plane as we shot over the enemy ship.

More shells tore at us, then the tracer was arcing over our wings. One by one the lights disappeared—I think our gunners got two of them—and, mercifully, we exited the flak.

The port engine was missing, I was standing on the rudder trying to keep the nose straight, and Modahl was bleeding to death.

He coughed black blood up his throat.

Thank God he was off the controls!

Blood ran down his chest. He reached for me, then went limp.

Three hundred feet, slowing . . . at least we were out of the flak.

The gyro was smashed, the compass frozen: The glass was broken. Both airspeed indicators were shot out, only one of the altimeters worked . . .

Everyone was babbling on the intercom. The cruiser was on fire, someone said, bomb blasts and flak had damaged the tail, one of the gunners was down, shot, and—

Modahl was really dead, covered with blood, his eyes staring at his right knee.

The port engine quit.

Fumbling, I feathered the prop on the port engine. If it didn't feather, we were going in the water. Now.

It must have, because the good engine held us in the sky.

We were flying straight at the black peninsula on the western side of the bay. We were only three hundred feet above the ocean. Ahead were hills, trees, rocks, more flak guns—I twisted the yoke and used the rudder to turn the plane to the east.

We'll go down the channel, I thought, then it will be a straight shot south to Namoia Bay. Some islands north of there—if we can't make it home, maybe we can put down near one.

The gunners lifted and pulled Modahl out of the pilot's seat while I fought to get the *Sea Witch* to a thousand feet.

Varitek had caught a piece of flak, which tore a huge gash in his leg and ripped out an artery. The other guys sprinkled it with sulfa powder and tried to stanch the bleeding . . . I could hear the back-and-forth on the intercom, but they didn't seem to think he had much of a chance.

Dutch Amme climbed into the empty pilot's seat. He surveyed the damage with an electric torch, put his fingers in the hole the shell had made that killed Modahl. There were other holes, five of them, behind the pilot's seat, on the port side. Amazingly, the destroyer hadn't gotten him—someone we had passed had raked us with something about twenty-millimeter size.

"Searchlights . . . That's why Joe Snyder didn't come back."

"Yeah," I said, refusing to break my fierce concentration on the business at hand. I had the Cat out into the channel now, with the dark shape of New Ireland on my left and the hulk of New Britain on the right. From the chart I had seen, that meant we had to be heading south. Only 450 nautical miles to go to safety.

"The hull's tore all to hell," Amme said wearily. "When we land we'll go to the bottom within a minute, I'd say. You'll have to set her down gentle, or we might even break in half on touchdown."

Right! Like I knew how to set her down gently.

Amme talked for a bit about fuel, but I didn't pay much attention. It took all my concentration to hold the plane in a slight bank into the dead engine and keep a steady fifty pounds or so of pressure on the rudder, a task made none the easier by the fact that my hands and feet were still shaking. I wiped my eyes on the rolled-up sleeve of my khaki shirt.

The clouds were gone, and I could use the stars as a heading reference, so at least we were making some kind of progress in the direction we wanted to go.

"Tell radio to send out a report," I told Amme. " 'Searchlights at Rabaul.' Have him put in everything else he can think of."

"Varitek is in no shape to send anything."

"Have Pottinger do it. Anybody who knows some Morse code can send it in plain English."

"You want to claim the cruiser?"

"Have him put in just what we saw. People saw fire. Leave it at that."

"With Mr. Modahl dead . . . it would look good if we claimed the cruiser for him."

"Do like I told you," I snapped. "A hundred cruisers won't help him now. Then come back and help me fly this pig."

Ten minutes later Amme was back. "Some flak hit the radio power supply. We can't transmit."

FIVE

When the sun rose Varitek was dead. The mountains of New Britain were sinking into the sea in our right rear quarter, and ahead were endless sun-speckled sea and open, empty sky. Right then I would have appreciated some clouds. When I next looked back, the mountains were lost in the haze.

Dutch Amme sat in the left seat and I in the right. Both of us exerted pressure on the rudder and worked to keep the *Witch* flying straight. We did that by reference to the sun, which had come up over the sea's rim more or less where we thought it should if we were flying south. As it climbed the sky, we tried to make allowances.

I also kept an eye on the set of the swells, which seemed to show a steady wind from the southeast, a head wind. I flew across the swells at an angle and hoped this course would take us home.

Our airspeed, Amme estimated, was about 80 mph. At this speed, with a little head wind, it would take nearly seven hours to reach Namoia Bay.

Fuel was a problem. I had Amme repeat everything he had told me as we flew down the strait, only this time I listened and asked questions. The left wing had some holes in it, and we had lost gasoline. We were pouring the stuff into the right engine to stay airborne. The upshot of all this was that he thought we could stay up for maybe six hours, maybe a bit less.

"So you're saying we can't make Namoia Bay?"

Amme thrust his jaw out, eyed me belligerently. This, I had learned, was the way he dealt with authority, the world, officers. "That's right, sir. We'll be swimming before we get there."

Of course, the distance and flying time to Namoia Bay were also estimates. Still, running the *Witch* out of gas and making a forced landing in the open sea was a surefire way to die young. I knew just enough about Catalinas to know that even if we survived an open-ocean landing in this swell and were spotted from the air, no sane person would risk a plane and his life attempting to rescue us. Cats weren't designed to operate in typical Pacific rollers in the open sea.

If we couldn't make Namoia Bay, we needed a sheltered stretch of water to land on, the lee of an island or a lagoon or bay.

There were islands ahead, some big, some small, all covered with inhospitable jungle.

Then there was Buna, on the northern shore of the New Guinea peninsula.

"What about Buna?" I asked Amme and Pottinger, who was standing behind the seats. "Can we make it?"

"The Japs are still in Buna," Amme said.

"I heard they left," Pottinger replied.

"I'd hate to get there and find out you heard wrong," Amme shot back.

So much for Buna.

I had Pottinger sit in the right seat while I took a break to use the head. The interior of the plane was drafty, and when I saw the hull, I knew why. Damage was extensive, apparently from flak and the bomb blasts. Gaping holes, bent plates and stringers . . . I could look through the holes and see the sun reflecting on the ocean. The air whistling up through the wounds made the hair on the back of my head stand up. When we landed, we'd be lucky if this thing stayed above water long enough for us to get out of it. Hell, we'd be lucky if it stayed in one piece when it hit the water.

As I stood there looking at the damage, feeling the slipstream coming through the holes, I couldn't help thinking that this adventure was going to cement my reputation as a Jonah with the dive-bomber guys. They were going to put me in the park for the pigeons. Which pissed me off a little, though there wasn't a damn thing I could do about it.

Varitek's and Modahl's corpses lay in the walkway in the center compartment. I had to walk gingerly to get around. Just seeing them hit me hard. The way it looked, this plane was going to be their coffin. Somehow that seemed appropriate. I had hopes the rest of us could do better, though I was pretty worried.

When I got back to the cockpit I stood behind Amme and Pottinger, who were doing as good a job of wrestling this flying pig southward as I had. Still, they wanted me to take over, so I climbed back in the right seat. Amme suggested the left, but I was used to using the prop and throttle controls with my left hand and the stick with my right, so figured I would be most comfortable with that arrangement.

Someone opened a box or two of C rations, and we ate ravenously. With two guys dead, you think we'd have lost our appetites, but no.

Amme:

We were in a heap of hurt. We were in a shot-up, crippled, hunk-of-junk airplane in the middle of the South Pacific, the most miserable real estate on the planet, and our pilot had never landed a seaplane in his life. Jesus! The other guys pretended that things were going to work out, but I had done the fuel figures, and I knew. We weren't going to make it, even if this ensign was God's other son.

I tried to tell the ensign and Pottinger; those two didn't seem too worried. Officers! They must get a lobotomy with their commission.

Lieutenant Modahl was the very worst. Goddamned idiot. The fucking guy thought he was bulletproof and lived it that way . . . until the Japs got him. Crazy or brave, dead is dead.

The truth is we were all going to end up dead, even me, and I wasn't brave or crazy.

Pottinger:

The crackers in the C rations nauseated me. The only gleam of hope in this whole mess was the right engine, which ran like a champ. Not enough gas, this little redheaded fool ensign for a pilot, a damaged hull . . .

Funny how a man's life can lead to a mess like this. Just two years ago I was studying Italian art at Yale . . .

Searchlights! The Japs rigged up searchlights to kill Black Cats. They probably nailed Snyder with them, and miracle of miracles, here came another victim. Those Americans!

Modahl. A braver man never wore shoe leather. I tried not to look at his face as we laid him out in back and covered him with his flight jacket.

In a few hours or days we'd all be as dead as Modahl and Varitek. I knew that, and yet, my mind refused to accept the reality. Wasn't that odd?

Or was it merely human?

"We're going to have to ditch somewhere," I told everyone on the intercom. "Everyone put on a life vest now. Break out the emergency supplies and the raft, get everything ready so when we go in the water we can get it out of the plane ASAP."

They knew what to do, they just needed someone to tell them to do it. I could handle that. After Amme got his vest on, I put on mine and hooked up the straps.

I had Pottinger bring the chart. I wanted a sheltered stretch of water to put the plane in beside an island we could survive on. And the farther from the Japs the better.

One of the Trobriand Islands. Which one would depend upon our fuel.

We were flying at about a thousand feet. Without the altimeter all I could do was look at the swells and guess. The higher we climbed, the more we could see, but if a Japanese fighter found us, our best defense was to fly just above the water to prevent him from completing firing passes.

I looked at the sun. Another two hours, I decided, then we would climb so we could see the Trobriand Islands from as far away as possible.

As we flew along I found myself thinking about Oklahoma when I was a kid, when my dad and sister and I were still living together. I couldn't remember what my mother looked like; she died when I was very young. I remembered my sister's face, though. Maybe she resembled Mama.

The island first appeared as a shadow on the horizon, just a darkening of that junction of sea and sky. I turned the plane ten degrees right to hit it dead on.

The minutes ticked away as I stared at it, wondering. Finally I checked my watch. Five hours. We had attacked the harbor five hours earlier.

Ten minutes later I could definitely see that it was an island, a low green thing, little rise on the spine, which meant it wasn't coral.

Pottinger was in the left seat at that time, so I pointed it out to him. He merely stared, didn't say anything. About that time Dutch Amme came down from the flight engineer's station and announced that the temps were rising on the starboard engine.

"And we're running out of gas. An hour more, at the most."

I pointed out the island to him, and he had to grab the back of the seat to keep from falling.

In less than a minute we had everyone trooping up to the cockpit to take a look. Finally, I ran them all back to their stations.

That island looked like the promised land.

Pottinger:

A miracle, that was what it was. We were delivered. We were going to make it, going to live. Going to have some tomorrows.

I didn't know whether to laugh or cry. The island was there, yet it was so far away. We would reach it, land in the lee, swim ashore . . .

Please God, let us live. Let me and these others live to marry and have children and contribute something to the world.

Hear me. Let us do this.

Hoffman:

I was so happy I couldn't stand still. I wanted to pound everyone on the back. Sure, I had been fighting despair, telling myself we weren't going to die when I really figured we might. The hull was a sieve—when the ensign set the *Witch* in the water we were going to have to get out as it sank. I knew that, everyone did. And still, *now* we had a chance.

"Fighter!"

One of the guys in the blisters saw it first and called it.

"A float fighter."

I rolled the trim over a bit, got us drifting downward toward the water. The elevator control cables had been damaged in the bomb blast. The trim wheel was the only reason we were still alive.

"He hasn't seen us yet. Still high, crossing from starboard to port behind us, heading nearly east it looks like."

After a bit, "Okay, he's three miles or so out to the east, going away. Never saw us."

The Japanese put some of their Zeros on floats, which made a lot of sense since the Zero had such great range. The float fighters could be operated out of bays and lagoons where airfields didn't exist and do a nice job of patrolling vast expanses of ocean. The performance penalty they paid to carry the floats was too great to allow them to go toe-to-toe with land or carrier-based fighters. They could slice and dice a Catalina, though.

"Shit, it's coming back."

I kept the Cat descending. We were a couple hundred feet above the water, far too high. I wanted us right on the wavetops.

"He's coming in from the port stern quarter, curving, coming down, about a half mile . . ."

I could hear someone sobbing on the intercom.

"I don't know who's making that goddamn noise," I said, "but it had better stop."

We were about a hundred feet high, I thought, when the float fighter opened fire. I saw his shells hit the water in front of us and heard the fifty in the port blister open up with a short burst. And another, then a long rolling blast as the plane shuddered from the impact of cannon shells.

The fighter pulled out straight ahead, so he went over us and out to my right. He flew straight until he was well out of range of our gun in the starboard blister, then initiated a gentle turn to come around behind.

"Anybody hurt?" I asked.

"He ripped the port wing, which is empty," Dutch Amme said.

"Good shooting, since he had to break off early."

I was down on the water by then, very carefully working the trim. I didn't have much altitude control remaining—if we hit the water at speed our problems would be permanently over.

I thought about turning into this guy when he committed himself to one side or the other. The island dead ahead had me paralyzed though. There it was, a strip of green between sea and sky. Instinctively, I knew that it was our only hope, and I didn't want to waste a drop of gas in my haste to get there.

Perhaps I could skid the plane a little to try to throw off the Zero pilot's aim. I fed in some rudder, twisted the yoke to hold it level.

And the lousy crate began sinking. We bounced once on a swell and that damn near did it for us right there. We lost some speed and hung right on the ragged edge of a stall. Long seconds crept by before we accelerated enough for me to exhale. By then I had the rudder where it belonged, but it was a close thing. At least the plane didn't come apart when it kissed the swell.

Pottinger was hanging on for dear life. "Don't kill us," he pleaded.

On the next pass the Zero tried to score on the starboard engine, the only one keeping us aloft. I could feel the shells slamming into us, tearing at the area just behind the cockpit. Instinctively I ducked my head, trying to make myself as small as possible.

I could hear one of the waist fifties pounding.

"Are you gunners going to shoot this guy or let him fuck us?"

With us against the water, the Zero couldn't press home his attacks, but he was hammering us good before he had to break off.

"He holed the right tank," Amme shouted. "We're losing fuel."

Oh, baby!

"He's streaming fuel or something," Hoffman screamed. "You guys hit him that last pass."

They all started talking at once. I couldn't shut them up.

"If he's crippled, the next pass will be right on the water, from dead astern," I told Pottinger. "He'll pour it to us."

"Naw. He'll head for home."

"Like hell. He'll kill us or die trying. That's what I'd do if I were him."

Sure enough, the enemy fighter came in low so he could press the attack and break off without hitting the ocean. He was directly behind, dead astern, so both the blister gunners cut loose with their fifties. Short bursts, then longer as he closed the distance.

Someone was screaming on the intercom, shouting curses at the Jap, when the intercom went dead.

I could feel the cannon shells punching home—the cannons in Zeros had low cyclic rates; I swear every round this guy fired hit us. One fifty abruptly stopped firing. The other finished with a long buzz saw burst, then the Zero swept overhead so close I could hear the roar of his engine. At that point it was running better than ours, which was missing badly.

I glanced up in time to see that the enemy fighter was trailing fire. He went into a slight left turn and gently descended until he hit the ocean about a mile from us. Just a little splash, then he was gone.

Our right engine still ran, though fuel was pouring out of the wing. As if we had any to spare.

The island lay dead ahead, but oh, too far, too far.

Now the engine began missing.

We'd never make it. Never.

Coughing, sputtering, the engine wasn't developing enough power to hold us up.

I shouted at Pottinger to hang on, but he had already let go of the controls and braced himself against the instrument panel. As I rolled the trim nose up, I gently retarded the throttle.

Just before we kissed the first swell the engine quit dead. We skipped once, I rolled the trim all the way back, pulled the yoke back even though the damn cables were severed, and the *Sea Witch* pancaked. She must have stopped dead in about ten feet. I kept traveling forward until my head hit the instrument panel, then I went out.

Pottinger:

The ensign wasn't strapped in. In all the excitement he must have forgotten. The panel made a hell of a gash in his forehead, so he was out cold and bleeding profusely.

The airplane was settling fast. I opened the cockpit hatch and pulled him out of his seat. I couldn't have gotten him up through the hatch if Hoffman hadn't come up to the cockpit. The ensign weighed about 120, which was plenty, let me tell you. It was all Hoffman and I could do to get him through the hatch, then we hoisted ourselves through.

The top of the fuselage was just above water. It was a miracle that the Jap float fighter didn't set us on fire, and he probably would have if we had been carrying more fuel.

"What about the others?" I asked Hoffman.

"Huntington is dead. The Zero got him. So is Amme. I don't know about Tucker or Svenson."

We were about to step off the bow to stay away from the props when a wave swept us into the sea. I popped the cartridges to inflate my vest, then struggled with the ensign's. I also had to tighten the straps of his vest, then attend to mine—no one ever put those things on tightly enough. I was struggling to do all this and keep our heads above water when I felt something hit my foot.

The ensign was still bleeding, and these waters were full of sharks. A wave of panic swept over me, then my foot hit it again. Something solid. I put my foot down.

The bottom. I was standing on the bottom with just my nose out of the water.

"Hoffman! Stand up!"

We were inside the reef. A miracle. Delivered by a miracle. The ensign had gotten us just close enough.

The *Sea Witch* refused to go under, of course, because she was resting on the bottom. Her black starboard wingtip and vertical stabilizer both protruded prominently from the water.

When we realized the situation, Hoffman worked his way aft and checked on the others. He found three bodies.

We had to get ashore, so we set out across the lagoon toward the beach, walking on the bottom and pulling the ensign, who floated in his inflated life vest.

"He took a hell of a lick," I told Hoffman.

"Maybe he'll wake up," Hoffman said, leaving unspoken the other half of it, that maybe he wouldn't.

Hoffman:

The only thing that kept me sane was taking care of the ensign as we struggled over the reef.

Maybe he was already dead, or dying. I didn't know. I tried not to think about it. Just keep his head up.

Oh, man. I couldn't believe they were all dead—Lieutenant Modahl, Chief Amme, Swede Svenson, Tucker, Huntington, Varitek. I tried not to think about it and could think of nothing else. All those guys dead!

We were next. The three of us. There we were, castaways on a jungle island in the middle of the ocean and not another soul on earth knew. How long could a guy stay alive? We'd be ant food before anyone ever found us. If they did.

Of course, if the Japs found us before the Americans, we wouldn't have to worry about survival.

Pottinger:

Fighting the currents and swells washing over that uneven reef and through the lagoon while dragging the ensign was the toughest thing I ever had to do. The floor of the lagoon was uneven, with holes in it, and sometimes Hoffman and I went under and fought like hell to keep from drowning.

We must have struggled for an hour before we got to knee-deep water, and another half hour before we finally dragged the ensign and ourselves up on the beach. We lay there gasping, desperately thirsty, so exhausted we could scarcely move.

Hoffman got to his knees, finally, and looked around. The beach was a narrow strip of sand, no more than ten yards wide; the jungle began right at the high-water mark.

At his urging we crawled into the undergrowth out of sight. The ensign we dragged. He was still breathing, had a pulse, and thank God the bleeding had stopped, but he didn't look good.

The *Witch* was about a mile out on the reef. The tail stuck up prominently like an aluminum sail.

"I hope the Japs don't see that," Hoffman remarked.

"If we can't find water, it won't matter," I told him. "We'll be praying for the Japs to come along and put us out of our misery."

After some discussion, he went one way down the beach and I went the other. We were looking for fresh water, a stream running into the sea . . . something.

At some point I became aware that I was lying in sand . . . in shade . . . in wet clothes . . . with bugs and gnats and all manner of insects eating on me.

My head was splitting, so I didn't pay much attention to the bugs, though I knew they were there.

I managed to pry my eyes open . . . and could barely make out light and darkness. I thrashed around a while and dug at my eyes and rubbed at the bugs and passed out again.

The second time I woke up it was dark. My eyes were better, I thought, yet there was nothing to see. I could hear waves lapping nervously.

The thought that we had made it to the island hit

me then. I lay there trying to remember. After a while most of the flight came back, the flak in the darkness, the Zero on floats, settling toward the water with one engine dead and the other dying . . .

I became aware that Pottinger was there beside me. He had a baby bottle in his survival vest, which he had filled with freshwater. He let me drink it. I have never tasted anything sweeter.

Then he went away, back for more I guess.

After a while I realized someone else was there. It took me several minutes to decide it was Hoffman.

"Are we the only ones alive?" I asked, finally.

"Yes," Hoffman said.

SIX

The next day, our first full day on the island, I was feeling human again, so Pottinger, Hoffman and I went exploring. Fortunately, my head wasn't bleeding, and the headache was just that, a headache. We had solid land—okay, sand—under our feet, and we had a chance. Not much of one, but a chance. I was still wearing a pistol, and all of us had knives.

We were also hungry enough to eat a shoe.

We worked our way east along the beach, taking our time. As we walked we discussed the situation. Hoffman was for going out to the plane and trying to salvage a survival kit; Pottinger was against it. There was a line of thunderstorms off to the east and south that seemed to be coming our way. Still hours away, the storms were agitating the swells. Long, tall rollers crashed on the reef, and smaller swells swept through the lagoon.

Watching the swells roll through the shallows, I thought the wreck of the *Sea Witch* too far away and the water too dangerous. Then we saw a group of shark fins cruising along, and the whole idea of going back to the plane sort of evaporated. We certainly needed the survival kits; we were just going to have to wait for a calmer day.

I had seen the island from the air, though at a low angle, and knew it wasn't small. Trying to recall, I estimated it was eight or nine miles long and a mile wide at the widest part. Probably volcanic in origin, the center of the thing reached up a couple hundred feet or so in elevation, if my memory was correct. I remembered the little hump that I flew toward when we were down low against the sea.

The creeks running down from that rocky spine contained good water, so we wouldn't die of thirst. There was food in the sea, if we could figure out a way to get it. There were things to eat—birds and snakes and such—in the jungle, if we could catch them. All in all, I figured we could make out.

If there weren't any Japs on this island.

That was our immediate concern, so we hiked along, taking our time, looking and listening.

On the eastern end of the island the jungle petered out into an area of low scrub and sand dunes. It was getting along toward the middle of the day, so we sat to rest. After all I had been through, I could feel my own weakness, and I was sure the others could also. But sitting wasn't getting us anyplace, so we dusted our fannies and walked on.

The squall line was almost upon us when we found the first skid mark on the top of a dune.

"Darn if that furrow doesn't look like it was made by the keel of a seaplane," Hoffman said.

I took a really good look, and I had to agree.

I took out my pistol and worked the action, jacked

a shell into my hand. The gun was gritty, full of sand and sea salt.

"Going to rain soon," Pottinger said, looking at the sky.

"Let's see if we can find a dry place and sit it out," I said, looking around. I spotted a clump of brush under a small stand of palms, and headed for it. The others were in no hurry, although the gray wall of rain from the storm was nearly upon us.

"Maybe it's Joe Snyder's crew, where he went down in *Charity's Sake.*"

"Maybe," I admitted.

"Let's go look." If Hoffman had had a tail, he would have wagged it.

"Later."

"Hell, no matter where we hide, we're going to get wet. If it's them, they've got food, survival gear, all of that."

"Could be Japs, you know."

He was sure the Japanese didn't leave a seaplane mark.

The first gust of rain splattered us.

"I'm going to sit this one out," I said, and turned back toward the brush I had picked out. Pottinger was right behind.

Hoffman ran up beside me. "Please, sir. Let me go on ahead for a look."

I looked at Pottinger. He was a lieutenant (junior grade), senior to me, but since I was the deputy plane commander, he hadn't attempted to exert an ounce of authority. Nor did I think he wanted to.

"No," I told Hoffman. "The risk is too great. The Japs won't want to feed us if they get their hands on us."

"They won't get me."

"No."

"You're just worried I'll tell 'em you're here."

"If they catch you, kid, it won't matter what you tell 'em. They'll come looking for us."

"Mr. Pottinger." Hoffman turned to face the jaygee. "I appeal to you. All our gear is out in the lagoon. You know the guys in *Charity's Sake* as well as I do."

Pottinger looked at me and he looked at Hoffman and he looked at the squall line racing toward us. He was tired and hungry and had never made a life-or-death decision in his life.

"Snyder could have made it this far," he said to me.

"There's a chance," I admitted.

He bit his lip and made his decision. "Yes," he told the kid. "But be careful, for Christ's sake."

Hoffman grinned at Pottinger and scampered away just as the rain hit. I jogged over to the brush I had seen and crawled in. It wasn't much shelter. Pottinger joined me.

"It's probably Snyder," he said, more to himself than to me.

"Could be anybody."

There was a little washout under the logs. We huddled there.

"Hoffman's right about one thing," I told Pottinger. "We won't be much drier here than if we had stayed out in it."

While it rained I field-stripped the Colt and cleaned the sand and grit out of it as best I could, then put it back together and reloaded it. It wasn't much of a weapon, but it was something. I had a feeling we were going to need everything we had.

After the squall had passed, the fresh wind felt

good. We sat on a log and let the wind dry us out.

We were alive, and the others were dead. So the wind played with our hair as we looked at the sea and sky with living eyes.

For how long?

I had seen much of death these last few months, had killed a few men myself . . . and oh, it was ugly. Ugly!

Anyone who thinks war is glorious has never seen a fresh corpse.

Yet we kill each other, ruthlessly, mercilessly, without qualm or remorse, all for the greater glory of our side.

Insanity. And this has been the human experience since the dawn of time.

Musing thus, I kept an eye out for Hoffman. He didn't come back. After an hour I was worried.

Pottinger was worried, too. "This isn't good," he said.

We waited another hour, a long, slow hour as the rain squall moved on out over the lagoon, and the sun came boiling through the dissipating clouds. Extraordinary how hot the tropical sun can get on bare skin.

The minutes dragged. My head thumped and my stomach tied itself into a knot. I wanted water badly.

One thing was certain; we couldn't stay put much longer. We needed to get about the business of finding drinkable water and something to eat.

"I guess I fucked that up," Pottinger said.

"Let's follow the keel mark," I suggested.

We didn't walk, we sneaked along, all bent over, even crawled through one place where the green stuff was thin. Hoffman's tracks were still visible in places, only partially obliterated by the rain. And so were the scrapes of the flying boat's keel, deep cuts in the sand where it touched, skipped, then touched again. The plane had torn the waist-high brush out of the ground everywhere it touched. Still, there was enough of it standing that it limited our visibility. And the visibility of the Japs, if there were Japs.

The thought had finally occured to Pottinger that if we could follow Hoffman, someone else could backtrack him. He was biting his lip so tightly that blood was leaking down his chin. His face was paper white.

The pistol felt good in my hand.

We had gone maybe a quarter of a mile when we saw the reflection of the sun off shiny metal. We got behind some brush and lay on the ground.

"That's no black Catalina," I whispered to Pottinger, who nodded.

Screwing up our courage, we crawled a few more yards on our hands and knees. Finally we came to the place where we could clearly see the metal, which turned out to be the twin tails of a large airplane. Japanese. The rest of the airplane appeared to be behind some trees and brush, partially out of sight.

"A Kawanishi flying boat," Pottinger whispered into my ear. "A Mavis." He was as scared as I was.

"I'm sorry," he said, his voice quavering. "You were right, and I was wrong. Letting Hoffman go running off alone was a mistake."

"Don't beat yourself up over it," I told him. "There aren't many right or wrong decisions. You make the best choice you can because the military put you there and told you to decide, then we all get on with it."

"Yeah."

"You gotta remember that none of this matters very much."

"Ahh . . ."

"You stay here. I'll go see what Hoffman's gotten himself into."

I wasn't going to go crawling over to that plane. Hoffman had probably done that. His tracks seemed to go that way. I set off at a ninety-degree angle, crawling on my belly, the pistol in my right hand.

When I'd gone at least a hundred yards, I turned to parallel the Mavis's landing track. After another hundred yards I heard voices. I froze.

They were speaking Japanese.

I lay there a bit, trying to see. The voices were demanding, imperious.

Taking my time, staying on my stomach, I crawled closer.

I heard Hoffman pleading, begging. "Don't hit me again, for Christ's sake." And a chunk of something heavy hitting flesh.

Ooh boy!

When they were finished with Hoffman, they were going to come looking for Pottinger and me. If they weren't already looking.

I had to know how many of them there were.

I crawled closer, trying to see around the roots of the grass bunches that grew on the dunes.

The Mavis had four engines, one of which was blackened and scorched. Either it caught fire in the air, or someone shot it up.

Finally I got to a place where I could see the men standing in a circle.

There were four of them. They were questioning Hoffman in Japanese. A lot of good that would do.

I never met an American sailor who understood a word of it.

The Japs were taking turns beating Hoffman with a club of some kind. Clearly, they were enjoying it.

The Mavis was pretty torn up. Lots of holes, maybe fifty-caliber. It looked to me like a Wildcat or Dauntless had had its way with it.

I kept looking around, trying to see if there were any more Japs. Try as I might, I could see only those four. Two of them had rifles though.

About then they whacked Hoffman so hard he passed out. One of them went for water, dumped it on him to bring him around. Another, decked out in an officer's uniform, went over to a little pile of stuff under a palm tree and pulled out a sword.

They were going to chop off the kid's head.

Shit!

I should never have let him go trooping off by himself.

The range was about forty yards. I steadied that pistol with a two-hand grip and aimed it at the Jap with the rifle who was facing me. I wanted him first.

I took my time. Just put that front sight on his belt buckle and squeezed 'er off like it was Tuesday morning at the range. I knocked him off his feet.

I didn't have the luxury of time with the second one. I hit him, all right, probably winged him. The other one with the rifle went to his belly and was looking around, trying to see where the shots were coming from. I only had his head and one arm to shoot at, so I took a deep breath, exhaled, and touched it off. And got him.

The officer with the sword had figured out where I was by that time and was banging at me with a pistol.

I rolled away. Got to my feet and ran, staying as low as possible, ran toward the tail of the Mavis while the officer popped off three in my direction.

"How many of them were there, Hoffman?" I roared, loud as I could shout.

"Four," he answered, then I heard another shot.

I ran the length of the flying boat's fuselage, sneaked a peek around the bow. Hoffman lay sprawled in the dirt, blood on his chest, staring fixedly at the sky.

The Jap bastard had shot him!

I sneaked back along the hull of the Mavis, thinking the guy might follow me around.

Finally, I wised up. I got down on my belly and crawled away from the Mavis.

I figured the Jap officer wanted one of those rifles as badly as I did, and that was where he'd end up. I went out about a hundred yards and got to my feet. Staying bent over as much as possible, I trotted around to where I could see the Japs I had shot.

The officer wasn't in sight. I figured he was close by anyway.

I lay down behind a clump of grass, thought about the situation, wondered what to do next.

I had just about made up my mind to crawl out of there and set up an ambush down the beach when something whacked me in the left side so hard I almost lost consciousness.

Then I heard the shot. A rifle.

With what was left of my strength, I pulled my right hand under me. Then I lay still.

I was hit damned bad. As I lay there the shock of the bullet began wearing off and the pain started way up inside me.

I tried not to breathe, not to move, not to do

anything. It was easy. I could feel the legs going numb, feel the life leaking out.

For the longest time I lay there staring at the sand, trying not to blink.

I heard him, finally. Heard the footfall.

He nudged me once with the barrel of his rifle, then used his foot to turn me over.

A look of surprise registered on his face when I shot him.

Pottinger:

I heard the shots, little pops on the wind, then silence. After a while another shot, louder, then twenty minutes or so later, one more, muffled.

After that, nothing.

Of course I had no way of knowing how many Japanese there were, what had happened, if Hoffman or the ensign were still alive . . .

I wanted desperately to know, but I couldn't make myself move. If I just sat up, I could see the tail of the Mavis . . . and they might see me.

I huddled there frozen, waiting for Hoffman and the ensign to come back. I waited until darkness fell.

Finally, I slept.

The next morning nothing moved. I could hear nothing but the wind. After a couple of hours I knew I was going to have to take a chance. I had to have food. I tried to move and found I couldn't. Another hour passed. Then another. Ashamed of myself and nauseated with fear, I crawled.

I found them around the Japanese flying boat, all dead. The four Japanese and the two

Americans. The Japanese officer was lying across the ensign.

There was food, so I ate it. The water I drank.

I put them in a row in the sand and got busy on a grave. I shouldn't have let Hoffman go exploring. I should be lying there dead instead of the ensign.

Digging helped me deal with it.

The trouble came when I had to drag them to the grave. I was crying pretty badly by then, and the ensign and Hoffman were just so much dead meat. And starting to swell up. I tried not to look at their faces . . . and didn't succeed.

I dragged the two Americans into the same hole and filled it in the best I could.

I was shaking by then, so I set to digging on a bigger hole for the Japanese. It was getting dark by the time I got the bodies in that hole and filled it and tamped it down.

The next day I inventoried the supplies in the Mavis. There was fishing gear, canned food, bottled water, pads to sleep on, blankets, an ax, matches.

After I'd been on the island about a week I decided to burn the Mavis. The fuel tanks were shot full of holes and empty, which was probably why the Mavis was lying on this godforsaken spit of sand in the endless sea.

It took two days of hard work to load the fuselage with driftwood. I felt good doing it, as if I were accomplishing something important. Looking back, I realize that I was probably half-crazy at that time, irrational. I ate the Japanese rations, worked on stuffing the Mavis with driftwood, watched the sky, and cried uncontrollably every now and then.

By the end of the second day I had the plane fairly full of driftwood. The next morning at dawn I built a fire in there with some Japanese matches and rice paper. The metal in the plane caught fire about an hour later and burned for most of the day. I got pretty worried that evening, afraid that I had lit an eternal flame to arouse Japanese curiosity. The fire died, finally, about midnight, though it smoldered for two more days and nights. Thank God I had been sane enough to wait for morning to light it.

With the fire finally out, I packed all the supplies I had salvaged from the Mavis and moved four miles along the south side of the island to a spot where a freshwater creek emptied into the sea. It took three trips to carry the loot.

I never did try to cross the lagoon to the wreck of the *Sea Witch.* On one of my exploratory hikes around the island a few weeks later I saw that she was gone, broken up by a storm or swept off the reef into deeper water.

I fell into a routine. Every morning I fished. I always had something by noon, usually before, so I built a fire and cooked it and ate on it the rest of the day. During the afternoon I explored and gathered driftwood, which I piled into a huge pile. My thought was that if and when I saw a U.S. ship or plane, I would light it off as a signal fire. I had a hell of pile collected but finally ran out of matches that would light. The rain and the humidity ruined them. After that I ate my fish raw.

And so my days passed, one by one. I lost

count. There was nothing on the island but the jungle and birds, and wind and rain and surf. And me. Just me and my ghosts alone on that speck of sand and jungle lost in an endless universe of sea and sky.

Later I learned that five months passed before I was rescued by the crew of a U.S. Navy patrol boat searching for a lost aircrew. Not the crew of the *Witch* or *Charity's Sake,* but a B-24 crew that had also disappeared into the vastness of the great Pacific. The war was way north and west by then.

I must have been a sight when they found me, burned a deep brown by the sun and almost naked, with only a rag around my waist. My beard and hair were wild and tangled, and I babbled incoherently.

The Navy sent me back to the States. They kept me in a naval hospital for a while until I sort of got it glued back together. Then they gave me a medical discharge.

Cut off from human contact during those long nights and long, long days on that island, I could never get the ensign and Modahl and the other guys from the *Witch* out of my mind. They have been with me every day of my life since.

I have never figured out why they died and I lived.

To this day I still don't know. It wasn't because I was a better person or a better warrior. They were the warriors—they carried me. They had courage, I didn't. They had faith in each other and themselves, and I didn't. Why was it that they died and I was spared?

The old Vikings would have said that Modahl and the ensign were the lucky ones.

In the years that have passed since I flew in the *Sea Witch* the world has continued to turn, the seasons have come and gone, babies have been born and old people have passed away. The earth continues as before.

As I get older I have learned that the ensign spoke the truth: The fate of individuals matters very little. We are dust on the wind.

V5

DAVID HAGBERG

DAVID HAGBERG is an ex–Air Force cryptographer who has spoken at CIA functions and has traveled extensively in Europe, the Arctic, and the Carribean. He also writes fiction under the pseudonym Sean Flannery and has published more than two dozen novels of suspense, including *White House*, *High Flight*, *Eagles Fly*, *Assassin*, and *Joshua's Hammer*. His writing has been nominated for numerous honors, including the American Book Award, three times for the Edgar Allan Poe Award, and three times for the American Mystery Award. He lives in Florida and has been continuously published for the past twenty-five years.

ONE

MONDAY,
NEW YEAR'S DAY, 1945 • BERLIN

The part that bothered Sarah Winslow most wasn't the spying, it wasn't the sleeping with General Schellenberg, nor was it missing her husband back in London. It was the Allied bombs that rained down on Berlin day and night. She wanted the bombing to continue, to flatten the city to dust. But she was afraid for her life and the lives of some of her neighbors in the apartment buildings just off the Kudamm. She had come to know and respect them even though they were Germans.

She pushed back the covers and slipped silently out of bed. It was an hour before dawn. They'd left the Cowboy Keller at three and come back here because Walther thought that making love in his mistress's tiny apartment up under the eaves would be romantic. And it was.

The bombing was far away just now, on the other

side of the Tiergarten, or maybe out by Tempelhof. The general was sound asleep, one hand thrown across his forehead, the dueling scar down the side of his handsome face fluorescent in the dim nightlight.

Sarah felt an overwhelming sense of guilt. She didn't think that the stench would ever wash off her. When she finally got back home everyone would smell it on her, see it in her eyes, feel it on her skin. She was tan from skiing in the mountains, well-groomed, well clothed, well fed. A major general's whore never went without. Everyone knew.

She padded nude over to the window. A letter opener lay on the small writing table. She looked at it, then back at Walther. It would be so easy to pick up the thing, walk silently back to the bed, and plunge the narrow blade into his heart. One less Nazi on earth.

But she would be arrested and shot or hung. And she would no longer send intelligence home to defeat the bloody bastards. Sometimes she asked herself which would help end the war sooner: Schellenberg's death or her spying? She didn't have the answer.

Snow lay cold and white, masking some of the ugliness of the bombed-out buildings. They'd never turned on the lights, so she'd not put up the blackout curtains. To the northeast she could see flashes as bombs exploded. But there were only a few searchlights tonight. Most of them had been destroyed or damaged beyond repair. And the electricity for them was a problem. There was no petrol to run the portable generators.

She had spent the better part of twelve months in Germany. At twenty-five she felt like an old woman.

Used up. Mind-weary. Cynical. It was the constant fear that she lived with day and night. She was never able to sleep well. She woke several times a night, fearing that she was talking in her sleep. In English. She thought everyone could see the worry lines on her narrow, pretty face. But all they saw was blond hair and blue eyes.

Schellenberg stirred on the bed. "Marta?" he mumbled.

Her British MI6 code name was CECILE, but her work name was Marta Frick. She posed as an American from the Milwaukee Bund. The American-accented German was easy for her, because she'd studied to be a screen actress. A woman of many voices, a director called her. But to her German-born mother, she'd always been *kleine Liebchen,* little darling.

"I have to go to the bathroom, Walther," she replied softly. "Go back to sleep, darling."

Schellenberg turned over on his side and was soon snoring. He always slept for a couple of hours after lovemaking. It gave her time to deal with the guilt.

Serving her God and her King but not her husband. The same thought kept running in her head like a mantra.

Schellenberg was head of the RSHA VI, which was the Nazi Foreign Intelligence and Espionage Service, with offices on Berkaerstrasse here in the city.

He knew things, some of them very frightening things, especially now that the war was almost over and Hitler was becoming increasingly insane and increasingly desperate. When Walther was drunk, and they were in bed, he talked to her. Told her things. Valuable things to prove that he was an important man and to prove that he really did love and trust her. After the war was over they were going to be married, maybe go to America.

Sarah waited a full five minutes to make certain that Schellenberg was asleep before she threw a thin blanket over her narrow shoulders and left the one-room apartment. A dingy corridor ran to the back and up three stairs to the bathroom.

The house was silent. The other boarders lived in the basement, afraid of the bombs, but Sarah insisted on the top floor. Schellenberg thought she was being terribly brave. In actuality she needed the height for her radio aerial.

In the bathroom, she locked the door. She removed a wooden panel from the wall behind the claw-footed tub and pulled out the small suitcase that contained her radio. She worked quickly but efficiently.

One of her problems over the past year, and especially in the past few months, was finding replacement batteries. The last time she had stolen them from the rubble of a newly bombed-out electrical shop. The penalty for looting was immediate execution by firing squad, but so then was the penalty for spying. It was something she thought about constantly. She had almost no illusions left except that she desperately loved her husband, who was a major in the Secret Intelligence Service, and that she desperately missed home, especially at Christmas, with softly falling snow and a roaring fire on the grate, and in the spring, when the countryside came alive.

Sarah opened the suitcase, attached the headphones and telegraph key to the connectors, then opened the tiny window. She clipped the antenna lead to a bare spot on the drain gutter. The building's east–west orientation made the drain gutter a perfect long wire antenna pointing directly at England.

It took a few minutes for the valves to warm up. As she waited she listened for sounds. This was the most dangerous time for her. If someone came now, she would have no explanation for what she was doing.

With the window open, the bathroom became like an icebox. Sarah shivered and held the blanket a little closer with her free hand as she sent her recognition signal and the query that she was ready to send, were they ready to receive?

She switched the set to receive. Almost immediately she got the proper recognition signal and the go-ahead to send.

When they'd gotten back this morning she'd come up here to get ready for bed. Away from Walther for just a few minutes, she managed to encode the information she'd gotten from him. Not being able to send what she had learned last night until now had been frustrating, and she unleashed a torrent of Morse.

The scientists up at the rocket research station at Peenemünde in the Baltic Sea near the Polish border had come up with another wonder weapon. This one was very hush-hush. Even Schellenberg knew only some of the facts even though one of his jobs was to help protect the place from sabotage.

Sarah's fist was fast and very clean. Morse code was something she had taken to naturally. Only the best operators worked with her.

She did not understand some of the technical details that Walther had bragged about, but she had perfect recall. She could repeat lines of meaningless gibberish word for word if need be.

But she did understand enough to know that the Nazis were very excited about a new three-stage liquid-fueled rocket that they called A11. It could fly more than five thousand miles. Across the Atlantic Ocean to the American eastern seaboard.

The problem had been the small payload. The guidance systems had to be very heavy in order to give the rocket any accuracy, which limited how big a weapon could be delivered. Schellenberg's news was that the problem was nearly solved.

"Marta, are you in there?" Schellenberg called softly. He knocked at the door. "What are you doing?"

"I'm sitting on the pot," Sarah replied crossly. "Do you want to come in and watch?" She switched the set off and hurriedly disconnected the leads. Her heart pounded.

"You've been up here half the night. Are you sure that you're all right?"

"I think it's something I ate." She disconnected the aerial lead from the drain gutter, rolled it up, and stuffed it into a compartment in the suitcase. The telegraph key and headset fit next to it. She had to be careful not to make any noise. Her hands shook.

"Is there something I can get you, *Liebchen*?" Schellenberg asked. He knocked at the door again. "I think that you better let me in."

Sarah latched the suitcase, replaced it behind the tub, and set the panel in place. She threw off her blanket, flushed the toilet, waited a few seconds, then unlocked the door and opened it.

Schellenberg stood there, looking at her and the

toilet lid. His eyes went to the open window. "My God, it's cold in here," he said.

Sarah closed the window, then ran water in the sink to wash her hands. "It's either that or the smell, Walther." She smiled at him. "Ladies do it, too, you know."

Schellenberg laughed finally and shook his head. "I didn't know where you'd gotten yourself," he said. "Come back to bed. You must be freezing."

Same Day
Mittelwerke Rocket Factory
Harz Mountains

Benjamin Steinberg was a master machinist and precision parts designer, just as his father had been, and before him his father's father. It was the only reason that a troop transport truck was waiting for him and a few other Jews at the Mount Kohnstein entrance to the vast underground complex.

Most of the twenty-three hundred men and women getting off their ten-hour shifts had to walk eight kilometers back to Nordhausen in the snow and bitter cold because Allied bombing raids had knocked out all the rail lines. Most of those workers were not deemed critical to the war effort, even though some were Aryans, so they walked while Jews rode.

Steinberg stopped at the tunnel exit and looked up at the dull gray overcast morning sky. The war was nearly over. Even isolated here most of them knew it. The two tricks were to survive until the liberation, and to do whatever it took to accelerate the Nazis' defeat.

He had managed to survive so far by being very

good at what he did, and by working wholeheartedly on the new guidance system. He had become indispensable. Even the great Wernher von Braun had come in person to compliment Steinberg on his fine work.

And he was managing the second trick by spying for the Allies. All through the work week he would compile his notes in a day ledger that he and the other machinists and engineers were required to keep. The shift supervisors or key engineers would look over the ledgers on a regular basis to make certain that work was progressing as it should and to clear up problems that might be developing. Steinberg slanted his writing slightly to the left for items he thought would be of interest to the Brits. He had a terrible memory, so if he didn't do it that way, he knew that he would forget half of what he wanted to send.

On Sunday, late in his shift, he would transpose his notes into love letters to a nonexistent wife in Leipzig.

On Monday morning, when his shift was over, he made sure that he rode in the last truck and sat at the very back next to the tailgate. On the way to the workers' compound Steinberg would drop his bundle of love letters at a certain spot near a large tree one hundred meters from the highway to Göttingen.

The arrangement had been made eighteen months ago by one of the other Jewish workers, who disappeared a few weeks later on a Monday, *after* Steinberg had already made his drop. All that week Steinberg lived in fear that Frankel had been arrested by the Gestapo. Under interrogation, the poor man would tell the Nazis everything.

But nothing had come of it, and Steinberg sent his notes the same way the next week. After a while, when nothing happened, he learned to relax, as much as that was possible.

He was surviving, and he was doing his part to shorten the war. That's all he was capable of doing for now.

Steinberg hunched up his coat collar and trudged across the rubble-strewn staging area to the last of the waiting trucks. Most of the incoming shift were already inside, and most of the outgoing shift were on the way back to the camp. The few stragglers gave Steinberg and the other Jews sullen looks.

"Late as always," one of the German guards said crossly to Steinberg.

A couple of the men in the truck reached down and helped him up. He mumbled his thanks as the guard closed and latched the tailgate and signaled to the driver.

There was little or no talking on the drive back because the Germans demanded silence, and everyone was too tired to do much talking anyway. Ten-hour shifts seven days a week in the underground workshops and assembly halls, some of them unheated, sapped a person's energy.

This morning Steinberg had another reason to remain silent. He was frightened. The breakthrough that they'd been working on, the one that they'd hoped would never develop, finally came together by midweek. The lightweight A11 guidance system, which was the key to the entire program, was done. There were only three of them completed, but they were ready for immediate shipment to Peenemünde and installation in the gigantic three-stage rocket.

No one would be safe. Not the British, not the

Russians, not even the Americans. New York and Washington were within reach, and the new guidance system, code-named *Gefühlstoff*, would place the payload within a three-hundred-meter radius after an eight-thousand-kilometer flight.

Steinberg didn't know what the payload would consist of, but everyone, even von Braun when he'd been up here, was respectful when they talked around the subject. Whatever it was had to weigh something in the neighborhood of 350 kilograms, and it would be superdeadly. He got that much.

It was very cold sitting by the tailgate; the canvas flaps would not stay closed. It had snowed steadily for the past three days, and the road was slippery. The truck driver was an old man conscripted just last week, and he wasn't very good.

They topped the hill and started down into the valley. The truck was traveling far too fast for the conditions. A couple of the workers at the front of the truck started banging on the back of the cab for the driver to slow down.

Near the bottom, Steinberg casually let his right hand drape over the edge of the tailgate. As they careened past the tree he tossed his bundle of letters off the side of the road.

The truck lurched sharply to the left as the driver tried to slow for the intersection. Then it fishtailed wildly to the right, sliding toward the edge of the road.

For a breathless moment Steinberg thought that they'd be okay; but the truck's rear wheels caught the edge of the steep ditch, slamming the truck around and sending it over on its side.

Steinberg felt himself being ejected from the back of the truck. He hit the side of the road hard with his left shoulder and tumbled toward the ditch. Before the pain could register, he looked up in time to see the back bumper of the truck coming right at him with the speed of one of the rockets he'd helped build.

Two Days Later
Mosquito Flight 23R
Over the German Baltic Coast

At twelve thousand feet, the De Havilland D.H. 98 Mosquito F.B. Mk VI skimmed just above a solid deck of clouds that spread in all directions to the horizon. The midmorning sun cast weird shadows in the cloud valleys and lit the tops so brightly it was like reflections off a snowfield.

"We're not going to spot a bloody thing up here," Sergeant Tony Ricco, the navigator/photographer said into his throat mike.

Lieutenant Tony Leonard agreed, but orders were orders, and this had come from the brass in London. Churchill wanted pictures. "How near are we?"

"Peenemünde should be five miles to starboard unless my arithmetic is cocked."

The mission was critical, so the "two Tonys" had been slected to fly it. They were the only choice, actually. They had the rare combination of skill and luck. In forty-seven photo recon missions over enemy territory in France, Belgium, Norway, and finally Germany, they'd been attacked numerous times. But they'd never taken so much as a single hit. Not one nick. And they always came back with their pictures.

"In for a penny, in for a pound," Leonard said,

happily. He liked his job. He hauled the twin-engined broad-winged airplane hard to the right, reduced power, and shoved the wheel forward.

The all-wooden medium-duty bomber/recon aircraft responded crisply, almost like a fighter would. Capable of speeds in excess of 375 miles per hour, and with barn-door-sized control surfaces, the *Wooden Wonder,* as it was called, could outperform just about anything flying except for the new Messerschmitt and Heinkel jets. But there weren't many of them around, so running into one of them was generally just a matter of bad luck.

They plunged into the cloud deck and within a few hundred feet everything outside the cockpit turned as dark as night. Snow was thick. Leonard pulled on the carburetor heaters so that the engines would not ice up. Their rpms dropped a couple hundred revs, but they were safely cocooned for the moment, so it didn't matter how fast they flew.

The meteorologists told them that the ceilings could be as low as three hundred feet but certainly no higher than one thousand. Their best bet would have been to look for an opening in the clouds. Short of that they would either have to return home or duck below the clouds and take their chances just off the deck, where they faced the possibility of ground fire and enemy jets. In addition, flying that low did not allow their cameras to see very far. They would have to spend a lot more time searching for what they'd come to snap pictures of.

But the war was almost over. They were dancing in the streets in London. Air recon missions were becoming less hazardous every day, although conditions on the ground for Allied agents in Germany were getting increasingly tough. People were being shot on the spot or taken away to be hanged for the slightest suspicion of a whole host of crimes.

And then there were the wonder weapons. Their experimental designations began with A1, which turned into the V1 buzz bomb, A2, which turned into the V2 supersonic rocket, V3 and V4, which were special types of cannons, and finally to the latest, which was designated A11, for the V5 three-stage rocket. The Germans called them *Vergeltungswaffen*, or vengeance weapons.

Everyone was afraid of them. And that, it was said, included Churchill.

At four thousand feet, Leonard eased back on the stick. By now people on the ground would be hearing their approach. Antiaircraft gun crews would be alerted, and if there were any fighters available, the pilots would be scrambled.

"Stand by," Leonard warned.

"Right," Ricco responded. They didn't talk much during the acquisition stages of the missions. There was no reason for words. They knew their jobs, and they knew what the other would do at each critical moment.

They broke out of the overcast at eight hundred feet, but visibility was down to less than a half mile in heavy snow.

Ricco looked up from his camera eye-sight for just a second. "Shit," he said, then went back to work taking pictures.

Leonard made one pass directly over what was left of the large missile storage building, the oval earthenworks bunker where rockets were tested, and the machine shops and what was left of the research labs. There were people on the ground, scattering for cover. But there didn't seem to be any antiaircraft guns anywhere.

Then they were over a large stand of trees. There were barracks, dining halls, and administrative buildings scattered here and there. But those buildings had suffered a lot of bomb damage. Churchill's orders were to kill the scientists and engineers first, then hit the rockets and rocket factories.

Leonard hauled the Mosquito in a tight turn back the way they had come and made a second pass just east of the oval works. Still there was no ground fire, nor were any fighter aircraft rising off the runway just to the south.

But it might be a moot point, Leonard thought. In this filthy weather they might not get any worthwhile photos.

One mile south, Leonard made a hard turn to port, lining up for a pass a little farther east, where some of the remote test-firing stands had been set up over the past six months. The Germans were doing most of their rocket construction up around Nordhausen, but their static test firings were done down here in the middle of the dense woods.

A dark metal streak dropped out of the clouds ahead of them, turned on a wingtip, and headed right at their windshield at an incredible rate of closure.

Acting on pure instinct Leonard fired two short bursts from his four 20mm Hispano cannons, then broke very hard left as the Messerschmitt jet fighter turned away like a flash of lightning and disappeared back into the clouds.

The jet was very fast, but because of its speed its turning radius was well outside that of the Mosquito's. It was the only advantage Leonard figured they had. That and the clouds just one hundred feet above them. If they could make it that far. But why hadn't the German pilot fired at them?

Leonard spotted what looked like a long bed transport truck off to their right in a small clearing. He turned that way, while at the same time trying to keep an eye out for the jet.

"Looks like the jackpot," he said into his throat mike. "Stand by."

They came across the clearing. Whatever the truck hauled out here was covered by a long tarp. Its narrow, pointed shape was distinctive. And it was very big. A lot larger than the V2.

"I'm on it," Ricco said.

They were on the other side.

"Do you need another pass?" Leonard asked. The jet dropped out of the clouds a half mile off their left wing. "We've got company."

"Time to take the film home," Ricco replied, looking up. He spotted the jet. "Right now, like a chum."

Leonard turned toward the oncoming jet, and started firing his cannons in short, controlled bursts. This time the German pilot did not turn away, nor did he fire.

"He has no ammunition," Leonard said amazed. The bloody fool was trying to ram them. It meant that whatever was lying down there on the truck was important enough for the Messerschmitt pilot to give his life in a suicide crash.

Pieces of the German jet were coming off under Leonard's fire. Still the pilot did not turn away. He actually meant to ram them.

Suddenly, they were so close that Leonard could see the pilot behind his plastic canopy. He got the impression the German was just a kid.

At the last possible moment Leonard hauled back on the stick, and the Mosquito shot up into the cloud deck, the Messerschmitt missing them by less than five feet.

"Did you see the look on that kid's face?" Ricco asked.

"Yeah," Leonard said as he made a lazy turn toward the northwest, where they would cross the Danish peninsula before heading home. "I'm sure he saw the same look on my face."

TWO

Friday • Storey's Gate, Westminster, London

Storey's Gate was one of dozens of governmental and military command installations that had been hastily moved underground during the blitz. This one was the most important, however, because it was where Winston Churchill often worked and slept.

Nearly everyone who operated in these places had done so for four years. All of them had the pale white skin that came from seldom seeing the sun.

That was in sharp contrast to the rugged outdoors look of an American Army Air Corps captain who walked just behind a leaner and older man dressed in the uniform of a U.S. Army colonel.

It was midmorning, overcast and bitterly cold. Everyone moved fast. No one wanted to linger outdoors. Just inside the unmarked entrance of a nondescript building in the middle of the block, their credentials were checked, and both men were frisked for weapons by two tough-looking Scotland Yard heavies who looked as if they ate barbed wire for breakfast.

Captain Richard Scott, Scotty to his friends, had played football for Princeton, lettering all three years he was eligible. At six-foot-two, two hundred pounds, he was much larger than the Brits he worked with, but he admitted to himself that he would not want to go up against either of the guards, even though they looked old enough to be his father.

"Just downstairs to the left, sir," one of the guards politely told Colonel David Bruce.

"Yes, thank you, I've been here before," Bruce said. He was Chief of European Operations for the Office of Strategic Services, America's answer to MI6, Britain's Secret Intelligence Service.

Scotty came across as the typical, young, brash American, while the colonel was considered by the Brits to be a proper gentleman. He was a highly respected attorney, the son of a U.S. senator, and his former wife was one of the richest women in America.

As he'd explained earlier this morning, Scotty wouldn't be allowed through the front door on a mission of this importance without a bit of muscle behind him. The British intelligence establishment was very leery of their American cousins. After all the OSS could trace its roots back only since 1941 while British spies had been at the game nearly four hundred years.

Scotty was to be the field commander on this mission, if MI6 would accept him, and the colonel was to be his headquarters controller, watching his back so that he wouldn't be hung out to dry.

They were met three stories down by a second pair of equally rugged-looking guards, who checked their credentials and frisked them a second time. Churchill was in residence. Whenever he was there the already tight security got extra serious.

Through a steel door they stepped into what might have been a floor of extremely busy offices for a major corporation, except that there were no windows to the outside, and the air smelled like a combination of stale cigars and unwashed bodies.

A youngish, very handsome man with blond hair dressed in an RAF uniform, major's insignia on his collar tabs, bounded down the hall like a rugby player, all smiles, his hand out.

"Colonel Bruce, good of you to come so quickly, sir," he said, shaking hands. He gave Scotty a careful inspection. "This is the lad you've told us about?"

Bruce nodded. "He's my number two for Special Operations. Dick Scott."

"Donald Winslow," the major said. He and Scotty shook hands. "I do hope you know what you're letting yourself in for."

Scotty was mildly irritated by the major's condescending attitude, but he'd been warned. He shook his head. "I wasn't told a thing, except that it's something important to do that needs our help in Germany."

Winslow gave Bruce a look. "Yes, it's certainly important." His eyes narrowed a little. He was like a stage actor, his expressions and gestures all over the place. "On top of that we really don't have much time, I'm afraid. Do let's get on with it, shall we?"

He led them to the end of the long corridor, past large offices teeming with men and women in uniform and in civilian clothes, all busy on telephones or at typewriters, or marking large maps and studying various documents and papers.

They went down another flight of stairs and into a similarly busy group of offices. At the end of this corridor was a large room behind tall glass partitions. One side of the room was dominated by a huge floor-to-ceiling map of England and Europe, while the center of the room was taken up by a very large contour map of the same area. Markers showing ships in the Channel and up in the Baltic, as well as military units—German and Allied—dotted the contour map.

Winslow hesitated long enough for Scott and Bruce to get a brief look, then ushered them into a much smaller, quieter room, with a conference table and a dozen chairs.

Winston Churchill was seated alone at the head of the table, his ever present cigar clamped in his mouth. He looked like an angry bulldog.

Scotty thought that if the British were trying to impress their American cousins, they were doing a good job of it this morning. He stiffened and started to salute, but then noticed that neither the colonel nor Major Winslow was saluting.

"We don't stand on formality here, Captain," Churchill growled. "Have you been briefed on the mission?"

"No, sir," Scott said. Whatever they wanted him to do had to be big; otherwise, they would not have gone to this length to get his attention. Yet the colonel had intimated that the British might not accept him.

Churchill nodded impatiently for Winslow to get on with it.

"Well, the short version is that the Germans have

perfected a new rocket, one they're calling the V5. It's a three-stage monster that can fly nearly fifty miles up and five thousand miles out."

"All the way to Washington and New York," Bruce added.

"Yes," Winslow replied. "All that was holding them back was the guidance system. The old ones were too heavy and too unreliable. But we have two independent confirmations that they've solved that problem. Which leads us to where you come in. We sent a recon plane out to Peenemünde to take a few snaps. We've spotted what we're reasonably sure is one of the V5s on a flatbed truck just east of the research and development labs. It looks as if it's operational. We want you to lead a team over there to destroy the damned things."

"How many are there?" Scotty asked. This wasn't making much sense. Why him? Why an American to head the mission? Not that he minded going. Hell, he'd come over here to fight Germans. But there was more to this story than he'd been told so far.

"Only three of the guidance systems have been built and shipped so far, according to our source," Winslow said.

Scotty glanced at Bruce. "Even if three rockets made it all the way across the Atlantic and fell somewhere in Washington, they wouldn't do much damage. Not enough to end the war." He shook his head. "What do they carry? Five hundred pounds, maybe?"

Winslow looked at Churchill, then back. His face was long. "Actually a bit more than that."

"Of what?"

"Anthrax," Winslow said softly. "One of the little gems the German scientists came up with in the late thirties. It would probably be an aerosol burst of some sort. Quite effective from what I'm told."

Now it made sense. Scotty had graduated summa cum laude from Princeton with a degree in biochemistry. But he did not fit the mold of a scientist. He was more athletic than just about everybody in the field. He was not only to be the technical brains on this mission, he was going to be a part of the muscle.

If the aerosol canisters of germs were already loaded, it would be up to him to render them harmless before they blew up the rockets. There was no telling where the winds might blow the anthrax. But certainly there would be Allied and civilian casualties if they weren't careful.

"Will you do it, Captain?" Churchill asked. "Jerry will know that we're sending somebody."

Scotty looked up out of his thoughts, aware that they were watching him closely. He nodded. "Yes, sir. That's why I put on the uniform."

Churchill handed him a sealed envelope. "Take this; it might help you with our bunch."

FRIDAY AFTERNOON • BLETCHLEY PARK

Scotty arrived at the Government Code and Cipher School fifty miles northwest of London around three o'clock in a blinding snowstorm. Driving up on the wrong side of the narrow, slippery roads was a chore. But after six months in England, driving on the left seemed almost natural.

Pulling up at the gate, he was careful not to make any sudden moves as he rolled down his window. The colonel said that this was the most heavily guarded secret installation in all of England. He didn't want some guard getting twitchy on him. There was a lot of rivalry and pressure between the Brits and the Americans. Especially between the SIS and OSS.

A young kid who didn't look old enough to shave dressed in a Royal Marines uniform came out and checked Scotty's orders. "Just straight up the drive, sir. Someone'll meet you at the front door."

"Thanks," Scotty said.

"Don't stop your car on the way up," the young marine cautioned sternly. "They don't like that."

"I'll keep that in mind," Scotty said. He had a fair idea who the "they" might be. If the colonel was impressed by this place, it must be very important. Colonel Bruce didn't impress very easily.

Scotty liked England. London with its old buildings, rich traditions, and history with the royal family and all. The small towns with their quaint inns, eccentrics, and public houses. He was even getting used to warm beer. But especially he liked the people. They might be insufferable snobs half the time, but they had hung on against Hitler's army and air forces, which had overrun just about all of Europe. He was most impressed by tenacity.

Brits were stubborn. That made him feel right at home. An old spinster aunt called him the most contentious but lovely boy she could imagine.

The main operation of the school was apparently housed in an old Victorian mansion that rose like a pile of rubble from the woods as he approached. But the grounds were dotted with prefab huts, making the place look more like a refugee camp than an important part of England's war effort.

He came around the long circular driveway and stopped his lend-lease Chevy at the foot of broad stairs leading up to the house, just as a young, very attractive woman, lieutenant's bars on her shoulders, came out to greet him.

"You must be Captain Scott," she said warmly. She was small, with a fragile-looking, pretty, round face and very large dark eyes. But she moved with the strength and grace of a dancer or an athlete. "I'm happy you made it."

"If it would make you even happier, I could pretend to be Ike."

She smiled, and they shook hands. "I'm Lieutenant Miles. I'll be briefing you this afternoon."

"What do your friends call you?" Scotty asked, falling in beside her as she went back up to the house.

"Lieutenant Miles," she told him.

The place was a beehive of activity. People came and went as if they were in a footrace, but no one raised their voices. It was as if everyone was in a library, or in church. And another thing that struck Scotty was how young everyone was. Some of them looked like teenagers. Nobody he saw as he followed Lieutenant Miles back to a conference room at the rear of the mansion was much older then twenty-one or twenty-two.

At twenty-eight he felt like an old man.

They went in. Major Winslow, whom Scotty had just left back in London, was perched on the edge of a long table laden with fat file folders, maps, photographs, and what appeared to be engineering sketches and blueprints. Winslow was languidly stuffing his pipe, as if he had been here all afternoon. He looked up in irritation.

"It's about time you got here, Captain," he said. "Took your time about it, I must say."

Scotty held his temper in check. "Couldn't help but stop for a pint on the way up."

"Oh, don't let him tease you," Miles told Scotty. "He only just got here himself, all out of breath."

Scotty was taken by surprise, and he laughed. Winslow grinned as well.

"I had to pull your chain, just a little," Winslow said. "Can't quite tell about some of you Yanks, strangest damned sense of humor. But it seems as if we might be related in an offhanded way."

"Oh?" Scotty couldn't imagine what the major was talking about.

"Our grandfathers were chums. *Very* close, if you catch my drift." Winslow glanced at Miles. "There is a certain resemblance to some of the family, don't you think?"

"Get on with you," she said. "We have a lot of work to do before the weekend. Mother is expecting us to be prompt for a change."

Winslow stuck out a hand. "Call me Donald. And may I call you Richard?"

"Sure," Scotty said. He turned to Miles. "My friends call me Scotty." They shook hands.

She blushed. "Actually it's Lindsay—"

"Linds," Winslow corrected her. He waved a hand at the piles on the table. "You have two hours to digest as much of this as you can. But if you will pay attention, like a good lad, Linds and I will give you a leg up. None of this rubbish can leave here, I'm told. And you wouldn't want to stay the night."

"Fine," Scotty said. He took off his coat. "You may talk to me while I'm reading. But what about personnel?"

Winslow gave Lindsay a glance. "There'll be four of us, plus you and four of your own chaps. Who they are is up to you. But I do have a few suggestions."

"Later," Scotty said. He sat down and opened the first file folder, which contained several dozen aerial reconnaissance photographs of Peenemünde. They were keyed to a sketch map of the rocket research installation. Some of the shots had been taken at low altitudes and were very good, showing lots of detail. Others weren't so good. The images were grainy and hard to make out.

"Perhaps we should wait until you're finished," Lindsay suggested.

Scotty looked up. "No, it's okay. Really. Start your briefing. I can do both things at the same time." He set the photos aside and opened a thick file folder that detailed the missions that had already been conducted against Peenemünde.

"Well," Winslow began. "The Germans started what they call the A Program to develop a liquid-fueled rocket. That was at a research facility in Kummersdorf near Berlin. A1 never got off the ground."

"Was that the V1 buzz bomb?" Scotty asked without looking up. *South Dakota I* and *II* were the code names for two missions in which agents were placed at Peenemünde late last year. They were never heard from again.

"No," Lindsay said. "That was a different series."

"What about A2?"

"That was back in 1934, on the island of Borkum in the Baltic. Von Braun managed to get two of the things off the ground, but not much else."

When Scotty was ten his mother discovered that he had a photographic memory. The teachers at the private school he attended encouraged him to develop skill at speed reading to see just how far his memory could take him, along with the intelligence to understand what he was taking in. He was reading the material in the files at more than twenty-five hundred words per minute. Most of it was easy-to-digest intelligence and engineering details, but to anyone watching him it looked as if he were merely flipping through the pages looking for something.

He put the missions file aside and opened a third file, this one on German code words for all the research equipment and exotic chemicals used in their rocket program. *A-Stoff* was liquid oxygen, *Blaulicht* was a radar homing device for missiles, *Messina* was a radar transponder for missile guidance systems, and so on.

"A3?" Scotty asked, looking up.

"A3 was the original research model for what became A4 which was the service weapon V2. A4b was equipped with wings, which never worked, and A5 became the new research test weapon for further development of the V2 which was already in the field."

Scotty opened a second file filled with engineering materials.

"Are you getting any of this?" Winslow asked, obviously frustrated. "Or am I just wasting my time?"

Scotty looked up. "I'm getting it. What about A6?"

"Their numbering system gets a little confusing. But essentially A6 through A9 were test projects to work out various fuels and fuel systems. In the meantime, V3 and V4 turned out to have nothing to do with the A series program. They were some other vengeance weapons. One of them was a cannon, I believe. But A10 was the design for a multistage intercontinental missile that was to become V5."

Scotty looked up again. "A11 must be the combat-ready model?"

"Right," Winslow said. He glanced at the file folders now stacked in neat piles. "We'll assemble the team on Monday and push off no later than Friday morning next. But first you'll have to read this material."

"According to this, the first V5 is scheduled to be fired one week from tomorrow. Leaving next Friday will be pushing it too close," Scotty said. "We'll leave on Wednesday. Thursday A.M. at the very latest." He got up and put on his jacket. "But what are we doing this weekend? Why aren't we getting started sooner?"

"It'll take until Monday to assemble our chaps, and we assumed that it would take just as long for you."

"I can have my people ready in two hours," Scotty promised. "If I can use the telephone, I can have them ready by tonight."

Winslow shook his head. "Telephones are out. This is too sensitive. In the meantime, I suggest that you take off your blouse, sit down, and get back to work."

Scotty glanced at the files and gave Winslow a vicious grin. "I've already read these. Are there more?"

"Listen here—"

"Trust me, Donald," Scotty said, patting the major on the arm. He turned to Lieutenant Miles. "Now, Linds, what do you have planned for the weekend that might include one incredibly lonely American boy? Far from home. Pining for company. Crying himself to sleep every night for the lack of a human touch—"

Lindsay laughed. "We were warned about you," she said.

"Yes, we were," Winslow agreed, but he, too, was chuckling.

"You're coming with me," Lindsay said. "To meet my father and mother."

"So soon?" Scotty asked. "We've barely met."

FRIDAY EVENING • MANSFIELD SHERWOOD FOREST

There was nothing to do until Winslow could round up his team. Scotty was left with the choice of going with Lindsay or returning to his quarters in London. It was an easy choice.

Lindsay rode up with Scotty, chattering all the way about her family, about the war, and about the mission. He didn't mind. In fact it felt good to be this close to a beautiful woman. He couldn't get enough of her voice, her appealing looks, and her scent, which was soapy and warm and feminine all at once.

"My mom, Anne, is a dear, but my father the brigadier can be a bit on the stuffy side at times," she said. She immediately smiled and gave Scotty a conspiratorial look. "Don't tell him that I said anything like that, for goodness sake. He'd take both of our heads off."

"Is he actually a brigadier?"

"World War One variety, but he keeps his old contacts. They listen to him in London. Actually he's Brigadier *Sir* Robert, so you better call him that, I suppose."

"Will they mind me showing up unannounced?"

"Heavens no," Lindsay assured him. "They're after me all the time to bring home an eligible bachelor."

She suddenly thought of something and shot him a worried look. "You are, eligible, I mean?"

"Was that a proposal?"

"Goodness no. It's just that I don't want to drag a married man home with me. Dad would see right through the ruse in a second."

Scotty held up his left hand. "No ring. No missus and kiddies waiting for me back in the States."

"Good. Er, I mean—"

"I know what you mean," Scotty said. "Or at least I think I do if you're telling me the whole story. But what about siblings? Brothers, sisters?"

"One each. Kevin's the oldest. He's thirty. The Germans have him in a POW camp somewhere around Munich, I think. And my sister, Sarah—she's married to Donald—is working as a spy in Germany. She's twenty-five and has been there almost a whole year now. We're all worried about her."

Scotty had a good idea what Sarah had to be doing in order to survive for so long. "Why doesn't she come home?"

"Because she's sending back damned good intelligence," Lindsay flared.

"Sorry, I didn't mean anything. It must be tough on your parents. But at least you're safe here in England."

Lindsay gave him an odd glance, but then changed the subject. "Peenemünde might not be our biggest problem," she said.

"Are you talking about Mittlewerke?" he asked.

She nodded. "Did you actually read all those files? Donald thinks that you might be a fraud. He's checking up on you."

"I'm a speed reader," Scotty told her. "And I don't forget anything. They call it a photographic memory. It's a pain in the neck sometimes, but most of the time it comes in handy."

She was impressed. "The factory is under a mountain, so our bombers can't get at it. But that's where they're producing not only the V5's guidance system, but the rocket itself, along with the V2. We might have to get over there and see what damage we can do. That's why the mission code name is *Coalmine.*"

"Getting out could be a problem," Scotty said. He'd studied the maps and the diagrams of Mittelwerke's layout and security systems. Getting into Fort Knox might be easier. But getting back out in one piece would be a couple of thousand times harder.

"The other problem is the launchers," she continued. "They're mobile. The bloody rocket can be launched from the back of a truck, or a flatbed railroad car that could be just about anywhere one day and two hundred miles away the next." She shook her pretty head. "We only got pictures of one of them near Peenemünde. But Sarah said that there were three of them operational. And our contact at Mittelwerke confirmed the number."

"Can't your Mittlewerke man gum up the process somehow?"

"He was killed last week in a truck accident, and his pickup man has disappeared," she said. She shook her head again. Her face was narrow but not angular. Her shoulders and hips were tiny, like a boy's. But her neck was long and graceful, and from what he could guess about her legs covered by trousers, they would be long and graceful, too. Like a dancer's.

It was very dark by the time they passed through

Nottingham and continued on the A60 to Mansfield on the edge of Sherwood Forest, but the snow had finally tapered off. A few miles later Lindsay directed him to turn onto a narrower road that wound its way through a dense stand of trees. They came out finally on a hill that ran down into a shallow valley at the bottom of which was a manor house right out of an old British novel about the landed gentry.

"You didn't tell me that you were rich," Scotty said.

"Poor as church mice, actually," Lindsay replied, her shoulders straight. "But we do have the house and the grounds. Been in the family for three hundred years."

Scotty parked in front and followed Lindsay across the gravel drive to the massive iron-strapped oak door, where she let herself in.

A beautiful woman who was an older carbon copy of Lindsay came across the vast entry hall, a warm smile on her face. Lindsay went to her, and they embraced.

Massive oak beams crisscrossed the tall ceiling, underneath which were stained-glass windows and huge oil paintings of what were probably the Miles ancestors. A fire was burning on the immense grate, and fabulously ornate and large oriental rugs were scattered everywhere on the stone floors.

"Mother, I'd like you to meet Captain Scott. He'll be leading our little jaunt," Lindsay said. "Scotty, this is my mother."

"I've already learned a great deal about you from my son-in-law," Mrs. Miles said. "All of it quite good." She offered her hand. She had a very slight German accent.

"And I've learned a great deal about your family, Lady Miles," Scotty said. "All of it *very* good." He brushed his lips against the back of her hand.

She smiled faintly. "Quite the chatterboxes, our children," she said. "The brigadier would like to have a few words with you, and afterward we're having just a light supper, I'm afraid. Tomorrow evening we'll dine formally."

"I didn't bring anything—"

"It's all right, Captain. You're about the same size as our son. We'll find something suitable for you."

"I'll show him the way," Lindsay said, and led Scotty across the hall and down a wide corridor.

"Your mother is as beautiful as you are," he said.

"I think you've got it the wrong way round, but thanks," Lindsay said. She stopped. "It's the door at the end." She smiled. "Remember, his bite is definitely much worse than his bark."

"Thanks," Scotty replied glumly.

THREE

MONDAY MORNING • OSS TRAINING BASE, FISHBOURNE

The mission briefing room was in a rebuilt barn two hundred yards from the old manor house. The place wasn't nearly as grand as Winacres, Lindsay's parents' estate; it had been in rough shape when the OSS took it over three years ago, and there wasn't enough time or real need to refurbish the place to its former glory. A hundred agents were processed through here each month for missions to the Continent, and they had other things on their minds than the decor.

Scotty had placed four telephone calls to London on Sunday with the brigadier's wholehearted permission, and in response the four OSS agents he'd briefly spoken to had shown up here, no questions asked. Thinking about the weekend with Lindsay and her parents, Scotty smiled. In the first ten minutes he'd been taken under the brigadier's wing and become an instant member of the family.

His four operators were lounging in front of the small stage, their feet up on folding chairs, the air thick with smoke, when Scotty walked in. They looked up, but no one stood to attention or saluted. Everyone who went into the field was a volunteer. They were, for the most part, well educated, highly motivated, and very egotistical. That's why they had earned the nickname Cowboys early on. And each new recruit was determined to live up to the reputation of his predecessors. That meant an almost total disregard for the rules. But no one bothered the OSS because they were getting the job done.

"We're going to Germany on Wednesday or Thursday," Scotty said. "The place is called Peenemünde. It's off the Baltic coast near the Polish border, and it's where the Nazis design and test their rockets. There's too much activity going on around the place, so we'll have to go in by submarine. Someone is working on the landing sites for us. But no matter how you slice it, it could get a little dicey. They might be expecting us."

His four volunteers watched him with feigned indifference. He could have been discussing tomorrow's entertainment at the USO in London. But they were his friends, and he could tell that they were interested.

"Judging by the disreputable nature of my colleagues, I'm guessing that we're going over to blow up a rocket or two," Sgt. Douglas Ballinger said. He was tall, slender, and very dark. He was an electronics expert and probably the brightest man Scotty had ever met. Ballinger, whose nickname was NMI, because he had no middle name, wasn't shy about letting people know just how smart he was.

"That took a stroke of genius to figure out," Sgt. Stuart McKeever, Mac, said through his bushy walrus moustache. He was an explosives expert.

"We're going to destroy *three* rockets, as a matter of fact," Scotty said. "You'll get the full briefing later today. But that won't be our biggest concern. We'll have to find them first, and at some point we might have to break into their factory and destroy the guidance systems on the assembly line, or better yet kill the engineers working on them."

"Why all the fuss?" Sgt. Donald Smith asked. He was a rocket expert. His dad worked with Robert Goddard, the American rocket pioneer, and as a young man Smith, whose nickname was Kilroy because his last name was so common, helped out. "The V2 isn't causing much harm now."

Scotty nodded. "You're right. But the rocket we're after is a brand-new one. The V5. It's a three-stage monster than can make it all the way across the Atlantic."

They all sat up. He had their attention now. "How big a payload does it carry?" Smith asked.

"It's not the size that counts, its what it'll carry that has everyone worried. Anthrax."

"What's that?"

"It's a germ that could kill a lot of people if it was released over Washington or New York City."

"Hell," Lt. Vivian Leigh said. He was their combat expert. He knew nearly every weapon carried by all sides, he was brutal in hand-to-hand, and his German was nearly perfect. He was a huge man, with a perfectly bald head and large, deep-set, dangerous eyes. Under normal conditions he was as mild-mannered as they came. He was a Harvard Law School graduate and a standout football player, the only venue other than Special Forces Training School where he showed his vicious side. He could blindside you, break a couple of bones, and afterward visit you at the hospital bringing candy and even flowers. But he didn't like bugs.

"The rocket factory is not at Peenemünde," Scotty continued. "It's at a place called Mittelwerke, dug into the mountains near Nordhausen. That's a couple of hundred miles south."

"That's just dandy," Ballinger said. "Can we ask who came up with this brilliant idea?"

"Winston Churchill," Scotty replied. "Which means we'll be getting some help. Four MI6 operators, whom we'll meet this afternoon, are tagging along."

"Who'll be the field commander?" Leigh asked.

"Yours truly."

His people nodded in satisfaction. They would take orders from a Brit, but they wouldn't have liked it. This way was much better.

Monday Afternoon • Bletchley Park

Scotty and his team were driven over to the Code and Cipher School in a windowless van marked with the logo of a grocery supplier. The trip was nearly one hundred miles, and snow lay slippery on the narrow roads. The going was slow, which gave Scotty a long time to ponder what might prove to be an impossible job, the task of reaching the Mittelwerke factory and damaging it.

The solution, of course, was to break their mission into two separate parts. By submarine to Peenemünde, then by air to somewhere near Nordhausen.

He thought about hijacking a truck and perhaps

some German uniforms to make the overland trip. But even if they did make it that far without being stopped, and even if they did somehow manage to damage the underground factory, they wouldn't have one chance in ten million of getting out alive.

He rode in the passenger seat and stared at the passing countryside, figuring their options. He wanted very much to return to England. Especially now that he had met Lindsay.

One of the Royal Marine guards on the gate peered into the back of the van, but he gave no outward indication that he'd seen anything other than groceries. He stepped back, raised the barrier, and let them through.

On the way up the long driveway through the woods, Scotty tried to get himself into a better mood. It was bad business beginning a mission in the dumps. But he thought it was an even worse business going into a mission from which you knew you wouldn't return.

They were directed to the kitchen pantry entrance in back, where under the cover of an overhang the five of them went inside. They'd brought their personal gear with them, but no weapons or other equipment. A man identifying himself as the charge of quarters brought them to their rooms in the west wing of the main house, where they dropped their things and went back downstairs and outside to one of the Quonset buildings.

It contained a typical briefing room, with several rows of chairs facing a slightly raised platform, at the back of which was a large map of England, the Channel, and most of Europe.

Major Winslow and Lindsay were there, along with two men who looked so pale and weak that

Scotty wondered why they weren't in the hospital. Their civilian clothes hung on them as if they'd just been released from a POW camp and not had a decent meal in a year. One was blond with long hair, and the other was frizzy dark brown and short.

Winslow introduced the blond man as Sgt. Talbot St. Lo, the Saint, who was MI6's leading expert on electronics, especially pertaining to avionics and missile guidance systems. The dark-haired, slightly smaller man was Sgt. Thomass Beddows-Smythe, a hand-to-hand combat instructor with more than two dozen missions behind enemy lines since 1940. His nickname was Bedfella, and Scotty's people visibly held back sniggers.

Winslow smiled midly. "Don't let their size deceive you, gentlemen."

Scotty introduced his people, and after they'd all shaken hands he turned back to Winslow. "I thought there were four of you? Where are the others?"

"We're it," Winslow said.

It took a moment for that to sink in, and when it did, Scotty shook his head. He understood now what the weekend at Winacres had been all about. "We're not taking a woman with us."

"Oh?" Lindsay said, raising an eyebrow. "Just why might that be?"

"It's just the way it is," Scotty shot back. "The chance that we'll all get home in one piece is slim to none. And you're not coming along. I need somebody who can shoot, somebody who can speak German, and somebody who knows something about rockets or electronics."

"*Ja, denn warum nicht eine Fraülein?*" Lindsay snapped. "I'm an expert marksman, I've gone through the MI6 training course twice, both times with Thomass, and I graduated with honors last summer in biochemistry at university." She looked at him with amusement. "If something happens to you, the team will need another biological expert."

"We'll get someone else," Scotty growled. He didn't like this at all. He didn't want the responsibility of any woman coming with them, but especially not her.

"There *is* no one else," Winslow said. "Sorry old boy, but my sister-in-law seems to be our man." He gave Scotty a look as if to say I should have warned you about her. "Shall we get sarted then? We need to be fully briefed by 2000 hours, after which we have a field drill in the woods. They've produced a mock-up of the rocket for us to practice disarming and destroying."

Scotty took out the letter that Churchill had given him at Storey's Gate. It gave him absolute authority over every aspect of the mission, including the right to commandeer or reject any piece of equipment, any plan, or any individual. The letter was signed by Churchill and by Eisenhower.

Lindsay refused to look at the letter in his hand though it was obvious she had an idea what it might be. Her shoulders were back, her tiny jaw set.

Scotty was seething inside. This wasn't what he wanted. But another part of him understood that Lindsay might be perfect for the job.

"Either I go, Captain Scott, or the mission will have to be scrubbed," she said. "We cannot afford to send only one biological expert. The risk of doing more damage than good is simply too great."

Beddows-Smythe, the MI6 combat instructor, watched with an amused expression. "Might I suggest you give the lieutenant a chance tonight on the practice range before you make a final decision?" His voice was as soft as a woman's.

Scotty considered the suggestion. It was a reasonable one, but he didn't like this kind of bickering. He glanced at them all, Lindsay included, and nodded. "Major Winslow will give the briefing, Sergeant Beddows-Smythe will conduct the training exercise, but I will be in overall command of the mission. Questions?"

There were none.

He looked pointedly at Lindsay. "No consideration will be given to your sex," he told her harshly. He thought she was beautiful.

She grinned like a vixen. "Well, that's certainly a refreshing change of attitude, Captain. Though I think that my sex, as you put it, might come in handy at the least expected moment."

That Evening • Bletchley Park Grounds

Their afternoon briefing went without a hitch, though everyone on the team understood the near impossibility of the Mittelwerke part of the mission. But a plan had formed in Scotty's mind, which more than ever made him determined to knock Lindsay off the team.

No calls were allowed from the Park, but Major Winslow managed to rustle up a messenger to take a letter to Colonel Bruce at OSS Headquarters in London. The messenger was instructed to wait for a reply.

After a decent supper of bacon and eggs with fried potatoes and fried tomatoes and beer, they were kitted out in winter battlefield dress with white coveralls and hoods. In addition they carried the tools they would need, the blank explosives and M3 forty-five caliber submachine guns, various pistols and other weapons.

They were not going to Germany as spies, or even as saboteurs, but as commandos striking a specific set of targets. Not that the Geneva Convention held much water in Germany these days, but going over in uniform might help if they were captured alive.

"We're after destroying three missiles," Beddows-Smythe told them.

They were assembled in what was turning out to be a very strong snowstorm, just below the crest of a long, low hill. The main house was far enough away that they could not see it, nor were there any lights anywhere on the grounds. They could have been on another planet, or on the island of Usedom in the Baltic, where Peenemünde was located.

"They're bloody big things, so they'll be hard for the Jerries to hide. But the bad news is that we only know where one of them is, or was, as of several days ago. Nor does it look as if this weather will clear up in time for another reconnaissance flight."

"We'll start with the one, and go looking for the others," Winslow said. "They'll be close."

"Just right, sir," Beddows-Smythe agreed. "Since Jerry is planing on launching all three of these rockets this weekend, there'll be SS and Wehrmacht along with scientists and technicians all over the place." He held up his razor-sharp knife for emphasis. "We kill no one unless it's absolutely bloody well necessary. And if we do it, it'll be this way. Minimize the noise."

"Throat or heart?" Lindsay asked, and Scotty thought that the question was for his benefit.

Beddows-Smythe grinned at her. "The throat's the best bet, Lieutenant. With the heart stab you sometimes have to be lucky or you'll miss. It hurts, and they tend to make a terrible ruckus."

She nodded but did not look over at Scotty.

"We cannot simply blow the things up, of course, because of the payloads. So I suggest that we split up into two teams, one with Captain Scott and the other with Lieutenant Miles. It'll be their jobs to safely remove the anthrax tanks from the nose cones so that we can take them far enough away that when the rockets explode, sending burning fuel all over hell and back, the tanks will not be compromised and release the germs."

He waited for Scotty to voice an objection, but there was none. Short of coming up with another bug man, they were going to be stuck with a woman. It wasn't that Scotty thought she couldn't handle the job. He had a couple of aunts who had flown airplanes in the twenties, gone exploring in the Antarctic, and even crossed the Pacific in a small sailboat. Women were capable of just about anything. But dammit, they did not belong in combat.

"Once all three rockets are dismantled and the charges set in place, we'll set the timers for a brief delay, then hotfoot it out of there before they can guess which way we've gone."

"A lot can go wrong," Scotty said.

Beddows-Smythe nodded. "Everything, sir."

It dawned on Scotty that the sergeant did not trust or like him and his American team. The Americans had come over to England with their fancy uniforms and abundant money, sweeping the British women off their feet. He could see how Beddows-Smythe looked at Lindsay. He was in love with her. It explained a lot.

"We're not going over on a suicide mission," Scotty said. "Destroying the missiles is important, but the war will be over in a few months whether they fly or not." He shrugged. "The damned things will probably blow up on takeoff anyway. They haven't had enough time to test them. So we're going to stay as safe as possible. I want to bring everyone back."

"Right—" Beddows-Smythe smirked.

"Do you have a problem with that, Sergeant?" Scotty demanded. If he wasn't accepted as a leader right now, he might as well step aside and let Winslow do the job.

Beddows-Smythe glanced at Winslow, but then shook his head. "No, sir."

"Fine. We'll take this one step at a time. The Peenemünde operation tonight, and the Mittelwerke mission tomorrow, for which I have a couple of ideas. Unless there's a hitch, I'm pushing our departure to Wednesday, the day after tomorrow."

"We might have a problem with transportation," Winslow said.

"I'll take care of it," Scotty said. "Now, Bedfella, let's get on with it, I'm freezing my ass off. And captains don't like that."

Beddows-Smythe laughed, the tension suddenly evaporating. "No, sir, neither do sergeants."

"Or women," Lindsay added.

They spread out on Beddows-Smythe's signal and began working their way over the hill and down into the woods. The mock V5 had been set up on a long, narrow platform to simulate a truck trailer. The Royal Marines were guarding the weapon. They knew that the intruders were coming, though not exactly from what direction. Scotty and his team, however, did not know where the guards were located, nor how many there were.

Halfway down the hill Smythe held up his hand, then urgently motioned them down. They all dropped to the snow. Smythe was slightly ahead and to Scotty's left, and Lindsay was somewhere off to the right.

Effective visibility was down to about fifty feet at best. A hundred feet out everything was lost in the swirling snow.

But then Scotty spotted two men in marine uniforms, their rifles slung barrel down over their shoulders, trudging from right to left, as if on a patrol path.

Smythe looked back. He'd spotted them, too. He gave Scotty the signal for: Do you see them? When Scotty gave the affirmative, Smythe motioned for the two of them to move down the hill while the others remained where they were. Smythe would take the guard on the left, Scotty the one on the right.

Scotty slipped his knife out of its sheath low on his right leg and scrambled down the hill with Smythe until they intersected the footsteps of the guards in the snow.

Smythe gave him a nod. They rose at the same time and made the final silent rush to the patrolling marines like a pair of lions closing in for the kill.

Scotty hit his man a second before the sergeant, pulling the man's head back and simulating a throat cut.

"Bloody hell," the young marine swore under his breath.

"Sorry, son, but you're dead," Scotty said. "So kindly keep your mouth shut."

The marine grinned wryly and shook his head. "Right you are, sir. But you've already lost, haven't you?"

Smythe's marine was also down. Scotty motioned that he was returning to the others. He turned and headed up the hill in a dead run, but keeping low, all his senses alert for trouble.

The figures of his team materialized out of the blowing snow. Two Royal Marines were sitting down, Lindsay and Vivian Leigh over them.

"It was a trap," Leigh said. He nodded to Lindsay. "She spotted them."

She gave Scotty a sweet smile.

"Are they both dead?" Smythe asked.

"This one isn't," Scotty said before Lindsay could reply. He dropped down beside the young marine guard who was grinning, shoved the kid's head back with force, and brought the point of his razor-sharp knife to within an inch of the marine's right eye.

"How many other guards are there?" Scotty asked.

The marine reared back in alarm. He appealed to Smythe. "Hey, sarge, c'mon. What's with the Yank?"

"This is Germany, son, and you're the bloody SS," Smythe told him.

"First your right eye, then your left," Scotty said, pressing.

"Just the four of us."

"Where are the other rockets?"

"I don't know about any other rockets."

Scotty moved the knive closer. "Where are the other rockets?"

"Bloody hell, Sarge, tell this bloody bastard that I bloody well don't know."

Scotty withdrew the knife, got up, and helped the marine to his feet. "No harm done. This is just a drill."

"Yes, sir."

"And I don't much like your language in front of the lady," Smythe cautioned.

FOUR

TUESDAY MORNING • BERLIN

It was almost dark, though Sarah Winslow couldn't detect any light in the gray overcast and swirling snow from the open bathroom window. She connected the antenna lead on the drain gutter, then hunched her blanket closer around her while she waited for the radio set to warm up. Her rendezvous time with London Station was approaching, and she didn't want to miss her schedule after cutting off her transmissions twice since New Year's Day. Both times radio-direction-finding trucks had rumbled up the street, but then had passed.

Walther had come over only once since New Year's Eve, to make love and stay the night. That was yesterday. He'd gotten up suddenly a couple hours ago and asked her to make him breakfast. He had an extremely urgent early appointment in the *Führer* bunker, and it didn't pay to be late.

He talked all the while she cooked the eggs, sausages, and spinach he'd brought over. Bragged, actually.

"The war is all but won," he told her. He laughed and slapped his hands in exuberance. "Just a few more days, now, and you'll see." He stopped and looked at her as if he were seeing her for the first time, and he smiled warmly. "Ah, *Liebchen,* if you only knew. If only I could tell you." He shook his head. "But then, you'll see soon enough. The entire world will see."

That wasn't like him, to brag so much. She didn't want to press her luck just then by asking him questions. He wasn't unusually suspicious, but there was something different about him. She couldn't put her finger on just what it was, but she was feeling an increased sense of isolation and danger.

The war was nearly over, and she wanted very much to get out of Germany right now.

She looked at her watch. It was six o'clock. She checked out the window to make sure the street was empty, then tapped out her recognition signal and got the go-ahead immediately.

She hurriedly told London what Walther had said to her just two hours ago, omitting nothing, but adding nothing either. Her job was to report facts, not to draw conclusions.

When she was finished, London Station sent the code that they had traffic for her: Was she ready to copy?

She replied in the affirmative.

EXTREMELY URGENT THAT YOU FIND OUT PRECISE LOCATIONS OF ENTRANCES AND AIR SHAFTS AS WELL AS SECURITY POSTS AT STANISLAW. BY NEXT SKED.

Stanislaw was the code name of the Mittelwerke factory near Nordhausen. But how in heaven's name London thought that she could get such information from General Schellenberg in twenty-four hours was beyond her. She was about to ask if they were joking, but then she thought better of it. London *never* joked.

She sent her will-comply signal, then added five words in a very slow, precise hand before she signed off.

I WANT OUT NOW PLEASE

London sent its acknowledgment, and she switched off.

She sat back, hunched practically into a little ball because of the cold and because she was truly and deeply more frightened than she'd ever been since arriving in Germany. She could think of little other than her husband, She knew every laugh line around his eyes, even though they'd only been married for two years before she'd been sent over. She could smell the scent of his clothes, hear his voice, and see his stupid habits, like how he put on his socks and shoes before he put on his trousers. He was forever pulling out the hems of his cuffs, but she couldn't make him stop it. Now she wished that she was there to watch him.

She reached out the window and unclipped the antenna wire as a tremendous bang hit the bathroom door. It burst inward with a crash that shook the entire house.

Sarah spun around, her heart going into her throat. The large man in a long black leather overcoat who'd broken in the door stepped aside, and

Schellenberg walked in, a faint smile on his face.

His eyes went from the antenna lead in her hand to the radio and back to her face. "Good morning, Marta. Or should I call you Cecile? Which do you prefer?"

She'd always known that this could happen, though she'd been too busy or too frightened to give it much thought. But now that the shoe had actually dropped, she found that she was calm. The only problem was the L pill, the cyanide capsule that all Allied spies carried. She'd left it downstairs in the apartment.

"The general's whore, will be fine," she said, amazed at how steady her voice was.

Schellenberg's smile was a little forced. "We have a new role for you, Marta."

She saw that she had gotten to him, and her lips curled into a nasty smirk. "I faked it, Walther. Right from the beginning. You're a rotten lover."

"When it's over, you'll regret that remark."

"I regretted it every time you were on top of me grunting like a pig."

Schellenberg wanted to hit her. She could see the effort it took for him to maintain his composure, while for her it was becoming easier by the minute.

"Let's go, my dear," Schellenberg said.

"I need to get dressed first, unless you mean to freeze me to death."

"Of course. But we've already found your cipher book and your suicide pill." He shook his head. "I think that you will wish that you still had it when we're finished."

"Where are you taking me, Gestapo Headquarters?"

"No, not at all," Schellenberg said. "In fact by this

afternoon you will have seen firsthand everything that London wants you to report on."

Sarah frowned. She didn't know what he meant. He could be elliptical at times.

"Mittelwerke, my dear. I'm taking you there this morning so that you can see it for yourself. And then you will send your message to London."

A cold shot of fear went directly into her heart. She shook her head. "No—"

"Oh, yes, Marta, you will cooperate with us." He smiled evilly. "You'll see."

TUESDAY EVENING • LONDON

The call from London for Scotty came a few minutes before four in the afternoon. He'd been in the training hut with the team, studying the relief map model of the Mittelwerke installation in the Harz Mountains.

There wasn't much to see except for the steep, heavily forested hills, the two entrances they knew about, and the various paved roads and narrow dirt tracks through the woods, along with the town of Nordhausen and the nearby concentration camp of the same name.

The best bet would have been to destroy the entire installation. But the workshops and assembly halls had been carved out of the living rock deep within the mountains, making the place impervious to air attacks.

And Scotty's team could not carry enough explosives to do the factory anything more than superficial damage.

The next best bet was striking at the engineers and scientists. The people who worked on the crucial bits of the rockets and guidance systems. MI6 had managed to piece together a work schedule and one critical piece of information. Most of the workers walked back and forth from the underground entrance to their quarters in the concentration camp.

But the engineers and some of the scientists, the people most important to Mittelwerke, were picked up in six trucks.

It was Scotty's intention to knock out the trucks and kill everyone aboard.

Riding down to London on the train, Scotty was looking forward to talking to Colonel Bruce. The colonel was one man over here whom he could trust implicitly. If Bruce said that the sun wouldn't rise until noon tomorrow, his people, Scotty included, would set their clocks to him, and not the Greenwich time tick.

In the letter he'd sent by messenger yesterday he'd asked Colonel Bruce's feelings about his plan for the Mittelwerke engineers. Some of the people riding in the trucks were friends of the Allies. Spies, some of them. Most of them Jews, who would be killed when their usefulness was at an end. But unless word could somehow be gotten to them to miss the trucks Wednesday night, Scotty couldn't see any other way out.

He had backed himself into a corner that he hadn't managed to get out of by the time the cabbie dropped him off at OSS Headquarters on Grosvenor Street, and he walked upstairs to the colonel's office.

It was approaching eight in the evening, but headquarters was very busy. The organization's main thrust had become focused on getting agents into

Germany. But Bill Casey, who'd been brought over to head up the effort, was finding that getting his people into place in Germany was nearly impossible. There was no effective underground in Germany as there had been in France. There were no fields lit on schedule by farmers with lanterns or torches. There were no safe houses. No underground railways. Nearly everyone in Germany was so traumatized by the assassination attempt on Hitler last summer that they had become informers. Anything real or imagined that was out of the ordinary, no matter how tiny or insignificant, was reported to the Gestapo.

The entire country was on the verge of imploding. It was becoming almost as dangerous for the average citizen in Germany as it was for an Allied spy.

Colonel Bruce, his jacket on and buttoned, his tie snugged up as usual, came around from behind his desk when Scotty was shown in.

"Come with me," he said. He marched out of his office and down the corridor to the rickety elevator. "Something has cropped up that you'll have to consider."

They took the elevator to the top floor, where the colonel had to vouch for Scotty in order to bring him into the headquarters' communications and analysis center.

The operation took up most of the floor under the eaves. It was the job of the young clerks, mostly women, to listen to broadcasts of any sort coming out of Germany. In another section of the top floor, analysts, mostly men, tried to figure out what was happening over there. A large part of their efforts involved messages from OSS and MI6 agents.

"One of our primary sources for your mission is

a woman code-named Cecile, who is the mistress of General Walther Schellenberg," Bruce said, leading Scotty back to the analysis division. "It was from her that we got the first word about the three rockets at Peenemünde, about the new guidance system, and about the payload."

"One of ours?" Scotty asked.

Bruce shook his head. "MI6. We think that she's in trouble, and you could be walking into a trap."

Scotty's lips compressed. "Maybe we should simply bypass Mittelwerke and concentrate on knocking out the rockets before they become operational. There won't be that many more of them, and the war can only last a few more months."

"There's more to it than that. If only one guidance system is mated to one rocket, which could be hidden anywhere in Germany, we'd be in serious trouble." Bruce gave Scotty a trust-me-on-this-one look. "President Roosevelt has taken a keen interest."

Scotty thought about the problem under these new circumstances. "Even if it is a trap, we can still hit the trucks carrying the engineers."

"Some of those people are our friends."

Scotty refused to look away. "I know."

"Yet you would go ahead?"

"Hell, I don't know any other way, Colonel. Especially if they know that we're coming and expect us to hit the factory. Anyway, who's Cecile?"

"Her real name is Sarah Winslow."

It took several seconds for all the ramifications of that news to sink in. "Major Winslow's wife?"

Bruce nodded. "Lindsay Miles's sister." Bruce looked away for a moment.

This was a bad business. Scotty could see that the

colonel was just as affected by it as he was. The brigadier and his wife had their only son in a German POW camp, one of their daughters captured as a spy, and yet they were willing to send their remaining daughter into harm's way.

"We realized that something was drastically wrong when she broke her schedule to tell us that she was visiting Mittelwerke with Walt. She's never called Schellenberg by that name. And then she sent the information we asked for. *All* the information. Which was utterly impossible for her to come by so quickly."

"I'm pulling Major Winslow and Lieutenant Miles off the team—"

"No," Bruce said. "Nor will they be told about this until you're in-country and only if it becomes absolutely necessary." Bruce gave him a stern look. "I'm counting on you."

Scotty didn't like it, but he nodded. "What do you want me to do?"

"Your plan for an airdrop near Nordhausen should work. We'll send you over as part of a bomb group. Your plane will stray off course for a bit, and once your team bails out, it'll catch up with the others in its group.

"You'll parachute just after dark, which will give you eleven hours total before dawn. Eight hours to reach the target, destroy it, and return to your rendezvous point, where you'll signal for a pickup. A plane will come in on your lights, pick you up, and get you down to the vicinity of Peenemünde in time for you to find someplace to hide for the day.

"That night you will find and destroy the three rockets on the ground. We believe they'll be in the vicinity of the V2 firing stands."

"What about afterward?" Scotty asked.

"There'll be a submarine waiting for you just offshore. You'll be given the signal codes."

"There'll be a lot of confusion after we hit Mittelwerke. But if we're not going after the engineers, then how do we pull it off? How do we hurt them so badly the Nazis won't recover in time to do us any damage before the war is over, and yet not risk the lives of our friends?"

There were at least fifty people busy at work up here, but none of them so much as lifted an eye toward Bruce and Scotty. People came and went at a furious pace, as if they were in a race, which in a way, Scotty thought, they were.

A large-scale map of the state of Thuringia north of the city of Erfurt was pinned to a large standup drafting table. Nordhausen was at the top of the highly detailed topographic map. The concentration camp and Mittelwerke factory were marked in red. Above the factory, about five kilometers to the north, a symbol like a parenthesis was marked across a small branch of the Aller River that flowed away from Brocken Mountain.

Bruce pointed a delicate finger at it. "A small dam. If it were to be destroyed, the resulting flood wouldn't cause terribly much damage, nor would it likely cause much loss of life. Merely an inconvenience to the Germans."

Scotty saw the idea at once. "But it will flood the underground factory."

"Indeed. I'm told that it will take five or six hours, but the underground caverns will flood, and it will take the Germans at least four months to construct a temporary dam, pump out the water, and repair the damage to the machinery." Bruce gave Scotty a rare smile. "Four months, that is, if they have nothing else to keep them occupied."

Scotty felt protective of Lindsay and even her brother-in-law, and he felt sorry about Cecile, but *Coalmine* was now, in his mind, a doable mission.

Bruce read his mind. "I'm sorry about Sarah Winslow, but it cannot be helped. I'm sure that you can see why withholding the fact she's there from her husband and sister is vital."

Scotty nodded glumly. "We'll be ready to leave in twenty hours."

"I'm counting on you," Bruce said, shaking hands.

"Business as usual, sir," Scotty replied. It had become the British national expression.

FIVE

WEDNESDAY AFTERNOON • MITTELWERKE

Schellenberg was in a bad mood. His chief of ciphers, *Oberst* Hans Schmidt, told him that there was no way of telling for sure if Marta had sent an embedded code word in her message to London, warning them that this was a trap.

A special Gestapo team had come down from Berlin to interrogate her last night and again this morning, but neither her story nor her defiant attitude had changed. She was willing to cooperate. She would send whatever messages they wanted her to send. But she was certain that London would see through the ruse.

"They'll know that I'm sending with a gun pointed at my head," she told them with confidence.

Nor would she give them her real name. She wouldn't confirm or deny that her code name was Cecile. She was Marta Frick.

The Mittelwerke chief scientist and the commandant of Nordhausen shared a large hunting lodge in the hills between the factory and the concentration camp. It was where Schellenberg was staying.

His driver took him down to the camp before supper, the country road through the thick forest lovely under a fresh blanket of snow. *In happier times,* he started to think, but cut it off. There would be no happy times until this godforsaken war was over. He had seen the look of derision in Marta's eyes when she said that she'd faked her orgasms with him. She called him a grunting pig. It hurt that she had called him those names, and that she was a spy, all the more because he was sure that he was in love with her.

The guards at the front gate let him in, and they drove straight over to the commandant's office, behind which were the interrogation cells for what they called *special prisoners,* mostly Jews who were engineers or knew some science and were being selected to work in the factory.

In this case it was Marta housed there, under the horrible ministrations of the Gestapo. But she was a British spy. She'd come over here of her own free will, not as a soldier with a gun, but as a woman with her body for sale.

He went directly back to the interrogation cell block. The sergeant on duty was the only one there. The Gestapo men had gone into town a couple of hours earlier.

"I'm taking the woman with me," Schellenberg said. He took off his leather gloves and slapped them against the side of his leg. His great coat was thrown over his shoulders, his general's insignia gleaming dully in the dim light.

The sergeant jumped up and came to ramrod attention. "Sir, I was given direct orders by Captain Gestern to hold the prisoner."

Schellenberg was surprised by the sergeant's gumption. The man had to be very frightened of the Gestapo. "Do you have eyes, Sergeant? I outrank everyone here, including the camp commandant. So, unless you want to be shot for disobeying the direct order of a superior officer, bring the woman to me."

The sergeant hesitated only a fraction of a second. *"Jawohl, Herr General,"* he snapped. He grabbed some keys and hurried back to the cells, returning a minute later with a very battered Marta.

Both her eyes had been blackened, patches of hair had been pulled from her head, her scalp was oozing blood in spots, at least two of her teeth had been knocked out, and the way she held herself told him that at the very least she had cracked ribs and perhaps some internal damage. His heart sank when he saw her. But dammit, she was the dirty little spy, not he.

"What shall I tell them, *Herr General*?"

"That Six has retaken control of the prisoner," Schellenberg said. He put his coat over her shoulders and led her outside to his big Mercedes.

They headed back to the hunting lodge. Since it was likely that London Station knew that Marta was being coerced, they would have to suspect that they would be walking into a trap if they came here to sabotage the factory.

He had given that some thought. The only chance of success would be blowing up the place or killing the key personnel.

He also considered leaving that very minute for Berlin. Back in his own headquarters, he would have more control over Marta's fate than he did here. Yet something held him back.

He could not remember everything that he told her when they were in the act of lovemaking; it was very stupid of him in the first place. He'd acted like a smitten schoolboy. But whatever he'd told her was probably enough, along with the aerial photos taken last week of one of the V5s at Peenemünde and the possible links to the Jew engineer who was killed right here at about the same time, to alert the Allies to the full potential of what they were faced with. When the three rockets flew in less than seventy-two hours, all three targeted on downtown Washington, D.C., warfare would be changed forever. London Station had to know that. They also knew that aerial assaults on Mittelwerke were futile, and yet the factory had to be put of commission.

But how?

He'd pored over the engineering drawings of the installation, the reinforced entrances, the camouflaged air intake vents. In order to do the factory any serious damage, tons of explosives would have to be set in place and detonated.

He shook his head. Impossible, given the security measures in and around the place. Two hundred fifty Wehrmacht and SS troops were on guard twenty-four hours per day. No unathorized person could get in or out of the place.

Which left a strike on the personnel. But many of them were Jews. Friends of the Allies.

"Where are you taking me?" Marta asked, her voice barely audible.

"Back to Berlin tonight, or perhaps tomorrow."

"Will I be shot?"

"Yes, unless you start helping me," Schellenberg told her. He'd almost said *helping us*, but changed his choice of words. They had been lovers. Maybe she was lying, maybe she wasn't faking the whole time. He'd listened to her moans of pleasure. Maybe she did feel something for him after all.

"I'll never help you," she answered, gaining a little strength. "I'm the enemy. And in a few months Germany will lose the war." She looked out the window. "The Wehrmacht will be replaced by Allied soldiers. Right here."

Schellenberg shook his head. Not if the V5 program was successful, he thought. He just had to figure out how the Allies were planing on stopping them.

He handed Marta over to the chief of the house staff, a matronly old woman who cooed and clucked disapprovingly. Marta would be cleaned up, her injuries tended to, and if anyone asked about her, their inquiries were to be directed solely to the general.

The house was quiet at this time of the day. The commandant's three children were still in school, and his wife was probably in town, where she spent most of her time.

He drifted back to the library and poured a cognac. The engineering and architectural drawings of the factory were spread out over the leather-topped desk, along with several very-large-scale maps of the countryside immediately above and around the underground installation.

He sat down on the couch, put his feet up on the coffee table, and tried to think like an Allied commando bent on destroying Mittelwerke.

Later That Afternoon • RAF Base Farnham

It had been a rough slog all day, getting the team prepared for the switch in mission plans, making sure that they had the equipment they needed, and waiting to the last minute for Colonel Bruce to twist some arms in London and send them the go-ahead.

As it was, they were nearly an hour late arriving at RAF Farnham. The pilots' briefing had already started. Scotty sent Winslow with the rest of their team to get something to eat while he went over to the operations ready room.

A British major was conducting the evening's briefing for the pilots and copilots of the twelve Avro Lancaster heavy bombers that were scheduled to head for Berlin within the next twenty minutes. A big map of Germany was pinned to the wall at the back of the stage, with courses, speeds, and targets overlayed in red.

The team was supposed to ride over in one of the bombers, which would divert away from the squadron, as if lost, and fly south to the vicinity of Nordhausen. The *Coalminers*, as they had begun to call themselves, would make the jump, and the Lancaster would rejoin its squadron over Berlin.

It had been an imperfect plan from the beginning, one that Scotty had ranged around to improve. But it was Lindsay who had come up with the alternative late last night.

The major stopped in midsentence as Scotty walked in and went directly to the platform. Every eye in the room was on the Yank, and none of the crew seemed the least bit friendly.

"Sorry, Major, but there's been a last-minute change of plans," Scotty said.

"You're welcome to the ride, Captain, but you were not invited to this briefing," the officer said. His name tag read *Clarke.* He was short, sandy-haired, and looked as if he hadn't slept in a week. He also looked irascible. "If you'll get your arse out of here, I'll finish with my lads, and we can take off."

"Have a look at this first, sir." Scotty handed him Churchill's letter.

Clarke wanted to bite someone's head off, Scotty's first. But he took the letter, quickly scanned it, looked up in surprise, then read it again, slowly this time. When he was finished he handed it back.

"Listen up, gentlemen. There has been a change of plans after all," he said. He turned to Scotty. "You'll brief us now, Captain?" He was still mad, but he was impressed.

Scotty nodded. He went to the map, found a marker, and laid out the course across the Channel directly to Nordhausen. "My team will be in the last aircraft. We'll jump right behind the last bombs."

"If you're talking about Mittelwerke, it's been tried by your lot as well as ours," one of the pilots said. "No go."

"The bombing is a diversion. We're going in just after the midshift change. If you can hit some of the soldiers guarding the factory, then well and good. But my team is your primary load."

"Dropping bombs on Berlin makes more sense," another pilot said.

"Not this time," Scotty replied. "For now there is no other target in Germany with a higher priority." He turned to the major. "I suggest that you dig out your target objectives of Mittelwerke from your mission files. I'm sure there'll be photographs and way points you've already used."

Major Clarke nodded to a sergeant at the back of the room, who turned and left.

"Will there be anything else?" Clarke asked.

"No," Scotty said. He was tired, too, and a little irascible about taking Lindsay along. Very likely they were walking into a buzz saw. It was possible that they would never make their pickup point, which was nearly eight kilometers from the dam. In that case they'd be stuck in the middle of Nazi Germany with absolutely no hope of escape.

The RAF officer read some of that from Scotty's expression. "Why don't you get yourself something to eat at the officers' mess? This lot will take us a half hour to sort out."

"We can't be late. There's a lot riding on this."

"There has been all along, hasn't there?"

THAT EVENING • MITTELWERKE

"I'm sorry, *Herr General,* but this has become Gestapo business," Captain Gestern said.

They were in the soaring front stairhall of the hunting lodge. Schellenberg's left eyebrow rose. He held out his right hand. "Very well, Captain, let me see your orders."

The commandant had made himself scarce when he realized what the Gestapo wanted and what Schellenberg's position was. Gestern had only his sergeant as backup.

"My orders are verbal, sir," Gestern said. He looked Nordic, square chin, short-cropped blond hair. "Now, if you will have the prisoner brought—"

"Not good enough," Schellenberg cut in. "When you have written orders from Himmler, bring them to me."

Ordinarily the Gestapo had precedence over any German officer, no matter what rank. But the secret police was a branch of the RSHA, in which Schellenberg was head of counterespionage. Gestern was in a very tricky position, and he knew it. If he was right, Schellenberg might get his hand slapped. But if he was wrong, the ax would fall on his neck.

Gestern bowed slightly. "As you wish, *Herr General,*" he said. He and his sergeant left.

"Was that wise?" Marta asked from the head of the stairs.

Schellenberg looked up at her. "You're going to help me defend this place."

"Like hell," she said. "Maybe I'll escape tonight."

"I think Captain Gestern would find that more amusing than you can imagine," Schellberg replied. He went back to the library, where he hunched over the diagrams and maps spread on the desk.

The answer was here, he was sure of it.

But where?

LATER THAT EVENING • EN ROUTE TO MITTELWERKE

Colonel Bruce was arranging the pickup. He hadn't managed to get that confirmed before Scotty boarded the Lancaster with his team. But the rendezvous point was set. It was a narrow, sloping field northwest of Nordhausen in a valley called Unter-Harz. And the time was set for 0400. It was up to the colonel not to leave them stranded. And it was a measure of how much trust his people placed in him that the Coalminers left on what could be a one-way ride.

The Lancaster was an ugly-looking brute, with a gross weight of nearly seventy thousand pounds, powered by four 1,280-horsepower Rolls-Royce Merlin engines. It was slower and flew lower than the B-17 Flying Fortress, but all the American bombers were being used on daytime raids over the Third Reich. For all its size and muscle, however, with the addition of nine people and their gear, the cabin of the tail end Lancaster was extremely cramped.

They sat on the bare floor, their knees hunched up, in two rows, Scotty in the lead on the left and Winslow on the right. Smythe stood forward, above the empty bomb racks and bomb bay doors. He was the jumpmaster. When the time came for the drop, he would go out the bomb bay, his trajectory guided by the bombadier/navigator. They would follow him. Their Lancaster would come in lower than the others, at under one thousand feet. That was high enough to give the chutes time to open properly, yet low enough so that they would not drift off target on the winds aloft.

They were all thinking about the 165,000 pounds of bombs the other eleven Lancasters would be dropping right ahead of them. Scotty could imagine all kinds of disasters: landing on an unexploded bomb and setting it off, landing in the middle of a still burning crater, or somehow getting their signals mixed up and jumping out of the plane *before* all the bomb's were dropped. A bomb fell a lot faster than a man dangling beneath a parachute. The odds of getting hit that way were miniscule, but they were odds none the less.

Just the year before a trip to Germany entailed a

long swing out over the North Sea to avoid enemy fighters and radar in France and Belgium. But the American First Army had crossed the German frontier four months ago, so the direct route over Belgium was possible.

The Baltic Sea and the north German coast around Peenemünde were still socked in, and it was snowing, but meteorologists predicted that by morning the region would gradually start to clear. For now the way into Germany was moonless, leaving the landscape very dark. But there were some low-lying clouds, and what little light there was glinted like burnished silver off the snowcapped hills and frozen lakes and ponds.

Besides the two man-sized canisters filled with the TNT, detonators, and det cord they would use to blow up the dam, the team members traveled with heavy loads.

Each of them carried the American M3 forty-five-caliber submachine gun, a razor-sharp stiletto, a personal handgun, in Scotty's case a 9mm Beretta, three and a half feet of piano wire with handles fashioned into deadly garrotes, and a few pounds of Composition B explosive and several pencil fuses for taking out the rockets. In addition they carried three hundred rounds of ammunition for each weapon.

Scotty and Lindsay carried gas masks and surgical gloves for dealing with the anthrax payloads, along with compact tool kits to remove the canisters.

St. Lo and Ballinger carried small electronic multitesters and specialized tool kits to deal with the guidance systems. One of the last-minute tasks they'd agreed to take on was to try to bring back one of the electromechanical computers.

They wore standard battle dress uniforms overlaid with winter white camouflage suits. Any empty pocket was stuffed with food from C and K ration packets.

Smythe's first test of their capabilities at Bletchley Park was kitting them out with everything they would carry into the field, or at least the equivalent weights and shapes, and running the confidence course.

St. Lo, Smythe, Lindsay, and Winslow, the four weakest-appearing Coalminers, turned in the fastest times. But as Lindsay patiently explained to the vexed but impressed Americans, the Brits had a much greater motivation to do well against the Jerries than did the Americans.

The navigator in the lead Lancaster had been on two nighttime bombing runs to Mittelwerke, and one to the town of Nordhausen, so he knew the landmarks. Combined with his dead reckoning, they came in as if they were flying on a guidance beacon.

For the past fifteen minutes the tail end Lancaster had gradually reduced altitude. They could feel it in the back of the plane because of the decreased pitch of the engines and the popping in their ears.

Five minutes out the copilot, Lt. Harry Christiansen, came back to them. He had to shout to be heard over the tremendous din.

"We're nearly over the target. The bomb bay doors will open one minute out. Sergeant Smythe will give you the signal to hook up. The moment he's away, follow in his wake. You'll have just forty-five seconds to get out if you all want to be on target and not spread all over hell." He looked at them as if he thought they were insane, then he gave Smythe the thumbs-up and went back into the cockpit.

"Check your equipment, if you please," Smythe shouted.

They all checked their gear, especially their parachute straps, and then checked each other's equipment.

A large jeweled yellow light came on above the bulkhead in front of the bomb bay.

"Hook up," Smythe shouted. He hooked the carabiner clips for the rip cords of the two equipment canisters that had been positioned at the edge of the bomb bay, then his own to the steel cable that ran the length of the cabin.

Scotty and the others got to their feet and hooked their rip cords.

The bomb bay doors rumbled open, the already deafening noise rising in volume as a tremendous wind whipped through the aircraft.

They could hear the bombs detonating ahead of them as an almost continuous thunder with distant lightning pulsing in waves.

Smythe stood at the edge of the bomb bay, watching the light. When it switched to green he shoved the canisters over the edge, folded his arms over his chest, and stepped forward, dropping like a stone.

Scotty was next. A huge, cold fist of air slammed into his body as he dropped into the pitch-black night. Three seconds later his parachute opened, and he was violently pulled from 150 miles per hour to a near standstill.

Smythe's chute and the chutes of the two canisters were visible below and to the right. Scotty looked over his left shoulder, but he couldn't see anyone else. Already the Lancaster was lost in the distance as it did a climbing turn for the trip home.

Ahead, the hills were heavily pockmarked with

craters. Some areas in the forest were burning, and what looked like a small convoy of trucks had been hit and lay like toys on fire, scattered on and around the highway.

He tried to get his bearings, but with bomb flashes still going off like camera flashbulbs, fire coming from distant antiaircraft guns, and the small blazes lighting up the night, it was impossible. Suddenly the land came up very fast, and he was falling through the tree branches. He tucked his elbows in and bent his knees. Then he hit and rolled with his landing, just missing the bole of a large tree.

Winslow was down about fifteen yards to Scotty's left, and two others were down a little farther in the same direction.

Scotty got out of his parachute harness and was rolling the canopy and lines into a ball when Smythe, Lindsay, and Ballinger trotted over. Winslow joined them. Something was obviously wrong.

"You two okay, then?" Smythe asked. There was some blood on his hands.

"We're okay," Scotty said. "What about you?"

"It's Talbot," Smythe replied bitterly. "His bloody parachute didn't open. He went straight in."

"It was horrible," Lindsay said. "He didn't make a sound—"

"Easy," Scotty told her. "It's rotten luck, but we can't stay here discussing the man's death. Cover his body with snow, with anything you can find, and get the team together. We're moving out in five minutes."

Smythe gave him a tight look. But then he nodded. "All right, you heard the man, let's get on with it."

SIX

THE SAME NIGHT • MITTELWERKE

Schellenberg watched from the window of Marta's bedroom as the last of the bombs fell far to the south.

It made no sense to bomb the factory. They wouldn't hit the concentration camp, and there was nothing left of any strategic value in the city. So what were they trying to accomplish? Did London Station believe the message that Marta had sent them about the air vent locations?

The commandant's family had gone down to the shelter in the basement with the house staff, while the commandant himself hurried off to the camp. It was a foolish gesture on his part, though brave, Schellenberg thought.

Marta, on the other hand, refused to leave her upstairs bedroom. "Better that I die here than in some filthy Gestapo cell in Berlin," she said.

Another futile gesture? Captain Gestern would believe that she'd remained upstairs so that she could signal the incoming bombers, which was stupid. Signal the bomb crews to do what? Of course, stupidity had never hindered the Gestapo in the past.

Keeping Marta safe was going to be increasingly difficult after tonight. But he was determined to help her—at least keep her alive until the end of the war. And then they'd see if there could be some sort of a life for them.

But he was still left with the question about the bombing raid. What were the Allies trying to do tonight?

His driver appeared in the doorway. "Captain Gestern is on his way over from the communications center."

"Has he got his orders?" Schellenberg asked.

"I don't know, *Herr General.* But I'd guess he has them."

Schellenberg nodded. "Is there any word on casualties?"

"A convoy was hit, but they were mostly Jews killed. There was no damage to the factory where most of the bombs were concentrated."

"No damage to the camp, or the town?"

"No, sir."

Schellenberg reflected on the situation. The bombing accomplished nothing, if the aim was to take out the rocket factory. But the Allies knew that this raid would be useless. Yet they had gone ahead with it. Why? They weren't stupid.

They had a plan.

"Find out if any parachutists were spotted," he told his driver. "The bombing raid may have been a diversion. And find out how many of them there are and where they landed."

"Shall I alert security?"

"Yes, by all means, Hermann," Schellenberg said. "Now hurry. I'll be downstairs in the library."

Sergeant Kolst left, and Marta laughed.

"Maybe they're already here, Walther," she said. "Maybe you're already too late."

"Perhaps you're right," Schellenberg said. He took her arm, and they went downstairs to the library, just as Captain Gestern and his partner walked in.

"We'll take the prisoner now, *Herr General*," Gestern said. He held out a Gestapo Arrest Warrant, presumably signed by the *Reichsmarshall*.

"When I've finished with her," Schellenberg said. He directed her to sit down in an easy chair by the lamp.

"Are you going to defy direct orders, *Herr General*?"

"Don't be an idiot; you can do whatever you want with her once I'm finished," Schellenberg said calmly. "But at this moment I am in the middle of a delicate intelligence operation for which I need her help."

"What help—?"

"Unless you missed the noise, there was a bombing raid on the factory this evening," Schellenberg said. "But I think it was a diversion."

Gestern was interested. "For what?"

"Security is looking for evidence that parachutists have landed. Probably from the last bomber. It did seem to come in much lower than the others."

"To try to destroy the factory?" Gestern asked disparagingly. "Well, I can tell you for a fact that they won't get very far. Security around this place is as good as anything I've ever seen." He glanced over at Marta. "If you're right, what part will she play?"

"They may be here because of the messages she sent to London."

"Here to attempt a rescue?" Gestern asked incredulously.

"Exactly. And I intend using her as bait, once we find out where they are."

"They won't get anywhere near the factory, sir."

"No, but they have a plan," Schellenberg said.

He went to the desk and shuffled through the factory blueprints and area maps. If the Allies had landed a raiding party, the answers would be right in front of him. He had to know where they landed.

THURSDAY,
TWO HOURS LATER • THE DAM

Scotty held up a hand for the team to stop just below the top of the last rise before the dam. He cocked an ear to listen. Earlier he was sure he'd heard something at a distance in the woods behind them. Soldiers, almost certainly, and a lot of them. Searching for something, or someone, like hounds on the trail of a fox.

But up here there was nothing except for the soft gurgling of water. If the Germans found St. Lo's body and the hastily buried parachutes and canisters, they would instantly realize that the bombing raid was a ruse. They might come here.

He crawled up the last few feet so that he could see over the top. There was no need for binoculars. He was less than thirty yards above the tiny earthwork dam and the small lake it had created. No more than forty feet across at the top, the dam plugged a narrow gap in a rock outcropping through which the river had once splashed.

A water race, about three feet in diameter, jutted out of the hill beside the dam and disappeared underground at the base. It probably carried water downstream to a small electrical-generating station.

There were no lights on the dam, nor was there a proper road, only a narrow track through the snow to a small hut in front of which was parked a German military motorcycle and sidecar. He was directly above the hut, which, as luck would have it, was on the far side of the river. Smoke curled from the tin chimney.

Scotty slid back down to the others. "There's a guard shack twenty-five or thirty feet on the other side of the hill. One, maybe two guards at the most. I didn't see any footprints in the snow across the dam, so they're probably inside keeping warm."

"It's where I'd be," Ballinger said. He was always bitching about something.

"Smythe and I will take care of the guards. As soon as I give you the all clear, Mac and Vivian will set the charges at the base of the dam. The rest of you make a perimeter."

"Expecting company?" Winslow asked. He was very cool. He could have been talking about a stroll across Trafalgar Square.

"Somebody was making a racket behind us."

"I heard it," Lindsay said. "Do you suppose they spotted us coming down?"

"It's possible," Scotty told her. He wished that she was safely back in England, but he could not worry about that now. "If they find our chutes and pick up the trail, they'll figure out what we're up to. So we have to shake a leg."

McKeever had already unslung the two packs of

explosives he'd taken from the canisters, while Leigh was unpacking the fuses they would need.

"Go," Mac said, without looking up. "We'll be ready when you are."

Smythe took out his stiletto, but Scotty took out his Beretta and screwed a silencer on the end of the barrel.

Smythe nodded, but did not sheathe his knife.

They crawled back up to the crest of the hill, then quickly made their way through the trees to a spot behind the guard shack before they started down.

The door faced the narrow track, but a window in the side of the guard hut faced the dam. Scotty motioned for Smythe to cover the door, then crept to the side of the shack and peered inside.

One German soldier, his jacket unbuttoned, his collar open, sat at a small table munching on a piece of dark bread. His rifle leaned against the table. A field telephone sat on a shelf by the door, and except for a dim lantern that hung above the table, and a tiny woodstove in the corner, the inside of the rough shack was bare.

Scotty hesitated for a moment. Something wasn't right, but he couldn't put his finger on it for several seconds. But then he saw it. There were two chairs at the small table.

Something crashed against the other side of the hut, and Smythe appeared, wrestling a very large German soldier to the ground.

Scotty broke the window with the muzzle of his silencer and fired two shots at the soldier, who'd grabbed his rifle. The man went down, but he started to bring his rifle up, his finger on the trigger. Scotty fired two more shots, one hitting the soldier in the jaw and the second his forehead just above his left eye. He was dead before he fell to the floor.

When Scotty turned back, blood was gushing from a large slit in the throat of the second guard, who was still thrashing around trying to bring his pistol to bear on his attacker. Smythe was trying to keep a hand clamped over the much larger man's mouth, while with the other shove the pistol away and still hold his bloody stiletto.

Scotty rushed over to them, put the muzzle of his pistol against the German's heart and pulled the trigger just as the man looked up at him in mute terror. His body stiffened, then went slack. He was just a kid. Probably still in his teens.

Scotty stepped back. He looked at Smythe, who was disentangling himself from the dead German. "Are you okay?"

Smythe nodded. "Thanks for the help. You?"

"He was just a kid."

"He was a German soldier who would have killed us both as was his duty," Smythe shot back sternly. "It's just rotten that he was only a baby boy, but that's one of the reasons we're here. To stop the bastards."

Scotty looked up to the crest of the hill. McKeever was watching. Scotty gave him the all clear sign, and he and Leigh came over the top and scrambled down the steep embankment to the base of the dam. Each carried large packs of explosives.

"Get the team down here," Scotty told Smythe. "We pull out in ten minutes."

"How long a delay on the fuses?" Smythe asked.

Scotty thought about it for a moment. If the Germans showed up there, they would be looking for the explosives at the base of the dam. Given enough time they would disconnect the fuses. He wasn't going to give them the time. "I want a ten-minute head start."

It was cutting it extremely close. But Smythe nodded and headed back up the hill.

That Same Moment • Mittelwerke

The night was made longer because nobody seemed to know what was going on except that an Allied bombing attack on the factory had failed to do any significant damage. By 1:30 A.M. an increasingly worried Schellenberg knew that the longer they waited to act, the more likely the raiding party, if one had landed, would be successful. But for the life of him he still could not think of what they meant to do. He had to know where they'd come down.

Half of the combined Nordhausen-Mittelwerke security forces was guarding the concentration camp and factory, while the other half scoured the countryside looking for parachutes. Nobody slept.

The house staff had brought food and drink to the study. Afterward, Marta had to use the bathroom. Gestern sent his sergeant to watch her, and Schellenberg did not object, though he wanted to.

There were two alternate possibilities. The bombing could have been a legitimate, though futile, attempt to destroy or at least damage the rocket factory. Or, the raid was a ruse for something completely different than a landing party of saboteurs.

Maybe they'd come to draw scarce fighter and antiaircraft resesources from somewhere else.

He called a friend at what was left of Luftwaffe Headquarters in Berlin, who informed him that he was too busy to answer every damned fool who called with stupid questions for which there were no satisfactory answers any longer. Schellenberg could hear bombs falling on the capital city over the long-distance telephone line, and the desperation in his friend's voice.

"There was an air raid on Mittelwerke tonight," Schellenberg told him.

"We know about the raid. But we didn't do anything about it because they can't hurt the factory."

"Did radar track the bombers afterward?"

"They went back to Belgium, then home across the Channel, we presume. What's your interest, Walther?"

"I think that something is going to happen down here."

"Well, if you want my advice, keep your ass covered. It won't be long now."

Sergeant Kolst appeared at the door. "You were right, *Herr General,* a raiding party did land. We found seven parachutes and one body. He broke his neck on landing."

"Good," Captain Gestern said.

"They're still looking, but just before I headed back up here, they found an equipment container and its parachute."

Schellenberg went to the desk and spread out the map. "Show me where they came down. Exactly."

Kolst studied the map to orient himself, then stabbed a blunt finger on a spot several kilometers to the north and west of the factory. In fact, not too far from the hunting lodge. Startled, Gestern looked up at Marta.

"Maybe they're coming here after all," she taunted.

"Which direction did they go?" Schellenberg asked.

"That's the bad news," Kolst said. "By the time they found where the parachutes and body were buried, the snow was heavily trampled. They had a large area to search."

"What about the factory entrances?"

"The SS are taking care of that, *Herr General,*" Gestern said. "Nobody will get in that way. If they're foolish enough to try, they'll be cut down."

Gestern was right, of course. But the Allies were not stupid. They had a plan. *They were here. For what? To do what?*

Destroy the factory? Or in some way hurt its operation or personnel?

Schellenberg looked at Marta sitting in the corner, a Mona Lisa smile on her face. He turned back to the map, and suddenly he had it.

The small dam above the factory. Directly below, in the the old riverbed, were several air vent shafts. If the dam were to be destroyed, the water would flood the shafts, leading directly into the factory. It would cause a lot of damage, and possibly even completely flood the place.

He looked up. "I know what they're trying to do."

"What is it?" Gestern asked.

"I'll tell you on the way. And if I'm right, I know how to stop them."

0230 • The Dam

Scotty waited at the top of the dam. He was becoming nervous. McKeever and Leigh were taking far too long with the explosives. But it looked as if they were having trouble digging deeply enough into the base of the dam because the ground was frozen rock hard.

The field telephone in the guard shack had not rung. There was no way of telling if the guards were supposed to report on a schedule. But even if they were not missed, St. Lo's body and the parachutes might be found. If they also found the canisters, the Germans might put two and two together. Not all of them were stupid.

Smythe had put Ballinger, Don Smith, and Lindsay on the hill across the river in the direction they would have to go to reach the drop zone. He and Winslow had gone a hundred yards down the narrow track and set explosive charges on several large trees. If someone tried to come up, they would drop the trees across the road, slowing any sort of a mechanized attack. With luck it would give them enough time to escape into the woods.

If that did occur, their biggest problem would be leading the Germans away from the landing zone and still giving themselves enough time to get back for the pickup.

He walked back to the guard hut. Nothing could be seen down the narrow road. Only a few puffy clouds obscurred the star-studded sky, but thankfully there was no moon. The night was deathly still and very cold.

Scotty started to turn when two sharp explosions echoed off the hills down the track. Almost immediately there was a third, then a fourth.

Smythe and Winslow had triggered the explosives to block the road. Someone was coming.

He ran back to the dam. Mac and Leigh had also heard the explosions. It was impossible to see exactly what they were doing, but it was clear that they were hurrying.

Lindsay stepped out from behind a tree at the

crest of the ridge across the river. She was fifty feet above the dam. She motioned toward the road with two fingers in front of her eyes, indicating that she was seeing something.

She held up one finger, made a steering wheel motion with both hands, then stopped.

Scotty cocked an ear to listen. He couldn't hear a thing.

Lindsay held up five fingers, and walked them up the hill.

Five people had shown up in one car and they were heading up the road on foot.

Scotty signaled his understanding.

Smythe and Winslow should have been up here by now. What the hell was taking them so long?

McKeever signaled from the bottom of the dam that they were ready to set the fuses.

They were running out of time.

Scotty signaled them to proceed, then get up the hill to where Lindsay and the others were waiting. He turned and headed past the guard shack and down the hill.

They had ten minutes, starting now, to get the hell out of here. If the dam blew while they were on this side of the river, it'd be all over for them.

Before he got twenty yards there was the sudden crackle of small-arms fire ahead. He scrambled off the side of the track and into the woods, where he held up to try to figure out what was going on.

The shooting stopped, and Scotty worked his way farther down the hill. Four large trees blocked the path. Below them, a large Mercedes sedan with general's flags on the fenders was stopped, its door open. Two people were down in the snow beside the car and not moving.

He couldn't see anyone else. The forest was deathly still. He knew that Smythe and Winslow had to be close, but he couldn't figure out why they had gotten into a shoot-out after they had dropped the trees.

He moved from tree to tree down the hill until he was within twenty or thirty feet of the Mercedes. Still he could see no one on either side of the barrier.

"Here," Winslow whispered urgently to his left.

Winslow was crouched beneath the low-hanging boughs of a fir tree, his M3 trained on the Mercedes.

Scotty scrambled over beside him. "What the hell are you doing? We have to get out of here. We've got less than ten minutes before the dam blows."

"Sarah is here. They've got my wife. I'm not leaving without her."

"Where's Smythe?"

"Here," Smythe said from a tree a few yards away. "I agree with the major. If we leave her here, they'll kill her."

"Go left, I'll take right," Scotty told Smythe. "Don will give us thirty seconds, then open fire on the middle of the blockade."

Without waiting for a reply, Scotty scrambled down the hill to the jumble of splintered wood stumps where the explosives had felled the trees. From his angle he could see the two downed Germans lying in the snow beside the car. One of them was a sergeant.

Something out of the corner of his eye caught his attention. A single set of footprints led away from the car straight down the hill toward the riverbed, disappearing into the dark woods. It was Winslow's wife. He'd bet anything on it. She'd taken her chance and run for it.

Her only hope would be to get across the riverbed and up the other side before the dam blew.

It was the only hope for all of them.

Winslow opened fire.

Scotty jumped up. He caught sight of two Germans, one of them with general's stars on his shoulder boards, crouching behind the barrier. He fired his M3, emptying the clip on full automatic, then ducked back to reload.

Smythe fired from the other side of the barrier.

Scotty popped back up, but both Germans were down and unmoving.

"Clear," Scotty shouted.

Winslow came running down the path. "Sarah," he shouted.

"She's gone Winslow," Scotty shouted back. "She took off downriver."

Winslow started over the downed trees, but Scotty pulled him back.

"We can't go after her now. We have to finish the mission."

"I'm not going with you—"

Smythe backhanded Winslow across the face. "You won't do your wife any good," he said sternly. "Are you hearin' me? She's survived for this long in Germany, she'll know more about escaping than we do if we're caught."

Winslow looked as if he wanted to bolt, but then some of the wildness drained from his eyes, and he shook his head. "Bloody hell. I actually saw her. She was right here."

"We've got less than five minutes to get across the dam, or we'll be stuck."

Winslow hesitated a moment longer before he turned away from the barrier and followed Scotty and Smythe back up the hill as fast as his legs could carry him.

They reached the guard shack and raced across the dam. The others at the top of the hill were frantically waving them on.

Smythe was first, but when Winslow slipped and fell, he went back. He and Scotty helped the major to his feet, and they clawed and scrambled their way up the steep slope.

At the top Scotty stopped to look back. He thought he saw a movement behind the barrier in front of the Mercedes. But then a deep-throated thump shook the ground. His eyes were dragged to the dam, which was collapsing in slow motion. Water began to stream over the crumbling top in a trickle, at first, that turned into a torrent, sending a wall of water down the dry riverbed.

He turned to Winslow, who was searching down river for as far as he could see. But there was nothing there except for a tidal wave of water moving at the speed of an express train.

0400 • The Landing Zone

They'd been obliged to march single file, doubling back to cover their tracks from time to time. Even so, they made it to their rendezvous point with several minutes to spare. Increasing cloud cover made the already black night even darker. The narrow, snow-covered valley between low mountains in the Harz range was deserted.

Ballinger, McKeever, Leigh, and Smith formed a line in the middle of the field. When they heard the airplane they would switch on their flashlights to guide the pilot in.

Providing Colonel Bruce was successful in rounding up transportation for them.

"Are you certain it was your wife back there?" Scotty asked Winslow. They stood huddled at the edge of the field.

"Yes," said Winslow. He was morose, and nobody could blame him. But once they reached Peenemünde, he would have to come back on track. The team needed him.

"Then the general we shot was probably Schellenberg."

Winslow's eyes widened when he realized the significance of what Scott had said. "You knew?"

"I knew that she was at Mittelwerke. But I never dreamed they'd bring her up to the dam. Schellenberg was going to use her to stop us."

"We should have gone after her—"

"If anyone can make it out, it's her," Smythe said, trying to be reassuring.

Lindsay, who was standing with them, averted her eyes, which were glistening. Her brother was relatively safe in a POW camp. But if they caught Sarah, the Germans would shoot her as a spy.

Smythe suddenly turned toward the west. "Here comes an airplane." He shook his head. "I don't recognize the sound. It might be German."

The others in the field had heard it, too, and they turned on their flashlights and aimed them straight up.

Scotty was listening intently. He recognized the sounds of the Pratt & Whitney twin Wasps. "It's one of ours. A Dakota."

But he was hearing something else as well. Someone was behind them. In the woods. He turned in time to see a disturbed pine bough drop its snow.

"We've got company," he warned. He pulled out his silenced Beretta and motioned for everyone to get down.

Smythe and the others pulled out their weapons. He looked over his shoulder at the Americans in the middle of the field with their flashlights. "What about the bloody airplane?"

"Wait," Scotty cautioned. Something wasn't right. If the Germans had followed them, they would have made noise. Something. And there was no way that the Germans could have known about this landing site ahead of time, to set up an ambush.

The Dakota DC-3 was very low now, coming in for a landing at the far end of the valley. They had run out of time.

"Who is it?" Scotty called out in English. He had to take the chance of drawing fire before the plane landed.

A slight figure in a very large coat of some sort stumbled out of the trees. It was hard to tell who it was, but then Scotty realized that it was a woman.

"My, God! Sarah," Winslow cried. He leaped up and ran to her before they could stop him. It could have been a trap.

But he grabbed her off her feet, the greatcoat falling off her shoulders, and they kissed and held each other, as the Dakota's front skis touched down with a puff of powder snow, the mission only half over with.

SEVEN

Before Dawn • En Route to Peenemünde

The Dakota was the lap of luxury compared to the Lancaster. A British medic and two crewmen had come along to render assistance. Sarah's wounds, none of them serious, were cleaned and re-dressed while the crewmen handed out hot coffee laced with brandy, and cheese and bologna sandwiches.

They flew very low and fast to keep out of the range of German radar, but still the two-hundred-mile flight up to Peenemünde off the Baltic coast was made half again longer because they had to avoid towns, military bases, and major highways. At one point they were less than thirty miles west of the Berlin outskirts.

They saw plenty of military convoys, and some tank traffic heading toward the west, but no air traffic whatsoever.

Many of the roads and even some of the smaller

towns were heavily damaged. Bomb craters in a corridor between Hamburg and Berlin were so numerous it was like looking down at a lunar landscape.

Another thing that struck Scotty was how dark the countryside was. There were almost no lights anywhere. Normally the sky glow of any big city such as Berlin would have been visible for miles. But the sky to the east was as pitch-black as it was in any other direction. There weren't many fires tonight.

At the start of this mission he never dreamed that Winslow's wife would show up the way she had. It was incredible. But now it was another problem he would have to deal with. The best solution would be to send her home on this airplane. But when he'd broached the subject to her, she'd completely ignored him.

She and her husband and sister had been huddled together ever since the medic had finished with her. They had a lot of catching up to do.

She was an extraordinary woman. She told them that she slipped away from Schellenberg and headed across the river not simply to escape. She knew that someone had come to blow the dam to flood the factory, and she wanted to draw Schellenberg, his driver, and the pair of Gestapo thugs to follow her, to lead them away from the dam.

After the explosion, she picked up the Coalminers' trail and followed them to the landing zone, always keeping a safe distance between her and them on the off chance that somehow Schellenberg was following her. She would provide an early warning if it came to that.

But nobody had followed, and when she heard the airplane coming in for a landing she'd made her presence known. For a few moments she thought that Scott might shoot first and ask questions later.

"I was petrified," she told them, which brought a laugh.

After everything she'd been through in the past twelve months in Germany the thought that she could be that frightened at the end was almost ludicrous.

Scotty got up and went back to them. Winslow held her in his arms, and Lindsay sat back against a bulkhead on her parachute pack, her legs stretched out in front of her. They looked up.

"We'll be over Peenemünde pretty soon. We have to start getting ready," he told them.

"I understand that you lost one of your people in the jump," Sarah said. Smythe had carried St. Lo's pack all the way through the operation. Sarah was kitted out with his spare uniform and jumper.

Scotty nodded. "How do you feel?"

She gave her husband a fond look. "Much better, thank you. I'm coming with you in place of Talbot to finish the job."

It was about what Scotty expected. "I don't suppose there's any use arguing with her," he said to Winslow.

"No," Sarah answered. "My husband does not make decisions for me. We make them together. I'm taking Talbot's place. We've already agreed."

"I am the team leader," Scotty shot back, even though he knew he was in a losing battle.

Sarah managed a smile. "Congratulations, Captain, you just inherited a new Coalminer. I only hope that you've secured us decent accommodations where we're headed."

Scotty couldn't help but return her warm smile.

Lindsay's family was something else. "The Ritz," he told her.

0900 • MITTELWERKE

It was full daylight by the time Schellenberg reached the main road and hailed a military supply truck. A stray bullet had passed through the Mercedes' radiator and shattered the distributor cap, making the car unusable. It had been a very long, cold walk down the mountain. But there was a lot of traffic here.

"You're bleeding, *Herr General*," the young Wehrmacht driver said.

"Just a flesh wound. Has the factory flooded?"

"Yes, sir. We're taking as much equipment out as fast as possible."

"Has a command post been set up?"

"Yes, *Herr General*, at the commandant's house."

"Take me there."

A steady stream of trucks filled with personnel and equipment headed toward the prison camp, while empty trucks, like the one he rode in, headed back toward the underground factory to help salvage whatever they could.

It was a disaster, in part brought on by his own stupidity for falling in love with a British spy. He never hated anybody more than he hated Sarah Winslow at that moment.

She had caused the Reich irreparable harm. And there was more to come. He'd heard them talking when they thought he was dead. One of them was an American; he recognized the nasal East Coast accent.

"We can't go after her now. We have to finish the mission."

Incredibly enough, one of the other men was Major Winslow, Marta's husband. He had been so close to his wife that he could touch her, and yet he agreed that the mission came before saving her.

Schellenberg's fists bunched so hard his shoulder wound twinged with an extremely sharp needle of pain, and he winced involuntarily.

The driver looked over in alarm. "Sir, I think you should go to the hospital."

He wasn't going to do anyone any good if he passed out, but even now the Allied commandos might be preparing to completely destroy the factory; or worse yet, kill their key personnel.

"Take me to the commandant's house. I'll see a medic there."

Traffic was also heavy to and from the hunting lodge. Stern-faced SS guards checked everyone one hundred meters below the house and again at the front door. They snapped to attention when they saw Schellenberg's rank, but asked to see his ID nonetheless.

The living room had been set up as a temporary command post now that the regular communications and control center in Mittelwerke was flooded. A lot of radios had been set up, aerials hastily strung up in the trees outside, and maps and charts pinned to the walls.

SS Major Karl Nebel, who was in overall command of Mittelwerke-Nordhausen security, looked up from the factory blueprints that he and several engineers were poring over. His rotund figure and narrow pig eyes behind steel-framed glasses made him look like a mean-spirited small-town banker, which he had been before 1939.

"Where have you been, *Herr General*?" he demanded "I have three squads out searching for you. We thought the commandos had kidnapped you."

"I was at the dam," Schellenberg said. "How bad is it?"

"We cannot stop the flooding. It'll take at least six months, perhaps longer, to divert the river and pump out the factory." Nebel's eyes narrowed even farther. "You were up there?"

"I had a fair guess what was about to happen, so I tried to stop them. I failed."

"You should have notified me," Nebel said angrily.

"It was my decision, *Herr Major*," Schellenberg shot back harshly. "But the raid is not over. There's more."

"I'm not the Gestapo—"

"There's more, Nebel. They might be right outside this house even as we speak."

"They've gone back to England."

"How do you know that?"

"One of my patrols spotted an airplane coming in about ten kilometers from here. By the time they could get close to the landing field, the damned thing took off. But they found evidence that at least a half dozen people, probably more, got aboard. Radar lost the plane heading west." Nebel glanced at the blueprints. "They're back in England by now, and we have this mess to clean up." He gave Schellenberg a bleak look. "And we have to determine how it happened. Someone is at fault."

"They're not in England," Schellenberg said.

"Oh?" Nebel asked, arching an eyebrow.

"They flew to Peenemünde to finish the job."

"I don't think so, *Herr General*," Nebel said. He shook his head. "No, I think that you are quite wrong again. Even the British wouldn't be that stupid. Perhaps you have been wrong about nearly everything."

1400 • Peenemünde

Scotty lay in the snow on a rise that looked out over the thickly wooded landscape that ran all the way down to the broad mouth of the Peene River. Two German soldiers, dressed in winter whites, their rifles slung over their shoulders, worked their way up the hill from where they'd left their VW. They were still nearly a mile off, and he could see through his binoculars that they were having a hard time in the deep snow. It would be a half hour before they got up here.

The open sea was a couple miles toward the northwest. The rocket research facility was spread out for several miles along the coast.

But the soldiers approaching were more than a security patrol. Something about them, about their being so far afield, led Scotty to believe that they were searching for something specific.

He pulled back below the rise, brushing snow across his tracks, then, making sure that he stayed on the tracks he'd made coming up, hurried down to the clearing in the middle of which stood the bombed-out ruins of what once had been a nice stone farmhouse. The Coalminers were staying in the fruit cellar.

The Ritz it wasn't, but secure it had been thus far. He expected that security would be tightened because of their attack on Mittelwerke. But if the patrol on the way up was looking specifically for them, it could mean that the pilot's ruse of flying west to fool German radar had not worked. It could also mean that the launch of the three V5s had been pushed up.

Ballinger stood lookout just within the ruins of the house. He was huddled out of the raw wind in the lee of the still standing chimney.

"Anything?" he asked.

"Two Germans are coming up the hill," Scotty told him.

"Shit, we've got another four hours before dark."

"We're going to set a trap. Keep a sharp eye out." Scotty went down the rickety ladder into the fruit cellar. The light from the one oil lantern they'd found was dim. Sarah was asleep in the corner, her head on Winslow's lap. The others were cleaning their weapons, organizing the Composition B and fuses they were going to use to blow up the rockets, going over their ammunition and other supplies, or just trying to relax and get something to eat. Tonight promised to be even longer than last night. Their rendezvous with the submarine wasn't until two in the morning, twelve hours from now.

"Okay, we have a problem coming our way," Scotty said. "Two Germans are coming up the hill from the road. There's just the two of them, and they've left their car on the road."

Sarah came instantly awake and sat up. "It's Schellenberg's doing. Are you sure you killed him?"

Scotty thought back to the moment just before the dam blew. He thought that he had seen a figure darting behind the Mercedes. But he wasn't sure. "I wouldn't bet my life on it. But he was hit, I saw the blood."

"So did I," Smythe said. "What makes you think that he's here?"

"He knows that Mittelwerke wasn't the only target," Sarah said. "He knows that we know about the three rockets." She looked at her husband. "He's in love with me. If he's alive, he won't give up so easily."

"If he wasn't killed at the dam, and if he *is* here, he can only suspect that we've come after the rockets," Winslow said. "And he'd be a perfect fool if he didn't love you."

"Once those soldiers find out about this place, he'll know for sure," Smythe said.

"We're going to kill them, switch uniforms, and two of us are going to take a little tour in their car," Scotty told them. "A rocket-finding tour."

"I'm coming with," Sarah said.

"Don't be a fool," Scotty told her flatly, and she reacted as if she had been slapped. But he grinned. "Anyway, you don't look like a German soldier. And if Schellenberg is here and happens to be at one of the launch sites, he could recognize you, and the game would be up."

Scotty was right, and Sarah knew it. She nodded, but it was obvious she didn't like the decision. She was used to living on the edge, living by her wits.

"They'll be at the top of the hill shortly," Scotty said. "Smythe, Mac, and Vivian will come with me. The rest of you pack up our gear and get ready to move out. If something goes wrong, you'll know it soon enough." He took out his silenced Beretta and checked the load. He had a full magazine plus one in the chamber.

"If they spot us first, and shoot, the game, as you

say, will be up," Smythe pointed out. "That kind of sound carries a long way."

"We'll let them come all the way into the house, then take them with garrotes. My pistol will be a last resort. I want as little blood as possible on their uniforms."

"Let's get on with it," Smythe said.

Ballinger was watching the crest of hill when they went up. "Nothing yet," he said.

"We'll hide in back until they get inside the front wall, then Mac and Smythe will sneak around front to get behind them, while the rest of us take them front on" Scotty said. "I want it quick and quiet."

They followed him to the rear of the house, where they spread out along the partially collapsed stone wall. From here they had a reasonably good view of the hill and excellent sight lines through to the front of the house.

Smythe spotted the top of a helmet at the crest of the hill. "Here they come."

Moments later both German soldiers appeared at the top of the hill. They spotted the partially brushed-out trail and the house at the bottom. They immediately unslung their rifles, said something to each other, and started down the slope.

It took forever for them to reach the house. But they were being cautious. As if they expected to find trouble. But if they were looking for a force of eight or nine commandos, they weren't being very smart about not first calling for reinforcements.

As they got closer, however, the mystery was solved for Scotty. He spotted the black collars of their uniforms beneath their winter whites. Twin lightning bolts gleamed. They were SS and arrogant.

Nothing could happen to them. They were the masters of the master race.

One of them came up the stone step into the house. He stopped short when he spotted the trapdoor to the fruit cellar. He beckoned for his partner to come quietly.

Mac and Smythe quickly worked their way to the front of the house.

Scotty gave them to the count of ten, then handed his pistol to Ballinger. He got to his feet and raised his hands over his head.

"I give up," he shouted.

The soldiers snapped around, bringing their rifles to bear.

"Don't shoot! Don't shoot, for Christ's sake," Scotty shouted. "I'm an American."

Mac and Smythe silently came up the step and entered the house. One of the Germans started to turn around.

"Nicht scheissen," Scotty shouted. *"Bitte, nicht scheissen!"*

Mac and Smythe looped the piano wire garrotes over the Germans' necks and pulled at the same moment.

Both Germans struggled violently, but they had no chance whatsoever. Gradually their struggles weakened, and they slumped to the floor, dead, their faces purple, almost black. But there was little or no blood.

Scotty and the others came from the back. "We have to hustle now," he said. They started removing the dead soldiers' uniforms. "Get Kilroy up here. He's coming with me to look for the rockets." Don Smith was their rocket expert.

Mac went to the fruit cellar door to summon Smith.

"What do we do in the meantime?" Smythe asked.

"Get ready to move out as soon as we get back," Scotty said, taking off his winter whites and uniform. "Two teams. I'll take one, and Lindsay gets the other. That's unless Don and I don't make it back. Then Major Winslow will take my team. Move out after dark."

The others clambered out of the fruit cellar, and Don Smith peeled out of his uniform and put on one of the German uniforms. He looked scared but determined.

"If we don't get back, it'll mean that the Germans will be at an even greater state of alert. All I can say is do the best you can," Scotty said to Winslow. "But those rockets must not be allowed to fly."

"Then you'd best find out where they're set up and come back here," Lindsay said. She kissed Scotty lightly on the lips, then Smith on the cheek. "Good luck."

1530 • Peenemünde

The ride down from Mittelwerke in the spider-legged Fiesler-Storch light spotter plane was rough. The air was bumpy, and the overcast had thickened as they neared the rocket research facility. By the time they touched down Schellenberg was bone weary, his shoulder wound hurt like hell, and he was in a foul mood.

A young Wehrmacht corporal picked him up at the airstrip and drove him over to headquarters in a battered VW *Kriegswagen.* The once impressive research center was now mostly in ruins. No building was without damage, and Schellenberg gloomily estimated that 70 or 80 percent were totally beyond repair.

The mighty Third Reich was grinding to a ponderous halt, choking on the dust rising from its bombed-out towns and factories. Sending three rockets loaded with anthrax to the American capital would kill a lot of people if they reached their destination and actually detonated on target. Maybe they'd even kill the cripple Roosevelt. But would it end the war in Germany's favor? Looking around him, Schellenberg sincerely doubted it.

Then why bother? Most soldiers out of the *Führer's* direct eye were merely going through the motions. German boys were being killed, but the high-ranking officers were fleeing to Switzerland or Portugal, or, for a lucky few, even Argentina and Brazil.

But this was no longer about Germany. This situation had been made personal. Not by him, but by Sarah Winslow, the dirty little British spy who had been nothing more than a lying whore all the time. He clenched his fists again, but this time it was more than his shoulder wound that hurt.

The four-story headquarters building was situated at the end of what once had been a pleasant tree-lined lane. Research and engineering laboratories were scattered in the woods like the sprawling campus of a modern university. Now all was mostly in ruins. Where once scientists and engineers strolled along paths, the facility looked deserted.

He instructed his driver to wait for him and entered the building, where he had to show his pass to an SS sergeant, who directed him to offices down a long corridor.

Peenemünde chief scientist Wernher von Braun

and chief of security SS *Oberstleutnant* Ernst Hofbauer were waiting for him in a littered conference room. Papers and diagrams were strewn everywhere, on the table, on chairs, on the floor, as if someone had been frantically searching for something.

Von Braun sat, looking moodily out a window, and he barely acknowledged Schellenberg's arrival. But Hofbauer got to his feet, an angry scowl on his narrow face.

"I understand that you are a general officer, and that you fill a vital function in State Security, but you are wasting valuable time by coming here and demanding to inspect us."

Schellenberg held his temper in check, to do otherwise would delay them even longer. "I have a car and driver at my disposal. Thank you for that, *Herr Oberstleutnant.* Now I require that you pinpoint for me the locations of the three rockets you mean to fire. I would like to inspect your security."

"As you wish, *Herr General,*" Hofbauer replied. "But security may be a moot point. The rockets will be launched at midnight."

"That may be too late. The saboteurs may already be here."

"I have patrols out searching the area. So far they've found nothing."

"In any event that may be another moot point, *Herr General,*" von Braun said. "The rockets will not be ready to fly *until* then." He looked away. "*If* then," he muttered.

1700 • PEENEMÜNDE

Scotty drove past the access road to launch site number three. The four SS guards on duty behind the barrier idly glanced at them, but made no motion for them to stop.

Finding the rockets had been ridiculously easy. Too easy? Scotty was becoming paranoid. No one had challenged them or asked to see their passes. It was almost as if a trap were being set for them. But that made no sense either.

Smith had found a facility map in the VW on which were marked *Spezial Sicherheit Zonen,* Special Security Zones, in red cross-hatchings. In addition to the cluster of engineering buildings around headquarters, one of the rocket assembly halls and the underground entrances to several exotic fuel storage bunkers, three areas in the woods northwest of the Central Works were so marked. They were all isolated and all within a couple hundred yards of each other, accessible by paved roads capable of handling heavy trucks.

Driving past, they were able to catch glimpses through the trees of the rockets on their launchers. None of them had been raised to the fire position yet. All of them were still protected by tarps. The casing around one of the rockets had been removed, exposing the motor. None of the V5s had been fitted with their nose cone payloads yet.

There were a lot of people around each of the rockets, most of them civilians, either engineers or technicians. A number of trucks and vans were gathered around each rocket, with wires and heavy cables snaking from what was presumably test equipment into the innards of each machine.

The Germans seemed to be working at a feverish pace. As if they were facing a fast-approaching deadline.

"How soon before they're ready to launch?" Scotty

asked, following the road that led back to the main north–south transport highway.

"No way of telling," Smith said. "But it'll take them at least six hours to add the nose cones, button all the panels, and fuel the rockets. That's if nothing's wrong."

"What'd it look like to you?" Scotty glanced in the rearview mirror, half-expecting to see a truckload of SS troops speeding after them. But no one was coming.

"It didn't look like they were making repairs," Smith said. "I'd guess they were simply getting three experimental rockets ready to launch." He gave Scotty a concerned look. "In a big hurry."

"They're worried about something," Scotty said. He grinned with more confidence than he felt. "Let's get back to the others."

The main highway that ran through the facility was like an artery connecting the various research and engineering areas with the assembly halls, test beds, launchpads, and storage dumps for everything from heavy equipment to fuels. The highway also ran straight up the length of the island. The snow-covered dirt road that led to the hill behind which the Coalminers were holed up was about five kilometers away.

Coming around a curve on the main route, they encountered a small canvas truck parked beside the road. Two SS soldiers got out of the cab and walked out onto the highway and waved them to a stop.

Scotty had worried about something like this. It was just rotten luck that it happened now, when they were so close to getting out of the facility's main security perimeter.

He eased the silenced Beretta out of his jumper,

felt for the safety, and switched it off as he slowed to a halt. He motioned for Smith to make no sudden moves.

The pair of security soldiers came up on either side of the car. The one on Scotty's side had not unslung his rifle, but the soldier on the other side had. Neither of them looked overly suspicious; in fact, they seemed bored. There wasn't much traffic this far out. Especially not today.

"What are you doing on this road?" the guard on Scotty's left asked.

"Checking security measures," Scotty replied in German.

The guard apparently suspected that something was wrong, probably with Scotty's accent, because he reached for his rifle.

Scotty levered himself up against the back of the seat and fired two shots past Smith, hitting the guard in the chest. Then he turned as the guard to his left was bringing his rifle to bear and shot the man in the face at point-blank range.

Both guards were down.

"We're taking them with us," Scotty said. He went around to the passenger side of the car. The second guard opened his eyes, and Scotty shot him in the forehead.

He and Smith loaded the bodies into the backseat of their VW and scraped snow over the blood that had leaked onto the road.

"Take the truck and follow me," Scotty said.

Smith glanced at the dead Germans in the back of the VW, then trotted over to the truck and got in.

They drove out into the countryside, turning down the dirt road in the deepening gloom. Now there were four German soldiers missing. It wouldn't be long before somebody came looking for them.

The clock starts now, Scotty thought.

1730 • PEENEMÜNDE

It was almost fully dark when Schellenberg's driver pulled up at the barrier guarding the road to rocket number three. Two SS guards were on duty. They came nervously to attention as the general got out of the car and walked over to them. They saluted.

"Who has come and gone past in the last couple of hours?" Schellenberg demanded.

"Technicians, *Herr General.* They're setting up the rocket," the SS sergeant answered.

"Anyone else? Someone perhaps passing by, maybe slowing down but not stopping? Someone on foot?"

A look of recognition dawned in the sergeant's eyes. "Yes, sir. They were driving a *Kriegswagen.* Two soldiers in white. They drove past."

"Did you recognize either of them?"

"No, *Herr General,* I never saw either of them before. But there are a lot of soldiers here."

"Which way did they go?"

The sergeant motioned toward the north. "The road returns to the Central Works highway."

"How long ago?"

The sergeant shrugged. "Twenty minutes, maybe thirty."

Schellenberg jumped back in the car, his heart pounding. It was them. He knew it was the American and his commandos. They were here after all.

With Sarah.

His driver headed to the main road while Schellenberg worked it out. The Allied raiders were hiding somewhere nearby. Somehow they'd managed to get two German uniforms and a patrol car so that they could find out the locations of the three rockets.

Presumably they went back to the others to get ready for the strike, which could take place at anytime after dark.

Even with double the number of security guards it might be impossible to stop the commandos from destroying at least one of the rockets and perhaps all of them.

The fools here, Hofbauer and especially von Braun, were relying on the thick overcast, which made an air raid impossible, and on the isolation of the facility, which made a raid by land unlikely.

They had grouped the rockets all within shouting distance of each other. That was Hofbauer's idea. It made security easier, he said. And they had set them up in very small clearings that were surrounded by dense forests. There were no perimeter fences.

But then another thought struck Schellenberg. Von Braun had been eager to take the Reich's money to develop his little toys, but he had never been keen on actually firing them as weapons.

Maybe he was stalling as he had been all along. Maybe von Braun was secretly hoping that a commando raid would make it impossible to launch.

Maybe that's why the rockets were still in the stages of preparation. They had not even been fueled yet. Nor had the anthrax canisters been attached.

Oberstleutnant Hofbauer was an idiot. Von Braun was anything but.

To the left, the road ran back to the research and engineering areas of the base. To the right it led straight north to the tip of the heavily wooded island. Schellenberg pointed north. "We'll go this way."

"Pardon me, *Herr General,* but shouldn't we get help first?" the corporal asked.

Schellenberg was impatient. "There's no time," he barked. "Move!"

"Yes, sir," the corporal said, and they headed north.

Within a couple hundred meters their headlights flashed across deep ruts in the snow on the side of the road and something dark on the pavement. Schellenberg ordered the driver to pull over.

He took a flashlight from the glove compartment and walked over to the dark spots on the road. At first he thought it might be oil. But someone had taken the effort to cover the stains with snow. He scraped some of the snow away with the toe of a boot. It was dark red. Blood. And it was not completely frozen yet.

His eyes went to the ruts off the side of the road. A security patrol had been stationed here. The two commandos had driven up, shot the guards, covered the blood, and stolen the second vehicle. They had probably taken the bodies with them.

Schellenberg sprang back to the car. "They came this way, and not very long ago."

"What would you like to do, *Herr General*?"

"Follow them," Schellenberg roared. "We'll find out where they turned off."

1815 • The Farmhouse

Scotty showed them the locations of the three launchpads on the map. The rockets had been grouped close together, probably for purposes of security.

"It actually makes our job easier," he told them. "We'll split into three teams instead of two. Sarah and Vivian will go with Major Winslow. Mac and Ballinger with Smythe and Kilroy and Lieutenant Miles with me."

"What about the anthrax?" Lindsay asked.

"It hasn't been loaded aboard the rockets yet," Scotty said. "And even if it had been, we'd never get close enough to grab it. There are SS and Wehrmacht troops crawling all over the place."

"Do they know that we're here?" Smythe asked.

"I think that they might have a fair idea. From what we could see they're bustin' their humps to get the rockets ready to launch. Which is why I want to go down there, ASAP, destroy the things, and get the hell out."

"They'll come looking for us with a vengeance afterward," Winslow said. "Mightn't it be better to wait until later in the evening? Closer to our rendezvous time with the sub?" He looked at the others. "I don't fancy being chased all over this island by a lot of irate Germans."

"No," Scotty said. "If we give them enough time, they'll eventually install the anthrax containers, and we'll be in big trouble."

"I'd say blow them in any event," Smythe said.

"If it comes to that, we'll do it. But I want to avoid the issue. We go now." He turned back to the map. "We'll be on foot afterward, so it'll be up to each team to get out to the rendezvous point on the beach without being followed. That's about three miles out."

"We can slow the Jerries down if we leave a few surprises in our wake," Smythe said. "We have enough trip wire to rig some Composition B and zero-delay fuses across our path. When they come stumbling through the woods, they'll be in for a nasty surprise. Should slow them down a bit."

"Good," Scotty said.

"That sounds like the easy bit," Lindsay said. "But how in heaven's name do you propose that we destroy the rockets in the first place if we can't get close to the things?"

"We're not," Scotty said. He turned back to the map and marked a pair of small Xs in each launch area.

"Fuel trucks," Don Smith said. "We saw them parked at one of the launch sites, so we're assuming they're at the other two." He looked up. "The white trucks will contain LOX—liquid oxygen. There'll be steam coming off the sides if they're loaded. And the dark trucks will contain the fuel. Hydrazine hydrate, or maybe something even more interesting. Whatever it is, it will be highly flammable."

"The point is, the ones we saw were parked at the edge of the clearing," Scotty said. "Which means we should be able to get to them without being detected."

"The trick will be to get both trucks to blow at just about the same time," Smith explained. "If we can get the fuel and the LOX to mix, it'll make a hell of a fire. Nothing is going to survive in those clearings. Certainly not the rockets."

"Nor the people," Sarah said with a vicious smile.

Scotty looked at his watch. "It's 1815," he said. "We'll take the truck back to the base perimeter and split up there. It'll be up to each team to get to their launch site, set the booby traps, place the charges under the trucks, set the fuses, and get out."

"Time?" Winslow asked.

"Nineteen-thirty."

Everyone reacted. "That only gives us an hour and fifteen," Ballinger said. "That's cutting it a bit thin."

"Then we'd best get started now," Scotty said.

1820 • The Main Highway

The corporal spotted the tracks leading off the main highway first. He slowed down. "There," he said, pointing off to the left.

"Stop the car," Schellenberg ordered. At first he couldn't see a thing. But then he saw what the corporal had spotted. A narrow dirt road led west off the highway. Clearly at least one vehicle had gone that way. Recently.

He jumped out and walked up the road and shined the beam of his flashlight on the tracks. There were more than one set. Two at least. One made by narrow tires, like those of a VW *Kriegswagen,* and the other superimposed set much larger. Perhaps a truck's.

He went back to the car. The headlights pointed north on the main highway, which disappeared a hundred meters away around a curve in the woods.

The Allied raiders knew where the three rockets were set up on their launch vehicles. They had killed four German soldiers and comandeered two vehicles. They would strike tonight.

The only thing Schellenberg didn't know was

from what direction they would be coming. His map did not show this dirt road, which had probably been used by farmers or perhaps fishermen during the summer. For all he knew it could curve back on itself in a large circle and approach the launch area from the south. Places like these were often honeycombed with tracks through the countryside.

Schellenberg switched off his flashlight and climbed into the car. "Turn off the headlights."

The corporal did as he was told. The night was suddenly pitch-black. "What are we going to do, sir?"

"We're going to find out where this leads," Schellenberg said. *"Gleich jetzt!"* Right now!

The corporal eased off the main road and headed west, maintaining a walking speed in first gear.

Within a few hundred meters they suddenly came out of the woods. A long, sloping hill rose to their left. A *Kriegswagen* and a small canvas troop truck were parked in the middle of the road two hundred meters away.

The corporal stopped without being told. Schellenberg grabbed the top of the windshield and pulled himself up. He studied the two vehicles through binoculars. It was obvious from the ruts in the snow around both vehicles that they had been turned around with some difficulty. They faced his way. Toward the east.

He scanned the side of the hill, spotting what appeared to be a well-used path to the top. The Allied commandos were just over the top of the hill. Hiding. Possibly in an old fishing shack, or perhaps a farmhouse or barn.

"Return to the highway," Schellenberg said.

"It'll be difficult to turn around. The road is too narrow. We might get stuck."

"Back up," Schellenberg ordered. "We'll wait for them on the highway."

1835 • Inside the Security Perimeter

Scotty drove the truck. Smythe and Winslow were in the cab with him, their weapons between their knees. Everyone else had climbed in the back.

He stopped twenty-five yards short of the main highway, and Winslow went the rest of the way on foot.

He came back on the run and climbed up into the cab. "No Germans. It's clear."

Scotty turned and knocked on the window to the rear of the truck. "Are you ready back there?" he shouted.

Sarah's face appeared in the glass. She gave a thumbs-up. She was eager. For her it was payback time for the hell she'd endured over the last year.

Scotty eased out onto the highway, switched on the headlights, and headed toward the launchpads. He was confused. Although there was a lot of security around the rockets, they'd not come across any patrols except for the two men on the hill and the two in the truck.

If the Germans were worried about a raid, there were no obvious signs of it. But more than one OSS mission had come to grief when they walked into what appeared to be a secure area and suddenly all hell broke loose as a trap was sprung.

He looked in his rearview mirror. There was nothing behind them.

There should have been search parties all over the island. The Germans were making a last-minute desperation play with the launch of the three rockets. And four of their people were missing. Who was in charge here?

Winslow noticed Scotty checking the mirror. "Anything?" he asked.

"We're still in the clear."

Winslow studied him. "But you're bothered."

Scotty glanced at him. "This place should be crawling with patrols."

"I agree," Smythe said.

"Not necessarily," Winslow disagreed. "For the past six months the Germans have been stripping anyone who can hold a gun from all noncombat assignments."

Scotty nodded though he wasn't satisfied with the answer. "I hope you're right. But that'd make them pretty stupid."

Winslow had to smile. "They were stupid when they drove out all their Jewish scientists in the thirties. They were stupid by not wiping us out on the beach at Dunkirk. And they were stupid by opening a second front." He shrugged.

Over a rise they came to the spot where Scotty and Smith had been stopped by the two guards in the truck. Just beyond it the highway curved to the left, and a couple hundred yards farther was the paved access road that led back to the three launch-pads.

"We'll leave the truck here," Scotty said, slowing down and pulling off the road. "If a patrol should come by, the empty truck might throw them off. They might think that the two soldiers just took off."

He switched off the headlights, and they all clambered out of the truck. No one was coming either way on the highway, but they couldn't afford to linger in the open.

Scotty led them across the road and into the dense woods until they had put the highway and the truck completely out of sight.

"Smythe and his team will take rocket one, Winslow number two, and I'll take three," Scotty told them. They'd made sketch maps from the original. They looked at them under the red beams of their flashlights.

"You know what has to be done," Scotty said. "So let's get on with it, and I'll see you on the beach. Good luck."

1845 • Launchpad Area Delta

After the raiders had entered the woods, Schellenberg waited a full ten minutes at his vantage point at the side of the road 150 meters behind the truck. He wanted to catch them unawares. But in order to do that he would have to drive over to one of the launchpads without their seeing or hearing his car pass by.

They were on foot. The perimeter around each rocket was guarded, and they did not know that they were being followed. The advantage, if it had ever been theirs, had switched.

At least one of the commandos was smaller than the others. He hoped that it was Sarah. Although he didn't know what he would do if he came face-to-face with her again, he wanted it with everything in his soul. She had hurt him.

He ran back to the car and got in. "Take me to launchpad three as fast as you can drive."

The corporal made no move to start the car. Something was wrong with the young man. He looked frightened. "If you're worried about the Allied commandos, don't be. They went into the woods."

"No, sir, it's not that."

"What then? We're running out of time."

"Sir, I was given a direct order by *Oberstleutnant* Hofbauer to take you wherever you wanted to go, but not to let you interfere with operations."

Schellenberg was dumbfounded. He wondered if it was the same in the British, American, and Russian armies. He thought not. They couldn't have come as far as they had.

"Why is that?"

"I don't know, sir."

"Well, nine of the enemy went into the woods no more than two hundred meters from here. They mean to kill some of our soldiers and blow up our rockets. If you allow that to happen, it will mean that you are a traitor. And you know what we do with traitors in Germany."

The boy was terror-stricken. He saw no way out.

"It's your choice, Corporal. But you might consider who would be the better officer to please, and *Oberstleutnant* or a *general*."

The corporal started the car and headed down the road, his expression a study in resignation. There was no way he could win.

They passed the deserted truck, rounded the curve, and turned onto the launchpad road. A minute later they pulled up at the barrier to launchpad three. Schellenberg jumped out and darted across the road to the SS guards.

"Do you have a field telephone?" he demanded.

"Yes, *Herr General*," the sergeant answered.

"Contact Hofbauer. I need to speak to him immediately."

"Yes, sir," the man said, and he went to the back of his patrol vehicle.

Schellenberg turned to the other SS soldier, a corporal. "Put your people on alert this insant. And turn on every light that you can. This area is about to come under attack at any moment."

The soldier was flustered. "Sir, I cannot give that order. We're not in charge of security here."

"Who is?"

"*Leutnant* Rauff."

"Where is he?"

"I don't know—"

The SS sergeant held up the field telephone. "*Herr General, Oberstleutnant* Hofbauer is on the line for you."

Schellenberg walked back and grabbed the phone from the man. "This is Schellenberg. Your launchpads are about to come under attack at any moment. Get extra security out here now, and order these idiots to do as they're told."

"How can you be so sure, *Herr General*?" Hofbauer asked with maddening slowness. "Did you see the attackers with your own eyes again?"

"Yes, you fool! There are nine of them, and they're here now!"

"I see," Hofbauer said. "Let me speak to Sergeant Siefert."

Schellenberg handed the telephone to the sergeant, who listened for a few moments, then nodded. "*Jawohl, Herr Oberstleutnant.* I understand." He hung up. He gave Schellenberg a sheepish look. "*Oberstleutnant* Hofbauer is on his way out to personally take charge, *Herr General.* He asks that we wait for him."

"*Gott in Himmel,*" Schellenberg said, stepping back a pace. He was in a lunatic asylum.

1910 • LAUNCHPAD THREE

The forest was quiet except in the direction of launchpad three, where someone was talking. Scotty, Lindsay, and Smith made their way from tree to tree toward the sound.

Before they had split up with the others they had synchronized their watches. It was 1910. The LOX and fuel trucks had to go up in flames in twenty minutes.

Unless something went wrong.

They saw a faint glimmer of light straight ahead. A few yards farther they heard someone laugh, and there was a faint clink of metal on metal.

Scotty stopped and raised a hand for Lindsay and Smith to hold up. The fuel trucks were straight ahead less than twenty yards through the woods. Steam misted off the white truck, which was parked only ten or fifteen feet from the fuel truck, Both faced inward, toward the V5 on its truck bed launcher.

He dropped down. "Don and I will set the charges under the trucks," he said. He took off his pack and removed the plastic explosive and an acid pencil fuse. Smith did the same thing.

"We'll strike north parallel to the highway, is that right?" Lindsay asked.

Scotty nodded. "We'll have to stay in the woods, there'll be patrols all up and down the highway. But I want to make them think that we're headed west toward the field where we came in. If we can divert some of them over there to wait for an air pickup, it'll help."

"I'll set the first booby trap to the north, which should push them west toward the highway. I'll lay the two others in that direction. Even Jerry ought to think he's got us figured out."

Scotty glanced at his watch. He crimped off all but twelve minutes of his acid fuse and shoved it into the block of explosive. It smelled like strong vinegar.

"I'll do the fuel truck," Smith said, crimping his acid fuse and arming his block of explosive. "These have to go off fairly close together."

"Let's do it," Scotty said.

They crawled toward the fuel trucks as Lindsay disappeared into the woods behind them. There were at least a half dozen technicians working on the rocket. The machine was bathed in strong lights. What few soldiers Scotty could see stood around a patrol car on the other side of the barrier.

There was something vaguely familiar about one of the figures, but the distance was too great for Scotty to tell much of anything except that he was an officer.

At the edge of the clearing they encountered a serious problem. The trucks were fifteen feet from the protection of the trees. Fifteen feet of open field in which Scotty and Smith would be exposed. Anyone looking their way would have to see them.

But all of a sudden he realized that wasn't true. The lights illuminating the rocket were so bright that by contrast the open ground between the woods and the trucks was in darkness.

"They won't see us because of the lights," Scotty told Smith.

Smith nodded his understanding.

Scotty crawled directly toward the LOX truck. Smith angled toward the truck that contained the fuel. If they were spotted, the game would be up. It would be impossible to set the charges on the trucks, then get out of there. The only other solution that Scotty had considered, though he hadn't discussed it with Smith or with the others, was to open fire on both tanker trucks in the hopes that the liquid oxygen and fuel might spill out, contact each other, and ignite.

Of course, they wouldn't get out alive in that case.

Scotty reached the LOX truck and crawled under it on his back. He stuffed the package of plastic explosive between the steel chassis frame and the support braces for the heavy tank above it.

Extremely cold air and fog rolled down around him from the sweating LOX tank.

He made sure that the acid fuse was in place, then crawled awkwardly back out from beneath the truck.

Smith came out seconds later, and the two of them crawled back to the edge of the clearing.

Smith reached the tree line first. He stood up and turned around.

Someone by the security barrier shouted, then opened fire with a pistol.

Smith stepped back, but someone else at the barrier opened fire with a submachine gun. Several shots stitched across Smith's chest, and one hit him in the forehead. He went down.

Scotty scrambled over to Smith to see if there was anything he could do, but the man was dead. A good portion of the back of his head was gone.

The Germans continued to fire indiscriminately, spraying bullets into the woods.

Scotty crawled into the forest on all fours as fast as he could move. He didn't think that he had been spotted. No one was shooting directly at him.

Twenty yards into the trees Scotty stood up. Shooting began somewhere in the distance to the south, toward one of the other launchpads.

Lindsay appeared out of the darkness, her face pale, her eyes wide. "Don?"

"Dead," Scotty answered. "Did you set the traps?"

She was shook, but she nodded. The firing behind them was decreasing. Very soon the Germans would realize that no one was shooting back, and they would be coming.

Scotty looked at his watch. It was 1927. The fuel trucks were set to explode in three minutes. "Lead the way," he told Lindsay.

She hesitated a moment longer, torn between wanting to leave and wanting to go back to see Don with her own eyes. But then she turned and headed back toward the highway, careful to avoid the trip wires she had strung between the trees at knee level.

1930 • Launchpad Three

Schellenberg held back at the barrier. There had been shooting at the other two launchpads, but the gun battles had not lasted very long. He couldn't tell if they had been one-sided like here, but alarms jangled all along his nerves. Something was wrong.

It should not have been this easy to repel the attacks. Unless the figure at the edge of the woods they'd opened fire on was finished with his task and was trying to escape, not come in.

The security troops had fanned out across the launchpad. The technicians had fallen back and were hiding behind the rocket. The SS sergeant turned and was about to say something when there was a bang somewhere near one of the trucks.

Schellenberg instinctively stepped back as a huge plume of white smoke billowed out from the LOX truck.

There was another bang, and for a long second nothing seemed to happen. But then a fireball erupted from somewhere between and above the two fuel trucks. It grew with incredible speed, and Schellenberg realized that he was flying on a carpet of extremely hot air.

1935 • The Forest

Scotty heard the fuel trucks at the other two launchpads explode. He'd been concerned that the other teams had failed. He had considered going back to help, but now that all three rockets had been destroyed, the mission was accomplished. It was time to get out.

The night sky behind them was aglow with the fuel-fed fires. There were other secondary explosions and smaller fireballs rising above the trees as the gas tanks on vehicles parked on or near the launchpads cooked off.

Lindsay stopped and checked her compass. She looked up to get her bearings, then without a word set off to the right.

The highway was less than fifty yards to their left. Scotty heard someone crashing through the brush from that direction, and he frantically motioned for Lindsay to take cover.

A German soldier appeared out of the darkness. He spotted Scotty, raised what looked like a

Schmeisser machine pistol, and opened fire.

Scotty fell back behind a tree but not before he was hit in the left arm just below his elbow.

Lindsay fired back with her submachine gun, hitting the German in the side, knocking him off his feet.

Scotty's arm was totally numb and useless, but there was no pain yet and not a lot of blood. He held his breath and cocked an ear to listen for someone else coming from the road.

A short, very sharp explosion came from somewhere behind them to the southwest. It was followed by three others in short succession. The booby traps were going off.

The chase had begun.

Lindsay was at his side. "My God, Scotty, you're bleeding."

"I'll live," he said. "We have to get out of here while the Germans are still stumbling around trying to figure out where we've gotten ourselves to."

EIGHT

Friday 0015 • On the Beach

A raw wind blew across the small cove, sending lines of nearly luminescent whitecaps marching out to open water. Steam rose in surreal wisps from the relatively warm ocean water.

Scotty leaned up against a rock, watching Lindsay and her sister Sarah work on Smythe. McKeever had been the last in, carrying the MI6 sergeant on his back. Ballinger hadn't made it, and from the looks of Smythe he wasn't going to make it either. He'd lost a lot of blood. His complexion was deathly white, and black fluid was leaking from a wound in his side.

Leigh hadn't gotten out from under his truck when it exploded, and counting Smythe, who would probably die any minute, they were down to five from the original nine plus Sarah. Winslow had received some flash burns on his face and hands when he pulled Sarah away from trying to find Leigh.

Scotty felt a sense of defeat. They had accomplished the mission, but he had lost half of his command. And he had let himself get shot. Halfway here he had fuzzed out, and Lindsay had to help him make it the rest of the way. He still felt weak.

Smythe suddenly cried out something, then was still.

Sarah got up. "Bloody hell," she said. She looked over at her husband and shook her head. "He's dead." She turned at length and headed up the beach.

Winslow got up and followed her.

After a while Scotty looked up. "I'm sorry," he said to Lindsay, who knelt on the rocks beside Smythe, holding his bloody hand in hers.

Her shoulders were hunched. She was crying. "It wasn't your fault," she said.

"I promised him that I'd get everybody home—"

"Don't be such a bloody Boy Scout," she flared. "This is the real world. People get killed."

"The young lady is correct, of course," Schellenberg said. He appeared out of the darkness holding a pistol on Sarah and Winslow. Their hands were raised over their heads.

Scotty reached for his pistol.

"I will shoot them both, husband and wife, and you will have two more deaths on your tender conscience," Schellenberg warned conversationally.

Scotty stayed his hand.

"I wonder if you feel any remorse over the German boys you killed? Especially my driver, who I sent into the woods to find out what direction you were heading. He was just a boy." Schellenberg shrugged. "But he was German, and we are the enemy."

"Yes, you are," Scotty said. "Your rockets have been destroyed, and you will lose the war. It's only a matter of months."

"We would have lost the war even if the rockets had been launched and hit their marks. The issue is what happens afterward?"

"Germany will be rebuilt—"

"To us, personally."

"Do you mean if we don't all die on this beach in a shoot-out?" Scotty asked. He glanced past Schellenberg toward the woods. But no one else was coming. The general was alone.

"Yes."

"Are you trying to make a bargain?"

Sarah slowly turned to face Schellenberg. "If the tables were reversed, I would not hesitate to kill you."

He looked at her for a long time, as if he was trying to memorize her face. His eyes strayed to Winslow. "You are married to an extraordinary woman, Major," he said softly.

Winslow turned. "Yes, I am."

Schellenberg looked at Sarah again, then lowered his pistol and started to walk away.

Sarah snatched her pistol from her jumper, but Winslow stopped her.

"The war is over," he said.

Scotty had his pistol out, but he lowered it, too. "We're taking Sergeant Smythe with us."

Sarah was shaking with rage. She watched Schellenberg's retreating figure until it was lost in the darkness, looked at her husband, then at the others. She lowered her head.

"Time to go home," Scotty said.

AFTERWORD

General Walther Schellenberg got his reward in the end. He survived the war, and at the War Crimes Trial in Nuremberg he was given a light sentence of six years in prison. He only served two before he was released.

Before that, however, at a lavish wedding ceremony at Winacres, the Miles estate in Sherwood, Richard Scott and Lindsay Miles were married. The matron of honor was Sarah Winslow, the sister of the bride, and the best man was Lt. Col. Donald Winslow, the husband of the matron of honor.

In attendance, besides Scotty's parents, who flew over from the States, were Winston Churchill and Gen. Dwight Eisenhower.

There was no press coverage.

Schellenberg never laid eyes on Sarah Winslow again.

FLAME AT TARAWA

BARRETT TILLMAN

BARRETT TILLMAN is the author of four novels, including *Hellcats,* which was nominated for the Military Novel of the Year in 1996, twenty nonfiction historical and biographical books, and more than 400 military and aviation articles in American, European, and Pacific Rim publications. He received his bachelor's degree in journalism from the University of Oregon in 1971 and spent the next decade writing freelance articles. He later worked with the Champlain Museum Press and as the managing editor of *The Hook* magazine. In 1989 he returned to freelance writing and has been at it ever since. His military nonfiction has been critically lauded and garnered him several awards, including the U.S. Air Force's Historical Foundation Award, the Nautical & Oceanographic Society's Outstanding Biography Award, and the Arthur Radford Award for Naval History and Achievement. He is also an honorary member of the Navy fighter squadrons VF-111 and VA-35. He lives and works in Mesa, Arizona.

ONE

I knew I was alive because I hurt so much. My nose and mouth held a horrible contagion of smell and taste that would have been unimaginable anywhere else on earth. Dimly, with effort, I sought to recall anything comparable in my twenty years. Nothing came close.

Through the throbbing in my brain I absorbed the absolute misery of my situation. Somehow—it wasn't at all clear—I had awoken to the wretched realization of my predicament before. Maybe more than once. Evidently I couldn't deal with it for more than several minutes at a time.

My stomach turned over again; I tried to vomit up whatever churned inside me, but nothing came. Only the dry heaves. The previous contents of my stomach were already strewn on my dungaree jacket or crusted on my mouth and chin. I gagged and choked out a small amount of saliva, but by now I had none to spare. If I'd been able to think more clearly, I'd have recognized the early stages of dehydration.

I groped around for something useful. My 782 gear—web belt with pistol, magazines, and canteens—was gone, evidently ditched during the past day or so. We flamethrower operators didn't carry packs because the sixty-pound M1A1 was all we could manage.

God in heaven, I need water. Just a little water . . .

I couldn't control my legs, but they twitched involuntarily in another spasm. I heard the splash of my spatted feet. Then the irony occurred to me: I was lying in water, about three inches deep. It was foul, putrid, awful. I lacked the ability or strength to move out of it.

At least I was out of the sun—the damnable equatorial sun, which made the coral sand so hot that you couldn't tolerate lying on it. But you had to, if you were on any of the four landing beaches of Betio Island in Tarawa Atoll during the third week of November in the Year of Our Lord Nineteen Hundred and Forty-three. If you stood up, you got nailed by a Jap sniper or stitched by a Jap machine gunner. If you stayed down, you still could get killed by a shell or grenade. Like Gunny Crouch said: If the direct fire don't kill you, the indirect fire will.

Okay, I was out of the sun. But that meant I was confined within the walls of some . . . place. What? Where was I? It was fairly dark, the only open spot visible to me being the large, irregular hole in the roof of—what? *Well, don't matter much. It's obviously a well-built place 'cause there's rebar sticking out of the cement, with coconut logs and sand or coral on top. Must be nearly impossible to see from the air. But the thick walls trap the heat. God a'mighty, it's hot, almost can't breathe.*

I opened my mouth more and tried to suck in some oxygen. A futile effort—I inhaled the horrible smell again. *What the hell is it?*

Lying on my back, I squirmed in the polluted water, trying to find drier ground. I bumped into something spongy soft, lodged against my shoulders. With my heels braced in the muddy pool, I shoved backward on my elbows. I was so damn weak that I lacked the will to turn my head and identify the obstruction. Something flopped beside my left shoulder. In the dim light I thought I recognized a hand, minus two fingers.

God, I'm hallucinating. I closed my eyes, shook my head a little, trying to focus. When I looked again the mutilated hand was still there. It was attached to an arm that was mostly attached to a torso. Gradually it dawned on me: I was up against a dead Jap, one of the naval infantrymen defending Betio against the Second Marine Division. He was what I was smelling—he and his pal. About ten feet away was the corpse of another *rikusentai,* wearing a shredded light green uniform. Even in semidarkness his face was a ghoulish Halloween mask. Both bodies were bloated in the extreme heat. Given much longer, they'd burst the confines of their remaining clothes.

I passed out again.

TWO

I only joined the Corps to impress my old man. By today's terms he was dysfunctional: a boozer who couldn't or wouldn't hold a full-time job. Heaven knows it was hard enough finding regular work during the Depression, but he seldom tried. The rest of us—my mother, two sisters, and I—did what we could to take up the slack, and somehow we scraped by. So did our entire generation—the one that somebody called the Greatest. Hell, we weren't the greatest. We just did what we had to do.

I didn't have to go to Tarawa.

In fact, I didn't have to be in the Corps. As an only son I could've remained exempt, especially since I was my mom's main breadwinner. Karen was married to a decent enough guy, but they had a baby of their own; Suzie was still in bobby sox and pigtails. Later I realized she had to be an "oops" since she was six years younger than me. Anyway, my mother understood me. When I told her I wanted to enlist she didn't try very hard to talk me out of it. She just asked why. I think that I looked over her shoulder—I was a good-sized kid for eighteen—and said something about doing the right thing. She knew what I meant. Besides, with a deferred entry I wouldn't be drafted by the damn Army.

Dad had been in the Army in the "First War," before we had so many that we started numbering them. In retrospect, I think he was embarrassed about his military service because after he died, I finally saw his discharge papers. He'd been gilding the lily for a lot of years with talk about France and Kaiser Bill. He'd been in a railroad supply outfit that arrived about a month before the armistice was signed in 1918. I was born five years later, two years after Karen. Anyway, he had an album with some clippings that included Floyd Gibbons's reports from Belleau Wood with the Fifth and Sixth Marines, which won a fighting reputation there. My old man was impressed; so was I.

After Pearl Harbor I was all pumped up to join the Marines—"first to fight." We knew about Wake Island, and we saw the movie with Brian Donlevy and William Bendix: "Send us more Japs." Man, that was for me—lemme at 'em. Suzie insisted I only joined because of the dress blues, and I don't mind saying that I was a pretty good-looking youngster with my cover set at a killing angle and a breezy confidence that I didn't really feel. Besides, a big brother wants to look good for his kid sister.

Boot camp was not like anything I'd experienced before. Yes, life was tough in the 1930s, but being part of a family made a big difference. At MCRD San Diego my family was a platoon full of fellow recruits and a couple of sadists with stripes: Sergeant

Connelly and Corporal Unger. Their first job was to make us terrified of them; they succeeded. Next they began teaching us, as Connelly said, "The easy way or the hard way, but you *will* learn the Marine Corps way." Hands-on instruction was normal, expected. You couldn't get away with it today.

A few years ago I read about "stress cards" so recruits can take a time-out like misbehaving kindergarten kids. You want to know about stress? Tarawa was stress. DIs might still yell at recruits today, but can't swear at them, let alone manhandle them. Wouldn't I like to hear what Connelly and Unger would say about *that*! I didn't like them much—Unger left bruises on my upper arms when I was snapping in with the M1 rifle—but after Tarawa I damn sure appreciated them.

Somebody—maybe a Roman—said, "The more you sweat in peace, the less you bleed in war." He must have been a Marine.

The key to understanding newly minted Marines is that they want to be regulation, squared away, salty. Of course, the only way to become salty is to log sea miles. Some would even dunk their covers (hats to civilians) in salt water so the green cloth and the metal adornments took on a nautical cast.

The Corps took about six hundred thousand people during the war, and I heard that about 97 percent went overseas. Almost exclusively, that meant the Pacific. (General Marshall, the Army chief of staff, would not permit a Marine in Europe. Like most Army officers of the Great War, he resented the hell out of us.) Some Marines were drafted, but the huge majority volunteered, for a variety of reasons both sacred and profane. Patriotism was a big part of it, but hell—anybody in uniform was considered patriotic. Most of the Army troops were drafted, and the Department of Veterans Affairs says the average age was twenty-six. Marines, on the other hand, were younger, leaner, meaner. More motivated, I guess.

I knew a few guys who joined because of the uniform. Dress blues were *the* sexiest outfit going—at least that's what some recruiters said. Maybe it was the choker collar—harkening back to the neck protectors in the War of 1812, hence "leathernecks"—or the red stripe on the trousers. (I'm sure that some recruits were disappointed to learn that only officers and NCOs got the red stripe.) However, in later years I preferred the Dress Blue Bravo option with "tropical long" khaki shirt, dress trousers, and white hat. DIs sometimes wore the same uniform with campaign hat. Man, that was *sharp,* with or without a field scarf. (That's a tie to you, Mister.) There's no mistaking it—that uniform belongs to a military man. But I remember in the 1990s when the Air Force used sleeve stripes like the navy—a three-striper was a major rather than a commander. Honestly, the first time I saw a USAF officer in that getup, I didn't know what he was. My first impression was an airline pilot. My second impression was a much-decorated bus driver. Finally, the blue-suiters had the good sense to be embarrassed and reverted to the previous system.

Most generals have far too much time on their hands, anyway.

I guess every Marine thinks that he was part of the Old Corps, when it was rough, brother, rough. My cousin's boy was an airborne trooper in Vietnam, and some of what he told me sounded familiar; I could relate to it. Today—forget it. They talk the same talk, but no way do they walk the same walk. In the 1980s when I heard that that the Commandant had approved camouflage *maternity* fatigues, I took off my gold eagle, globe, and anchor lapel pin. I was embarrassed; wouldn't wear it until 10 November the next year. In my era, camouflage was special; it set you apart as a member of an elite, even if it was the *Waffen* SS. Yet today pregnant females wear "cammies."

Recently I read that everybody in the Army now wears a beret because all soldiers are "elite." I'm still waiting for somebody to explain *that* to me. For one thing, a beret is an absurd garment. I'm sorry, in this PC era, but I never saw one that didn't look queer. Beyond that, how in the name of Chesty Puller can *everybody* be elite? If everybody is special, then nobody is.

Every 15 April I still grind my teeth at the thought that *my* tax dollars buy faggoty hats and maternity cammies. The day the Marine Corps issues berets is the day I take off my gold lapel pin. For good.

Until then, Semper Fi.

THREE

I can't tell what I thought and what I think I thought. But lying in that squalid space, lapsing in and out of consciousness, it's certain that I spent some time trying to think pleasant thoughts. Nothing was more pleasant than New Zealand. Nothing before; nothing since.

New Zealand was wonderful. The New Zealanders were even better. Especially Bonnie. Bonnie McKenzie, "A wee bonnie lass," her father insisted. I agreed. Trouble was, he didn't much like me. Well, maybe that's too harsh. I think that Andrew McKenzie did like me in his own way. He just didn't think that a Yank private was good enough for his daughter—not by half.

Bonnie was nineteen, a year younger than I. She had raven hair, blue eyes, and a fair complexion with freckles. We told each other that we were in love, and maybe we were. Several hundred guys in the Second MarDiv married Kiwi girls, and most of the relationships I knew of seemed to take, including those that lasted " 'til death us do part."

The Second Division was based in and around Wellington, mainly at Queen Elizabeth Park. My engineer battalion of the Eighteenth Marines pitched camp at Paikakarika, which I could hardly pronounce. Fortunately, I never had to remember how to write it because our location was classified during those eight months. My family only knew that I was "somewhere in the South Pacific."

I quickly learned that the division was full of experience and talent. We had officers and NCOs from the Old Corps who'd fought bandits in the banana wars, served in China, and a goodly number who'd fought in this war, on Guadalcanal. Our training was entirely practical, blissfully absent of the chicken stuff so common in the military, even in the Corps. Our commanding general, Julian C. Smith, was as fine a leader as the Marines ever produced. He genuinely cared about us, and he was frequently present on maneuvers, standing in his gray raincoat, watching his boys through rain-flecked spectacles.

Other than basic equipment and squad, platoon, and company tactics, we concentrated on two things: physical conditioning and marksmanship. There was a competition among the battalions and within the division generally as to who could hike the farthest the fastest with fewest dropouts. It was a real stigma if you didn't finish a hike—the corpsmen kept busy treating blisters.

We got a lot of trigger time in New Zealand—even built a couple of extra ranges ourselves. Marksmanship was a fetish in the Old Corps, something akin to mysticism. But it was hardly surprising, considering the backgrounds of our leaders. The CO of the Second Battalion, Eighth Marines, Major "Jim"

Crowe, had been a warrant officer before the war, a noted rifle coach and match shot. Major General Smith and his chief of staff, Colonel "Red Mike" Edson, also held Distinguished Rifleman ratings. In fact, Edson later was executive director of the NRA. His letter to the mothers of America probably wouldn't get printed today: Basically he said, "Mom, if you want your son to have the best chance of coming home alive, make sure he learns to shoot as a boy."

We engineers didn't shoot as much as the line infantrymen, though if we had, maybe I wouldn't have ended up humping a damned flamethrower. I had qualified as a high Marksman, which still put me in the lower tier of shooters. But if things went right (and of course they never did), we weren't supposed to use rifles very much. Our primary weapons were explosives and bridging equipment. We were expected to blow up obstacles blocking access to landing beaches, demolish enemy strongpoints, and erect crossings of rivers and canyons. All while under enemy fire.

After all, we weren't "the damned engineers" for nothing. The "damned" was less an insult than a curse; we were "damned" because we worked under very tough conditions. But regiment and division expected us to cope with the challenge, and we expected it of ourselves.

A couple of days after I sewed on my first stripe, I was so proud that I insisted on taking the McKenzies to dinner. It just about broke me, but it was worth it. Rationing had been in effect almost four years, but one thing about New Zealand—it has a lot of sheep. I never ever acquired a taste for mutton, but at least I could take Mr. and Mrs. McKenzie and Bonnie to a fairly nice place. My chevron definitely looked better than the previous "slick sleeve" appearance of my uniform blouse, but Andrew McKenzie had little concept of "private first class." He'd been in the home guard for a while, and understood "lance corporal," which sounded better, so I figured it was close enough. Ironically, the Corps adopted the lance corporal (E-3) rank in 1958.

I met Bonnie at a serviceman's club where she worked part-time as a volunteer hostess. Maybe it's the Scots-Irish influence, but it seemed that all the New Zealand girls were pretty, and many were downright beautiful. Naturally, I wasn't the only American she knew or dated, but we hit it off right away, mainly because she really liked to jitterbug. If I say so myself, I knew my way around a dance floor in those days—certainly more than most of the guys, who were issued two left feet. Bonnie and a couple of her galfriends admitted that their own feet took a beating most weekends, so anybody who could shuffle his boondockers in time with the music was ahead of the game.

Looking back, I thought that Bonnie and I had a torrid affair, but it was pretty tame by current standards. We didn't do much more than indulge in occasional (well, okay, frequent) heavy breathing, but she said I was the only one, and I believed her. When the division embarked for Tarawa it was "an understood thing" that we'd resume our romance when I returned. As things turned out, it wasn't possible.

I still think of her now and then.

FOUR

They told us that the Marine Corps didn't have many flamethrowers in late 1943, and the Second Division almost none. Therefore, we got sixty for Tarawa, all from Army stocks in Hawaiian warehouses. Since then I've seen different figures, but evidently no more than a couple of dozen made it ashore. At any rate, our combat engineer battalion assumed the flamethrower mission in addition to everything else: construction, demolition, and the like.

"Flame projectors" were highly useful for "reducing" enemy fortifications such as bunkers and pillboxes. Trouble was, we got them too late in our training cycle to integrate them into the twelve-man rifle squads. Later on, most infantry landing craft "boat teams" had a well-balanced platoon of riflemen, machine gunners, BAR men, explosives crew, and flame team, but that was in the future.

Marines and sailors don't always get along—they're like oil and water. To each other they're "jarheads" and "squids" because while Marines make their living running into machine-gun fire, sailors usually have it easy aboard ship, sleeping on clean sheets and eating hot meals. But there are exceptions, I'll tell you, brother: Seabees are mighty fine people, I learned that on Betio. To watch a bulldozer driver lower his blade and push a ton of coral and sand on top of a Jap bunker, with machine-gun rounds spanging off his cat, fills a leatherneck with admiration.

Then there's corpsmen—what the army calls medics. For some reason I never understood, the Marine Corps doesn't have its own medical personnel. They're all from the Navy, but you couldn't tell us apart on Betio or Saipan or Okinawa. They wear the same uniform, eat the same cold chow, sleep in the same mud, and get killed by the same ordnance. I never once saw a corpsman refuse to advance into fire to treat a wounded Marine. Hell, I don't think I even heard of it. If I ever got a slug of booze on any of those frigging islands, a corpsman could have half of my ration.

Because our flamethrowers were so late in arriving, we had no time to train properly. In fact, I didn't play with one until we sailed from New Zealand, bound for an en route rehearsal at Efate. When Platoon Sergeant Healey informed me of my new status (I was not consulted) I was pretty damn unhappy, not that it mattered. He said that because I only shot Marksman in boot camp, I was less useful as a combat rifleman, so it made good military sense to give me the flame gun. The Sharpshooters and exalted Experts got M1 Garands and BARs instead of flamethrowers, mortar tubes, or Browning heavy machine guns.

As a PFC I was designated a "flame gunner" with an assistant who carried a five-gallon jerry can of extra fuel, nitrogen propellant tank, and tools, plus his basic load with an M1 carbine. With my shoulders protesting beneath the weight of my burden I made damn sure that Private Dean, my A-gunner, also humped my shelter half, K-rats, and other gear. He wasn't very happy, not that it mattered.

The M1A1 weighed sixty pounds all-up, with two tanks of thickened fuel and the nitrogen propellant tank. Maximum range was fifty yards; we had at most ten seconds' firing time from five gallons of fuel.

Later in the war, as an NCO instructor, I learned the history of the weapon. The original model, the "mark one, mod oh," had serious problems, especially since the fuel often burned itself up on flight to target. A more viscous mixture was needed, one that burned slower and delivered more fire on target. Tests with fuel thickeners such as soap, rubber, and crankcase oil were unsat.

Standard Oil developed a rubber-based thickener, but it had poor shelf life. However, in late 1941 the National Research Council blended the fatty soaps of aluminum naphthanate and palmitate into a gelatinous substance that could be shipped in sealed containers. When mixed with gasoline the naphthetic and palmitic salts coagulated, lowering the flash point of the fuel. The new mixture, resembling applesauce, was called napalm.

However, the basic M1 flamethrower wasn't powerful enough to project the thicker fuel far enough. Changes to the fuel valve and pressure regulator solved the main problems, and the M1A1 had twice the range of the M1—about fifty yards. The "A1" was what we took to Tarawa Atoll.

We were told that the M1A1 often had unreliable ignition in the tropics owing to the battery spark system. The battery was supposed to ignite the small nitrogen supply in the wand, which in turn lit off the fuel. However, if the thickened fuel didn't flare, the gunner sometimes sprayed fuel on the target, which was ignited with tracers or phosphorous grenades.

Once acquainted with the theory of the damn thing, we set about learning how to use it. Mainly it was by guess and by God; standing on the fantail of the attack transport en route to our destination. The process was simple enough: Turn on the hydrogen and fuel tanks, check for adequate pressure, aim, then press the igniter switch and the flame handle. Gunnery Sergeant Crouch demonstrated for our benefit. When he spoke, we listened. He was an old guy—probably thirty-one to thirty-three—and we reckoned he'd had more women and booze than the rest of us combined. It was certainly true in my case: I was still two months from voting age. I could die a painful, violent death, but I couldn't buy a beer.

"The force of the propellant can push you backward," Gunny explained, "so you need to plant your feet and lean into it, like an automatic weapon." He took an exaggerated posture, bending at the knees and inclining his torso forward. When he lit off the device, a low *whooshing* sound emerged from the wand, followed by a long spurt of flame with thick, black smoke. He played the stream of fire back and forth, allowing the napalm to settle in the wake of our ship. It was damned impressive to notice how long the fire burned on top of the water.

"Another thing," Gunny said. "Don't any of you

sons a'bitches let fly with this thing at too high an angle. If you do, and you're not braced, you can get pushed backward, or downhill, and the flame will rise and fall on top of you." He glared at us as only a Marine Corps gunnery sergeant can do. "You're s'posed to burn Japs, not Marines."

As far as tactics, they were rudimentary. Basically, a squad would approach a target pillbox or bunker and shoot at the firing slits, keeping the gunners' heads down. That was supposed to allow the flame-thrower man to get close enough to douse the place with hell jelly, which would drive the Japs from their guns. (Nobody will continue fighting with his face on fire!) Then the demolitions men would toss in satchel charges or, failing that, riflemen would pitch in some grenades. The theory was that we'd regroup and advance to the next obstacle.

On Betio, though, it didn't work that way. The Japs had devised a very tough defense in depth, with interlocking fields of fire. Almost every strongpoint was covered by rifles or MGs from two more positions, so even if we suppressed the fire from one place and advanced to destroy it, we were exposed to the Japs on the flanks.

We spent the rest of that day and most of the next two taking turns, learning how to operate and maintain the wretched new weapon. Eventually there was a lot of prestige with being a flame gunner—they were very popular guys on the islands we visited. But even discounting the high casualty rate (66 percent on Betio alone), I'd have gladly dropped the honor. The damn thing scared me: bucking the force of the hydrogen propellant, feeling the searing heat on my face, watching what it did to structures and people. Lieutenant Anthony, our platoon leader, must have sensed my attitude because at one point he patted my shoulder, and said, "Just remember, Bertram, it's far better to give than receive."

FIVE

"Gentlemen, we are headed for the Gilbert Islands." Our operations officer, Major Harry Pelt, stood on the ship's deck, with an easel holding a large map of the Central Pacific. The *Arthur Middleton* was a 10,800-ton Coast Guard transport taking our Marine Corps landing team toward the equator. She and fifteen other attack cargo and transport ships comprised the Southern Task Force under Rear Admiral Harry Hill.

"Specifically," Pelt continued, "we are going to seize an atoll there, called Tarawa." He was careful to pronounce it correctly: *ta*-ra-wa. The Second Marine Division's destination had been kept semisecret since departing New Zealand.

"The Gilberts straddle the equator, running about a hundred miles north and south," Pelt added. He traced the archipelago, from Makin Atoll in the northwest to Arorae in the southeast. "Many of these islands were uninhabited, and Tarawa is like most atolls in this part of the world—a large lagoon surrounded by a coral reef. The place that interests us is this island." He tapped the map. "Betio." The spelling confounded the pronunciation, *bay*-shio.

"It looks like a pork chop," muttered a BAR man in the third row. Somebody laughed unconvincingly.

Pelt decided to ignore the wisecrack. "Actually, it looks more like a rifle," he said. "The stock is the west end, narrowing to the drooping barrel here on the east with the lock on the north. But it's very small: about two miles long by six hundred yards at the widest point. Betio covers less than three hundred acres, and apparently the highest elevation is only ten feet."

A squad leader raised his hand. "Sir, what's worth taking on such a small place?"

"I'm just coming to that," Pelt replied. "The Japanese have an airfield on Betio, about four thousand feet long. The brass says we can't allow them a bomber base to interfere with our shipping between the Gilberts and the Marshalls up here to the north. So we're going to take it and put our own planes in there."

Pelt paused for effect. He had no doubt that the Eighth Marine Regiment, with the rest of the Second Division, would seize Tarawa. The only uncertainty was what it would cost.

"Our flyboys have photographed Betio yard by yard." He did not mention that originally Rear Admiral Hill's staff relied on a century-old British map of the island. "We know pretty much what's there, and it's a tough nut. The Japs have about forty-seven hundred men, including construction troops. The others are mostly naval infantry. Jap marines."

A murmur skittered through the green-clad audience. American and Japanese marines had rarely clashed in the nearly two years since Pearl Harbor—the most notable exception being at Wake Island in December '41. The riflemen, machine gunners, flamethrowers, and corpsmen in the audience realized that they faced a serious enemy.

"Our force will enter the lagoon through this gap in the west side of the reef," Pelt continued. "On D day we'll embark in LCVPs and amtracks and assault the island, on these beaches." Again he tapped the map, ticking off the landing zones: Green Beach on the blunt west end; Red One, Two, and Three on the north.

"Most of the island is covered with palm trees, except for a section at the west end of the airstrip. There are pillboxes and bunkers all over the place, with preregistered fields of fire. Offshore there are obstacles—some with mines—intended to funnel our landing craft into artillery zones. We expect naval gunfire to eliminate much of those.

"Once you're ashore you'll find a three-to-five-foot seawall, probably coconut logs stacked up to prevent tracked vehicles from getting inland. Our engineers will handle those.

"Weapons include light and heavy machine guns, defiladed tanks with 37mm guns, antiaircraft weapons, and heavy coastal batteries up to 75mm or more. It's also reported that they have some 5.5- and 8-inch guns.

"Now then. Remember that at most the island is only about six hundred yards wide, which means you're never more than three hundred yards from the waterline. Defense in depth is just not possible for an invader, so expect determined counterattacks, especially after dark. The Japs aren't stupid:

They know that the best way to defeat a landing is to overrun the beachhead. That's where supplies come from.

"Another thing: This is the first coral atoll we've tackled. There are lots of others like it in the Pacific, so this operation will be studied closely. It's important that we get it right."

Pelt spoke for another ten minutes, outlining the complex evolution of an opposed amphibious landing: assault units, ship-to-shore movement, phase lines, communications, naval gunfire, and air support. The Marine Corps had taught and preached the amphibious gospel since the end of the Great War; graduates of the Basic School at Quantico became evangelists. They knew the 1915 British disaster at Gallipoli inside out.

"You'll get equipment checks on D minus one and on D day morning but briefly, check your weapons and ammo. No loaded weapons or fixed bayonets at any time unless you're ordered. You should carry three days' worth of rations. And another thing: Carry your gas masks. We know from previous landings that they're the first thing troops discard, but you need to keep them handy. We know a lot about Tarawa but not everything."

Finally, Pelt looked around. "Now, I know you fellows must have a lot of questions, probably some I can't answer. But I'll try." He nodded at a platoon leader in the front row.

"Sir, if Betio is so small with no civilians, why don't we use gas?"

The ops officer almost flinched. He had asked the same question of his regimental commander and was rudely rebuffed. Consequently, Pelt passed on the sentiment: "Earlier this year the president said the United States will not use poison gas in this war."

Somewhere in the dungaree-clad audience a Republican mortarman voiced a heartfelt sentiment. "Screw Roosevelt."

There was some nervous laughter, and it occurred to me that there didn't seem to be many Democrats in the Marine Corps. FDR's son James was exec of a Raider battalion, but I heard he later became a Republican. Anyway, it didn't matter very much. A lot of us weren't old enough to vote.

SIX

They blew reveille at a quarter 'til midnight—the unholiest wake-up call I ever had. Everybody including our platoon leader, Lieutenant Alexander, was peeved. "The damn moon isn't even up yet," he groused.

The swabbies fed us well, though: steak and eggs with plenty of coffee. There was the usual gallows humor about condemned men and hearty meals, though it didn't seem to be a major concern. We'd been hearing for several days how the Navy was going to obliterate Betio Island and the Jap defenders. There were three old battleships in the fire support group—*Maryland, Tennessee,* and *Colorado*—plus four cruisers and a bunch of destroyers. That didn't even include four carriers, though we learned that the fly-fly boys promised a whole lot more than they could deliver. Later on the airedales learned to do a fine job for the infantry, but it took a while for their performance to match the brochure.

Before reporting to our boat stations each squad

or platoon ran an equipment check. Our NCOs were good—several of them had been at Guadalcanal—and they knew what was important. As a flame gunner my loadout was unusual, even for so specialized a bunch as the engineers, but Sergeant Healey gave me the once-over just the same. "You got two full canteens?" he rasped.

"Yes, Sergeant."

I don't know why he asked because he hefted each canteen on my web belt just to be sure. He grinned like a wolf, and muttered, "When it comes to slaughter, you'll do your work on water, an' lick the bloomin' boots of them that's got it." I had no idea what he was talking about—I'd hardly heard of Kipling in '43—and I was astonished that Sergeant Healey had ever read poetry. But we had some odd birds in the Corps. He noted my .45 pistol, magazine pouch, and sheath knife, then asked, "Where's your ruck?"

I nodded to my A-gunner. "Dean has it."

Healey turned to Dean, who got to carry my gear plus his own. Fortunately, he was a big, strapping Dakota farm kid who could manage the burden: two shelter halves, both our allotments of K-rations, his own clean clothes plus a change of socks and skivvies for me, extra napalm fuel and hydrogen gas canister plus tools, not to mention his M1 carbine and ammo plus a couple of grenades. The riflemen all carried at least four Mk 2 "pineapples" with three-second fuzes.

The theory was that we could sustain ourselves for three days before we needed serious reinforcement or supply. That was the theory. In truth, the logistics people really screwed up, and what we needed most—M3 and especially M4 tanks—were loaded early aboard the ships rather than late. Consequently, the Navy had to move mountains of supplies to get at the Stuarts and Shermans rather than putting them ashore right away. The same applied to other essentials, including ammo, water, and medical supplies. Oddly enough, food wasn't a big problem for the first couple of days. Everybody ashore was too busy, too scared, or too dead to care much about eating. We lived on nervous energy.

Finally, we were herded to the ship's rail and went over the side, climbing down the cargo nets to the waiting Higgins Boats. Everybody was overloaded, but the flamethrower was bulky as well as heavy. I needed a couple of helping hands getting into the boat. From there we were delivered to the LSTs (Landing Ship, Tank, but "Large Slow Targets" the sailors called them) for reboarding in the LVTs (Landing Vehicle Tracked) that comprised the first three waves.

The LVT was a lot like the LCVP (Landing Craft, Vehicle and Personnel), better known as the Higgins Boat, in that it was designed by a civilian who foresaw the need before the Navy did. What Andrew Jackson Higgins of New Orleans was to wooden landing craft, Donald Roebling of Clearwater, Florida, was to the tracked variety. He devised his amphibious vehicle as the "Swamp Gator" in the wake of severe hurricanes in the early 1930s. At that time there was no purpose-built rescue vehicle for such contingencies, but the Marine Corps noted its potential for combat, and had it built by the Food Machinery Corporation. However, Mr. Roebling had to finance the military prototype himself, "betting on the come" that he'd be reimbursed. The Corps had no contingency funds for such things in 1940.

Militarily, LVTs were thought most useful for taking supplies to a hostile shore, but it wasn't long before their versatility included troop carrier duty and even combat support with integral howitzers and flamethrowers.

Anyway, we spent almost six frigging hours in various landing craft, finally with eighteen men crowded into an LVT-2. As far as I know, it was the first time that tracked vehicles had been used for an actual assault. But Tarawa was different from everything that happened before. As an atoll, it had a large reef that blocked the Higgins Boats unless there was at least five feet of water over the coral barrier, but our Water Buffalos and the earlier LVT-1 Alligators could cross the reef without much difficulty. However, they weren't optimized for combat assault: no armor and no ramp to allow fast unloading.

The Second Division did some fast modifications. Enough suitable armor plate was found in New Zealand to protect the fronts of the Alligators already on hand. The more capable Buffalos were shipped by LST from the West Coast and barely made the embarkation in time. Their armor was next to useless—rifle and machine-gun fire could penetrate it at a couple hundred yards or more—but it was better than nothing. Suitability tests confirmed that both types of amtracks maintained seakeeping quality with the extra weight, and off we went.

From the engineers' perspective, the LVT-1s and -2s still left something to be desired. Troops could disembark by jumping over the side or stern, but heavy weapons and other gear had to be lowered pretty carefully—a real problem on a defended beach. Mortar tubes and base plates, flamethrowers, fuel cans, and the like, were serious impedimenta. A lot of that hardware went to the bottom of the sea because it was just too heavy or took too long to offload amid incoming gunfire. A ramp in the stern of the tractor would've made things a lot easier and reduced casualties. That modification didn't arrive until the "dash three" model, called the Bushmaster. However, I hardly saw one until sometime before we hit Okinawa well over a year later.

We were hoisting ourselves and our gear into the amtracks when the LST skipper hailed all hands over the loudspeaker. He said the chaplain had some words of comfort for us: "This will be a great page in Marine Corps history," he intoned. "Wherever you are, stop and give a prayer . . . God bless you."

I don't remember how most of the fellows responded to that. I think I just cursed some more at the damnable weight of my flamethrower. I didn't really get religion until a couple of days later.

Our amtrack had just left the LST's bow, when somebody said, "Hey, lookit." He was pointing southeasterly, toward the island. I craned my neck, glancing over the gunwale, and saw a red light arcing into the dark sky maybe five miles off. It was a star shell fired from Betio. We didn't know it at the time, but it was a warning from the Jap naval infantry. They'd finally spotted us.

The "tracks" then churned away from the LSTs, arrived at the assembly points, and waited until each wave was organized behind its guide boat. I was in the second wave for Red Beach Three. We had a rough ride owing to a westerly chop, which hit us from astern during the transit to the lagoon, then broad on the starboard beam during the final approach. The LVTs rode fairly low, as they were basically smallcraft that pitched and rolled. Everybody was wet; several guys got seasick and puked over the side. A couple of demolition men just up and heaved without thought to the wind. They got their breakfasts back in their faces—and so did some others with stronger stomachs. Gunny Crouch's utilities were flecked with what looked like scrambled eggs; I thought he'd pull his KA-BAR and skin the private alive. Instead, the old-timer just flicked the mess off with one finger. I guess he knew that far worse was awaiting us.

Entering the channel through the west side of the reef, we assumed an east–west line of bearing prior to our turn toward the beach. My engineer company was attached to Major "Jim" Crowe's Landing Team Three, assigned to occupy Red Beach Three. That was the easternmost beach on Betio's north shore, on the left flank of Landing Team Two in the middle.

Just inside the lagoon we passed the yellow buoy markers designating the line of departure. From there we made a ninety-degree starboard turn and began our run to shore.

Our run to Red Three began six thousand yards from shore. That's three nautical miles, and it took almost an hour. There was no opposition that we could tell, and not much to see. The island was hidden beneath a cloud of smoke and dust, which looked impressive to amphibians like me, who'd never been exposed to combat. "Looks damn good," chirped Dean. "Maybe the swabbos got it right."

Gunny Crouch just pulled his helmet low over his eyes, pretending to appear bored. "Don't bet on it," was all he said.

Our amtracks reached the reef at low tide, which caused some adverse comment from the platoon leader and senior NCOs. They saw more of the big picture than we privates and PFCs, knowing what it meant. The Higgins Boats in the fourth, fifth, and sixth waves wouldn't have the clearance they needed over the accumulated coral. There would be no choice but to off-load the troops for a long, long walk to the beach in waist- or chest-high water. As it was, our track crawled over the five-hundred-yard-wide reef without difficulty other than a lumpy ride, the 200-hp Continental engine groaning along.

I remember thinking as we lurched across the reef and churned toward shore that I'd made it. *Now I'm really a Marine,* I thought. I was making an amphibious landing on an opposed beach, where I assumed I'd fight and suffer—and survive.

Some guys will do anything for their self-image. Nations and military recruiters rely on it, but of course I didn't figure that out until years later.

Once across the reef, churning toward shore, things were surprisingly quiet. I remember seeing red-and-white pilings at frequent intervals in the lagoon, and wondering what they were. "Maybe they're building a seawall," somebody speculated. We were still dumb boots in some ways. They weren't pilings; they were range markers. The Japs had us boresighted, and we didn't even know it. The reason so many of the first wave LVTs got ashore was that the Japs expected us to land on the south coast, and it took them a while to shift troops to the other side. God knows, the northern approach was bad enough with some obstacles, a lot of barbed wire, and more bunkers than we could count.

At that point the riflemen were told, "Lock and

load!" They had already applied the safeties on their Garands, so they locked the breeches open, thumbed in a clip of eight .30-06 cartridges, and nudged the operating rod handles forward. They were set to go. Same with the BAR men. The rest of us—especially us flamethrowers—couldn't do anything until we disembarked. By then I was getting itchy to be away from the LVT, with its stomach-churning motion and gasoline fumes.

Landing Team Three was supposed to disembark along the two-hundred-yard stretch of Red Three, east of the long pier bordering Red Two. However, because of the obstacles, our seventeen tracks mostly rolled ashore on the western half of the beach, a couple of hundred yards from the northern taxiway of the airfield. We got some MG fire as our Water Buffalos crunched out of the surf, and you could hear the high-pitched *pings* and more solid *whacks* as 6.5 and 7.7mm rounds impacted the armor plate.

Our second wave was ashore on Red Three, and the next wave of LVTs mostly got through. We thought things were going tolerably well, but didn't know what had happened six hundred or seven hundred yards offshore. Out there, the erratic tide that the planners were so worried about did in fact turn against them. LCVPs were unable to cross the reef, so coxswains dropped the ramps and unloaded the troops right there. The Marines in the fourth, fifth, and sixth waves had no choice but to wade hundreds of yards through waist- or chest-deep water while Jap gunners looked through their sights, noted the range markers, and opened fire.

Whenever Tarawa is discussed, there's always mention of the tides. It's odd how something like that takes on a life of its own—an historical conventional wisdom. The CW on Tarawa is that the "dodging" tide caught us by surprise, leading to so many casualties. But that's not so. The planners, and even some at the company level, knew that the information was risky, based on incomplete data. They realized that there was perhaps a fifty-fifty chance that we'd find the reef exposed, preventing the Higgins Boats from getting across.

Many years later I read that high tide was calculated for 1115 hours at five feet over the reef. The next best period was expected more than two weeks later, on 5 December. No other usable tide was forecast until January, which was out of the question.

It turned out that H hour and D day occurred on one of two days in 1943 with the lowest tides at Tarawa Atoll. That was the result of the moon's effect on the low (neap) tides; I don't pretend to understand the astrophysics, meteorology, and hydrodynamics of the situation. It's enough to know that the planners took a guess, and they guessed wrong. The average water level on 20 November was barely three feet—two feet less than the LCVPs needed to clear the reef.

In turn, that meant a gruesome walk through water for nearly half a mile in some places, under direct and indirect fire every step of the way. I was personally spared that nightmare because my engineer team rode an LVT. Thank you, Mr. Roebling. You probably saved this Marine's hide.

The only thing I can say in compensation is: It could have been much worse. But that's not much help to a thousand dead Americans.

SEVEN

As a kid I saw Lew Ayres in *All Quiet on the Western Front.* I never read the German novel; didn't much care for fiction unless it had guns and horses. But the movie made an impression on me, as it was meant to. Like most viewers, I thought the most memorable scene was the muddy shell hole where Paul Baumer kills the French *poilu,* using a boot knife. Ayres, who became a conscientious objector in the Next War—my war—portrayed the extreme ambivalence of the frontline soldier caught up in the frenzy of killing for survival with the grief of taking life. Now, trapped in my filthy, choking, waterlogged bunker, I thought about Paul Baumer.

I didn't feel anything like him.

Instead of a muddy, intact French corpse, I shared my hole with two filthy, putrefying Japanese cadavers. From what I could see of them, neither was very much like the erstwhile typesetter that Baumer grieved over. It didn't even occur to me to wonder what they'd done in civilian life. I didn't care how old they were, if they had families, or anything else about them. They were dead Japs—the best kind. Except they stank something awful.

I wasn't sure what killed them, but apparently not the large-caliber shell that penetrated the bunker. For all I knew there might be more of their kind buried in the water and rubble. Naval gunfire was one of the big failures at Tarawa, along with air support. The battlewagons like *Maryland* were too close to shore, so most of their sixteen-inch shells arrived in a shallow trajectory. Some men had seen them skip off of bunkers and splash into the lagoon on the south side. A couple of destroyers came in close enough for almost direct fire support, though. If I ever meet one of those tin-can sailors, I'll buy him a drink.

There were two holes: a small one in the front wall and a larger one overhead. Judging by the partial hole in the concrete, it was a 37 from one of the M3 light tanks that got ashore. We badly needed more M4 Shermans with their 75s because the Stuarts' guns hardly made a dent. Additionally, because the water level on Betio is barely eight feet, the larger explosion (undoubtedly from naval gunfire) had churned up enough coral to flood most of the floor. I wondered if the water was rising. If so, unless I regained some mobility, I was in danger of drowning.

The bunker seemed to be a machine-gun position, with firing slits on three sides and a door at the rear. I guessed it was large enough for three or four men—Japs, anyway. Somebody said the average Japanese male was about five-foot-two or -three; little guys with buckteeth and thick glasses who bowed and smiled a lot. A treacherous bunch of bastards who cut off prisoners' heads for sport and staked pregnant women to the ground. But even after what we knew of Nanking and Pearl and Bataan, and the stories our own guys had from the Canal, I don't think that I really hated the Japanese. I just wanted to kill my share of them as fast as possible and get the damned war over with. At age twenty I didn't have a plan, other than survival. I'd worry about a job, much less a career, back in civvy street. No way was I staying in the Corps, waiting for the War after the Next War. What would that be? World War Three or Four?

Of course, that was before the GI Bill, college, and the offer of extended service in the Reserves. After all, a Marine can change his mind, right?

God, it was miserable in there. I'd have sold my soul for a decent drink. I remember wondering if I'd go crazy enough to drink the foul water I lay in, with rotting, stinking flesh and guts strewn about. My head was clearing somewhat at that point, and I groped around, seeking some kind of weapon. That's when I must have begun thinking I'd rather kill myself than sink far enough to ingest that filth. Maybe I laughed at that point—a thin, choking laugh of two or three syllables. The Japs were supposed to be the suicidal ones, the *Banzai* boys who sought death before dishonor. Marines didn't work that way. Did they?

How had I gotten here?

I couldn't understand how I became semiparalyzed in the murky, stinking bunker. The smaller hole was in the wall before me, somewhat toward the top where the tank gunner had boresighted a firing slit. Okay, but how did that explain things? The entrance behind me seemed to remain closed, so evidently I didn't come in that way. Besides, why would I?

I tried to concentrate. What was I doing when I came here? Just when was that? This morning? The day before? Obviously I'd been without my flamethrower; apparently I had no gear with me at all unless I'd lost . . .

The carbine.

Dean's carbine. I had it with me when—what? When what happened? My head throbbed, my throat strained, and my stomach churned once more. I gagged and choked and heaved again. Maybe I messed my pants. I couldn't tell.

I didn't care.

Thinking back from the perspective of nearly sixty years, I guess I can be perfectly honest. Or at least try to be. I wouldn't want my children or grandchildren to know it, but I wanted just one of two things, lying in that wretched situation. I wanted out, or I wanted to die. Ha! I was a twentieth-century Patrick Henry: *Give me liberty or give me death!* But I was no longer living, just existing in a putrid, miserable purgatory with no point to staying alive. If I'd had my pistol I would have shot myself to end the misery, and that's a fact. Death would have been preferable to one more hour in that damned reeking place.

The odd thing was, I finally found a weapon after groping around. At first I just felt the metal at the edge of my fingertips. By stretching farther—so far it hurt—I dragged it a little closer. It was heavy, a Japanese Type 92 7.7mm machine gun, based on an old French Hotchkiss design. It fed from stripper clips laid on a tray. The barrel was bent about thirty degrees, though, and I probably couldn't have used it for suicide anyway—too cumbersome. What I needed was a Nambu pistol or even one of the light MGs. Weird thing, you know? It struck me there and then how odd the Japs were. Their infantry weapons were nowhere as good as ours, except their LMGs. If anything, they were better because the Type 96s were lighter and more portable than our air-cooled Brownings. The Nambus also were better than our beloved BAR; the Jap guns had thirty-round magazines versus twenty, and a quick-change barrel to boot. But the Japs didn't really understand firearms. They issued three-foot bayonets, and their officers carried swords. What can you say about people who put bayonet mounts on their light machine guns?

After a few moments I stopped thinking about weapon design. I just wanted something to end my existence.

How bad was it? Okay, I'll tell you. If my wonderful mother could have been there to hold my hand and plead for me to hang on just a while longer, for the sake of her unborn grandchildren, I'd have asked her to get me a gun or a knife. That's how far gone I was—awash in fouled water, bloated corpses, and self-pity.

Don't ever let anyone tell you that Marines don't cry.

EIGHT

During the last 150 yards or so, the amtrack gunners opened fire on the beach. It was comforting to hear the two pedestal-mounted Browning .50s *chug-chug* along, spewing hot brass into the troop compartment.

Later—much later—I read that only 53 of the 125 amtracks in the first three waves reached shore. The hard thing was to ignore the casualties in the water. Our briefing was adamant on that point—don't stop to pick up the wounded. The longer our landing craft were in the lagoon, the more time the Jap gunners had to zero in on them. It was the ultimate brutality of war, but still some of us groused about the order. Marines are trained to look out for each other, to work together. In fact, that's what *gung ho* means in Chinese. But the logic was inescapable: You could lose thirty men trying to rescue one, and we needed every single man on the island.

Betio's beaches averaged thirty to fifty yards wide, rising only five or six feet above the tide mark. On shore, the seawall was only twenty feet from the water. However, once we were ashore things quickly became too crowded. Men were lying shoulder to shoulder—a ragged green carpet on the white beach. Units got intermingled, command structures broke down, confusion reigned. It was a squad leader's fight with platoon leaders deciding strategy, when the lieutenants survived. Our company and battalion commanders were generally high-quality officers, but they had little radio communication because our gear wasn't properly waterproofed. The commanders were reduced to sending runners back and forth. Those guys took horrible losses; I heard that a dozen or so were shot down near Colonel Shoup's CP on Red Two.

Red Three covered the north shore from east of the long pier to the end of the four-thousand-foot runway. Approximately in the middle was the short Burns-Philip wharf, which was only accessible at high tide. The coconut log seawall was not complete along Red Three's right (westerly) flank, which permitted a couple of our tracks to move inland. But as soon as my team disembarked, many of us were pinned down near the seawall. People scattered, looking for cover.

I popped up behind the coconut logs for a quick look at the nearest bunker. I gauged it at forty yards—probably beyond effective range. Ducking behind cover again, I wormed my way several yards to the left, grunting from the physical exertion. The rest of the squad followed. Maybe five or six men—half the outfit. The senior NCOs were nowhere in sight; the confusion was incredible.

"All right," I wheezed. The riflemen stopped; Dean, Hardy, and Jaworski crayfishing to join me. I inhaled, trying to fill my lungs with air rather than smoke, sand, and a growing stench—a combination of dead flesh, burning things, and fear.

I looked around, constrained by the M1A1 on my back. "We gotta get closer to the bunker. Can't cross open ground, though."

"We need smoke," Hardy said. "Anybody got smoke grenades?"

Nobody answered. Looking around, I realized with a sudden chill that I was in charge. But we couldn't do much on our own. We needed more shooters and demolition men. I looked into Jaworski's wide eyes. *He's even more scared than I am. Give him something to do.* I said, "Jerry, scout around. See if you can find an NCO and tell him we have a chance here."

With visible reluctance Private Jaworski crawled backward, his spatted feet in the tide. Making the motion of a nesting crab, he edged rearward until his dungaree pants were darkened with water, then turned about and raced on hands and knees back where he'd come. The boy dragged his rifle in the sand and sea—a mortal sin at Parris Island, a misdemeanor on Betio Island.

Time crept past, every tick of the second hand with a separate beginning, middle, and end. The narrow beach became more crowded as additional amtracks arrived. I led my bobtailed squad farther along the beach, making room for the new men and staying well away from the amphibious tractors, which inevitably drew heavy fire. The noise—at first almost overpowering—by then seemed normal.

It's hard to remember everything in that much confusion, especially after so long. I do know I pulled myself up close behind the coconut logs, closed my eyes, and tried to blot out the appalling sights and sounds around me. *Think,* I willed myself. *Think about something good. Something from home.* Nothing came to mind.

Several minutes after leaving, Jaworski was back with reinforcements. Sergeant Healey was with him, and I've never been so glad to see anybody. Healey was wounded, with a bandage on one arm and pockmarks on his face, but he was still in the fight.

"Also got these . . ." Jaworski gasped.

Hardy reached out, scooped up two smoke grenades. "Where'd you get 'em?" he asked.

Jaworski inhaled, a loud gasp in the cloying air. He started to speak, then shook his head. He rolled on his back, trying to breathe again.

I pulled the wrench kit from my pocket; the tools had gouged a hole in my thigh. I nodded backward to Dean, indicating that we should withdraw down the shallow incline. "Need more room," was all I could say. God, it was hard to breathe.

At the waterline I gave the tool kit to Dean, and he turned valves and twisted handles, trying to stay low. A grenade launcher round detonating thirty yards away tossed water onto us, but finally he tapped my helmet. We crawled back to Healey.

"Okay, here's what we do," Healey said. "Copping, take your BAR about ten–fifteen yards to the right. Rest of you guys, between here and there. Shoot at the gun slits, keep 'em down. Jaworski will throw the smoke." He looked at me. "Then Bertram will . . ." He paused, realizing what he was about to say. I swallowed hard. ". . . do it." He glanced around. "Somebody go with him to cover his approach."

"I better come with you, Bert." It was Hardy. I looked into his eyes. They were hazel. *Never noticed that before. Bunked with the sumbitch eight months; never knew it.* No words came; words were inadequate to describe what I felt.

"Let's do it."

The BAR man and the other shooters opened up. Chips and dust flew from the two bunkers facing us. With a lunge of my legs that required every bit of muscle and energy I possessed, I willed myself over that log seawall into the beaten zone of two or three machine guns. My boondockers didn't seem to touch the ground; my mouth was wide-open, sucking in all the humid oxygen I could ingest. I was aware of my heart. It never never felt so stressed. I was sweating buckets; salty drops fell from my helmet band and eyebrows. A Jap machine gun threw up spouts of sand and coral around us.

We made it. Hardy and I flopped down about fifteen paces from the gun slit of the closest bunker. He rolled over into an uncomfortable prone position, guarding my right side. He hollered something that sounded like "Clear!"

The guys behind the log wall were still shooting, but the volume was noticeably lower. It occurred to me that they'd all opened up at once, which meant the Garands began running empty within a few seconds of each other. *Gotta talk about that,* I thought. *Need more fire discipline.* Only the BAR was still firing regularly, that 550-rpm *chug-chug-chug* tapping out two- and three-round bursts. He was a good man, that BAR guy. He must've had the fastest reload in the battalion.

Suddenly the high, fast chatter of a Nambu 96 erupted almost close enough to touch. The Japs were back in action after ducking the original fusillade of covering fire. I could feel the muzzle blast, but the Jap gunner didn't know I was there. I was just outside his field of view.

Hardy was shooting now, bad sign. He called something more, probably *What th' hell you waitin' for?* I reared up on one knee, braced myself, and aimed the tube at the firing slit. I distinctly remember thinking, *Boy is he gonna be surprised.* Then I pressed the handle.

The low, rushing sound of ignited gas merged with the rest of the sounds on Red Three. The squad behind the logs; the Jap MGs; Hardy's Garand. I heard *blam, blam, blam-blam,* then the unmistakable *piing!* of his ejected clip.

I seared the Japs without ever seeing them, just the muzzle of one 6.5 Nambu. The gunfire stopped immediately inside the bunker as the gunners fled from the embrasure.

Almost immediately the demolition guys were beside me. One of them, a kid named Janek, pulled the handles on his satchel charge, counted one-potato, two-potato, and tossed it through the port. Then he rolled himself into a ball behind me.

I thought I'd better get out of the way.

With the package on my back I couldn't roll over, so I just flopped forward like a beached flounder. I pulled my helmet down over my ears, turned my face away from the bunker, and opened my mouth to relieve some of the pressure.

The satchel charge exploded on the sixth potato with a loud, piercing *ka-BOOM.* God, I love Composition C. Dust, wood, palm leaves, and other debris erupted into the air.

Before the dust began to settle, the rest of the squad was there. A couple of them fired full clips through the gunport just to be sure, but it was wasted ammo. The BAR man risked a look inside. "Can't see much," he panted. "Two, maybe three guns in there."

That was Step One. The procedure was: Repeat as necessary.

NINE

Getting across the beach wasn't as hard for us as it was for most others. But our initial success was misleading. We cleared Red Three fairly quickly with relatively few losses and headed inland. When we crossed an open space among the blasted-out palm trees, somebody hollered, "Hit the deck!"

Without thinking, I dropped prone, even with sixty pounds of flame gear strapped on. That's what training does for you. I didn't know why the warning was shouted until a carrier plane rolled in on us. I still remember the blunt wingtips—a Hellcat, I thought. But it was an Avenger, a carrier-based bomber. I still remember seeing the white belly and that cavernous bomb bay with the doors opened. The pilot nosed down, and I remember thinking it odd that we didn't hear his engine, but there was a lot of other noise. Small-arms fire was snapping and barking all around.

We only saw the plane for a few seconds because of the tall trees. It's odd how your mind works at times like that. I thought, *I've got about five gallons of jellied gasoline on my back, and that bastard up there is gonna start shooting at me.* For no good reason, I rolled onto my side and looked up. It was contrary to what we learned about air attack because a white face shows up against most earth backgrounds. But I felt I needed to put something between those airborne guns and my napalm, even if it was *me.*

Then I heard that big radial engine. The Grumman was probably over a thousand feet up when it pulled out, but the low, steady rumble of the engine came to me amid the gunfire on the ground.

The pilot dropped a couple of bombs—probably 250-pounders—and most of us cursed the flyboys, their mothers, and anyone else remotely associated with them. The Japs were bad enough—we damn sure didn't need our own planes trying to kill us. However, the bombs didn't seem to do any harm because the pilot dropped "long." Maybe he wasn't even aiming at us. Anyway, the explosions erupted in some trees about seventy yards away, but what cohesion our landing team had up to then was mostly lost. Guys scrambled every direction to get out from under.

About thirty of us got to the eastern taxiway of the airfield and started to settle in. But we couldn't stay long; we were exposed, out in the open with no secure flanks. At that point we didn't have the numbers to hold an extended perimeter.

That was when we began to respect the Japs' ability to infiltrate. We made an orderly withdrawal past MG nests and bunkers that we'd overrun just several minutes before, then were fired upon from those same places. We didn't see many Japs above ground—they were like gophers.

Another thing: I'd always heard that most Japs couldn't shoot straight. If so, they put every one of their marksmen on Betio. They were everywhere—in bunkers, trenches, trees—even in the wrecked ship off Red One. Those naval infantrymen could hit almost anything they could see, with everything from Arisaka rifles to three-inch coastal guns. They blew LVTs and LCVPs out of the water more than five hundred yards offshore. And they seemed to have all the ammo in Japan.

Shortly after reaching the taxiway I heard a squeaking, clanking sound. I think some of us assumed it was one of our tanks or even a bulldozer, but that was just skylarking—the kind of optimism you overhear at the slop chute. Several of us were facing in the direction of the noise when a Jap light tank rolled into our position. We were stunned—we didn't expect naval infantry to have tanks though evidently division intelligence had some evidence. Reportedly there were seven or more on Betio, but this was the only one that actually attacked. Others were found dug into revetments, hull down so only the turret showed.

Some riflemen scrambled on top of the Type 95, which seemed almost comical. It was small and awkward-looking. It had a light cannon—a 37mm—and a machine gun. But there were no supporting infantrymen. Everybody knows that armor needs infantry to operate effectively. Maybe these Japs hadn't read the manual.

Anyway, our guys were trying to toss grenades inside the tank. But the Japs were buttoned up, and the Marines were badly exposed. A BAR man and one or two others were shot off the damned little thing. We didn't have many antitank weapons on

Betio—just towed 37mm guns that arrived too late. Toward the end of the three days there were some self-propelled 75s, and they were useful against bunkers, but what we needed were bazookas. There weren't any; I don't think any of us had ever seen one.

A captain ordered us to prepare to pull back, and that was a disappointment. We had just started making progress when we were told to withdraw. It was just as well, though. We were ordered back to the beach and set up a perimeter maybe 150 yards deep. Some guys griped about being run off by one little tin can, but as I said, our flanks were exposed, and we'd have had to pull back even without the tank showing up.

Carrier planes had already bombed us on the advance southward. Then they strafed us on the withdrawal northward, maybe thinking we were Japs making a counterattack. This time the planes were Hellcats. We weren't very impressed.

Nevertheless, the bombing and strafing really upset us, in more ways than one. I don't think that anybody who's never been under air attack can appreciate how it feels. The emotion is one of complete vulnerability, like a field mouse under a hawk. Repeatedly in memoirs, soldiers speak of feeling naked, unprotected. When I read of the panzers trying to reach the Normandy beachhead, I understood what those Germans must have felt. Actually, their ordeal was far, far worse than ours. They were under direct attack by fighter-bombers for hours, even days. On Betio I experienced a couple of incidents, then it was over.

For a long time I seemed to be the only flame gunner around—at least the only live one. The Japs recognized the danger we represented to their fixed defenses, and they made us combat engineers priority targets.

Man, I was frustrated, confused, angry—all at once. There was a lot of shooting, most of it inbound, and I wasn't doing any of it with my flamethrower. Finally, though, Sergeant Healey pulled me along with him. I grabbed Dean by the stacking swivel and took him in tow.

We scrunched into an abandoned MG nest, by the look of it. Sandbags were piled about four high and several deep. There were a lot of 6.5mm brass and some scraps of Jap gear. Healey pointed between two bullet-riddled bags leaking sand. "There," he said. "Burn it out."

I risked a glimpse. At first I didn't see anything worth igniting—just the usual debris, mostly shattered tree trunks and fallen palm fronds. Then I saw a muzzle flash. The Japs were tremendous at camouflage. A low-lying coconut bunker on a slight elevation had a good view of our sector. It was mostly covered with sand and foliage; amid the smoke and dust it was even harder to see.

Ducking back under cover, I called to Dean and had him turn on my fuel and hydrogen tanks. He fumbled a bit, then tapped my helmet. Then I turned to Sergeant Healey. "We'll all open up on that bunker," he said in a loud voice. He leaned close to me so I could hear him over the gunfire and other racket. "When they stop shooting, rush 'em and give 'em the hotfoot."

I said something that must have sounded like "Okay" (I thought I said "Shit!") because without another word the noncom shouted to his bobtailed squad. They all opened fire with Garands and carbines. Wood splinters and sand spouts erupted around the firing slit, but it was impossible to tell if the Nambu light MG had stopped shooting. Nothing to do but trust to luck.

I lowered my head like a fullback charging the Crimson Tide line and bolted from cover. It was one hell of a long way—about thirty-five, forty yards. I slumped behind a shot-off palm tree, leaned around the side, and pressed the firing lever with my right hand while activating the igniter with my left. *Ka-whoom!* The thing lit off with a low, rumbling roar and rocked me back. In my excitement and fear I'd forgotten Gunny Crouch's first lesson—I hadn't braced myself. The nozzle lifted, spreading the thickened fuel higher than I intended, but there was a residual benefit because it sent the flame stream across the top of the bunker and onto the far side. I adjusted aim, braced myself, and fired again. This time the stream went into the horizontal firing port. I held the lever down for a good three or four seconds.

From the corner of my eye there was movement: The sergeant and his team dashed forward, assault firing as they ran. One of them slid to a stop at the edge of the bunker, pulled the pin on a grenade, let the spoon go, and did a quick two count. Then he tossed the pineapple inside and rolled away. The thing went off with a hollow *bang*.

Healey and a couple of others were on top of the bunker immediately, watching the far side. I ran up beside them, not really sure what I'd do. What happened then is something I will never, never forget.

The door flung open and a Jap ran out. He was on fire. His clothes were burning on his back. So was his hair. It was so unexpected that none of us moved for a couple of seconds. Then everybody shot at once. The Jap pitched forward, facedown in the sand. "Damn," said one Marine.

I couldn't think of anything to say.

TEN

Finally, I thought I knew.

It was on toward nightfall, which would be a relief to the leathernecks still in the fight. Along the equator, evening fell quickly, and often it brought a breeze. Not much of one, but anything—absolutely anything—was a relief on that bitch of an island. Inside my bunker, though, I couldn't feel it.

What did I know? I thought: *Have to remember.*

Oh, yeah. Dean got it, and I went for fuel. But when?

Late on D plus one, before we left cover, I wanted to be sure that my A-gunner was nearby. I'd need a refill before long. Just as I turned to Dean, an explosion blew sand, coral, and debris over both of us. He was between me and the blast; I thought it was a mortar round. As it turned out, the Japs didn't have mortars on Betio, but they had plenty of grenade launchers. At first I didn't think much of it because it was a fairly small explosion, but Dean reeled, slumped to his knees, and dropped on one side.

I reached him after a hard, short crawl. He was breathing noisily, bleeding from the nose and mouth. He said something that I couldn't understand—a low gurgle. He repeated it a couple of times. I was scared and angry. With the flame rig strapped on, I couldn't do much for him. Somebody called for a corpsman—that went on for three days—but there were none near us. One of the other Marines rolled him over and pulled up his dungaree top. Dean had taken several splinters in his right side, apparently reaching the lung. A couple of other men dragged him to cover and did what they could, which wasn't much. Sulfa powder, bandages, direct pressure. Combat first aid.

I had one or two others pick up his spare tank, his carbine, and some magazines. We left him with another wounded man; I only saw him once again. At a reunion in the 1960s I learned he'd never fully recovered and died about 1955.

Each time I regained consciousness I seemed to think of something else. That is, other than my predicament and the fundamental need for water. For the longest time I tried to figure how the Japs had survived a direct shell hit on their bunker. They should have been shredded by a Sherman's 75mm gun, let alone a five- or eight-inch naval shell.

Then it occurred to me, something the company commander said in our briefing. "The Japs are masters at infiltration," he had said. He knew—he'd been on Guadal. "They train for it like nobody else, and they're about as good in daylight as at night."

The two corpses in "my" bunker had probably been a light machine gun crew, skittering through the wreckage and debris that was Betio to reoccupy the bunker after it was first shelled. Probably on D plus one. Maybe they found some of their friends spread across the overhead and bulkheads, maybe not. It didn't matter. Their position was now in the Marine rear, permitting them to back-shoot any unwary Americans advancing through the "secure" area.

I had no way of knowing how many Marines they ambushed that way, but finally somebody had tumbled to their game. Judging by the condition of the corpses, maybe they were killed by grenades. Certainly they had not burned, though I sort of wished they had.

How do you get people to do that? I wondered. I damn sure wouldn't have done it, and I don't think I knew anybody who would. Not for my buddies, not for the Corps, not for America. Damn sure not for Roosevelt. For one thing, it was a death warrant, without a ghost of a fighting chance. Trapped in a position of their own choosing, behind the deepening American perimeter, they had to know they were going to die there. But they stuck to their post. I'm here to tell you: Those Japs were absolute bastards as human beings, but they were the kind of troops every commander dreams of. "Run over to that bush, take two steps left, and get shot." *Hai! Banzai!*

No wonder we had to nuke them twice.

ELEVEN

The Japs began killing themselves on the second day.

It was late that afternoon, I think, when the Word filtered down. That was the thing about the Corps: somebody always had the Word: the poop, the scuttlebutt, the hot dope. Usually it was wrong, of course, but it filled a lot of slack time. In this instance, it was correct.

Very few of us can choose how we die, but many of the Sasebo Seventh Special Naval Landing Force exercised their options. Some Japs who'd been surrounded and unable to sneak away had committed suicide. A company runner who passed through our lines had seen a couple of corpses: They blew themselves up with grenades. Others took off those peculiar two-toed shoes, put their rifle muzzles beneath their chins, and pressed (or, actually, pushed) the trigger with their big toes. Hey, whatever floats your boat.

The odd thing was, if individual Jap marines had

decided to die, why not die fighting? Why not take another one or two or six Americans with them? It made no sense, personally or militarily. At least, not to us. Evidently it made a lot of sense to those Japs, and every one of us was glad of it. The others who fought it out were plenty bad enough.

Anyway, by evening of D plus one we had finally crossed the island, with elements of two battalions of the Second Regiment pushing south from Red Two. At least that's how it looked on the neatly drawn maps produced for the operational analysts and the history books. On my part of the perimeter, still inland from the Burns-Philip wharf, we only heard occasional snatches of info, but it was good to know that Marines now owned part of the south shore, called Black Beach. A battalion of the Sixth Marines was ashore on Green Beach at the west end, holding for the reserve battalion to land the next day and advance toward us.

We had spent most of the day trying to expand our perimeter southward and a little eastward. The whole area was full of bunkers, MG pits, and spider holes. You couldn't take anything for granted, and the battalion gunfire spotter had his hands full. I heard him talking to the destroyers offshore, and felt better for it. Our communications were erratic at best, but the lieutenant was able to call for naval gunfire in target grid 235, inside the eastern taxiway. For some reason I still remember the way he spoke—he was a Southern boy, and he had absorbed the careful enunciation they taught at artillery school. "Fahr mishun on gree-ud tu-oo, tha-ree, fahve. Ovah."

The first round impacted near the runway and the spotter called a correction, adding, "Fahr fur e-fay-ect." After the five-inchers pounded the area, he called to check fire, and we jumped off, taking advantage of the brief shock following a bombardment. But the Japs were resilient. That night they counterattacked.

My situation began when we tackled another batch of bunkers and rifle pits. I was getting low on fuel and propellant, and knew I'd be out of business shortly because we had no more refills. However, I thought there was enough firing time left to make it worthwhile for another effort, so I offered my team to a platoon from another company. The platoon leader—a first sergeant—had doped out the overlapping fields of fire and pointed to a well-camouflaged position to our left front, east of the taxiway. It appeared to be composed of coconut logs covered with palm fronds and sand. I poked my head over the fallen tree trunk for a quick look. There was no apparent shooting.

"You sure it's occupied?" I asked.

The NCO was an old-timer of about twenty-six. "Shit no, I'm not sure of anything on this frigging island." He spat out the words with grains of sand from his lips. Obviously, he'd been kissing the ground with the rest of us that day, which might have explained his candor. Ordinarily Marine Corps noncoms were dead-nuts certain about *everything*. Even when they were wrong.

"Well, I'm about out of juice," I replied. "Wouldn't want to waste it on an empty position."

The platoon leader regarded me for a long two count. Without turning his head, he barked an order. Something like, "Jones, draw fire."

Though Marine Corps discipline is different from Army discipline and damn sure different than the

Navy variety, I didn't really expect Private Jones to jump up long enough for some Jap to boresight him. But damned if that's not what he did. He staggered to his feet, clamped his helmet down on his brain housing unit with his port hand, grasped his M1 with the starboard, and sprinted about twelve paces. Then he flopped down, his boondockers flailing above him as if he was still trying to run nose first.

Nobody shot at him. At least, not specifically.

I was about to comment to the sergeant upon my tactical sense when he bawled another order. "Able, Baker, Charles! Draw fire!"

It would've been comical in other circumstances. Two of the riflemen cautiously arose to comply with the order when the third, obviously more committed, piled into them from behind. All three went down in a tangle. They thrashed around, bawling and cursing, while the NCO slowly shook his head like a mother hen disgusted with her brood. Finally, he hollered, "Shake the lead out!" They did so, scampering in different directions, zigzagging all the while.

A machine gun opened up from the position about sixty yards away. We all ducked as wood chips flew from our protective tree trunk. The MG chattered away at Larry, Curly, and Moe, cycling at about six hundred rounds per minute. Mostly the gunner zigged when they zagged, but in those few seconds shooter and target zigged simultaneously. One of the decoys went down with a grazing wound to one leg.

I looked at the platoon leader again, probably wide-eyed in surprise, admiration, or astonishment. He spat out more sand. "Some Japs got more fire discipline than others. You gotta remember that one man can be a waste of ammo, or shooting at him might give away a position. Two can be marginal. But at this distance, three's a worthwhile target."

We were out of satchel charges, so this bunker was going to be taken on the cheap. As before, the riflemen opened up a hot masking fire while I worked my way into position, hoping all the time that there wasn't some sniper tracking me from above. A lot of trees still had foliage that could conceal a Jap.

This NCO knew his business. He staggered the firing rate of his Marines so at least two or three were shooting all the time while others reloaded. Again, Hardy and I wormed our way close to the side of the bunker, which had a firing slit on that end. Amid the noise I glimpsed empty brass piling up inside. No time to lose. I went into a crouch, aimed the flame gun, and opened up. The heat and flames roiled inside the bunker.

I depressed the initiator trigger again—nothing. "I'm empty!" I dropped the wand and began shrugging out of the bulky harness. A strap caught on my web belt; I felt impotent. "Help me dammit!" Hardy slung his M1 and stepped behind me, lifting some of the weight off my shoulders. In seconds I was free, and Hardy set down the weapon with an audible *thunk.*

Meanwhile, another Marine dashed several feet to my left, covering the rear exit to the position, but nobody emerged. I realized that our covering fire had stopped, and sort of recall hearing high-pitched noises from somewhere. I didn't need to hear it, though. The smell was confirmation enough.

TWELVE

Damm it, something's wrong.

The thought just wouldn't go away. Without quite knowing why, I felt that my recent memories were all wrapped around each other, getting in one another's way.

Maybe I was hallucinating—I just don't know. But for some weird reason I couldn't remember when I'd left Dean or when I'd finally run out of fuel and hunkered down in our perimeter on D plus one.

I knew that we began consolidating our lines early that afternoon, but there wasn't much for me to do. I hauled my empty flamethrower to a convenient spot behind the main line of resistance, used the last of the water in my second canteen, and wondered about something to eat. With Dean gone, I'd lost my beast of burden and didn't feel like begging chow from the others.

Even if I'd had a refill, the M1A1 wasn't much use in a defensive situation, so I became a fifth wheel. Finally, I settled in with a light machine gun crew;

three Marines setting up their air-cooled Browning. With nothing else to do, I offered to haul ammo or fill sandbags—anything to keep busy. I watched the gunner run a field headspace check, the quick and dirty way without resorting to a guage. He opened the breech, pulled back the charging handle a minuscule amount, and saw the bolt move incrementally. "Good to go," he said. If it moved too much or too little, he could get a malfunction at a most inopportune moment. The A-gunner fed him a cloth belt with 248 rounds while the third man set a spare ammo box and some grenades within reach.

We had been damned lucky that the Japs didn't attack during the first night. If they had, I seriously doubt we could have held the shallow perimeter on Red Two and Three. Much later it was learned that the generally disappointing naval gunfire had done some good: It destroyed a lot of the phone lines buried in Betio's shallow soil; and it probably killed Admiral Shibasaki with most of his staff. He knew his business—the defenses proved that beyond any doubt—and if he'd been alive to coordinate the counterattack, we'd have been in severe trouble.

Analysts later said that Tarawa was the only landing the Japs had a chance of defeating. After all, we only outnumbered them less than two to one, and every military textbook says the attacker needs three to one. If anything, an amphibious operation needs better odds than that.

I still get the galloping willies thinking what it would've been like, trying to get *off* that frigging island. Getting ashore was damn near impossible as it was.

So when *did* I run out of fuel?

I definitely went dry that afternoon, taking down

the bunker with the first sergeant, but no way could one load have lasted me two days. And what about Dean's carbine? I didn't have it with me when I joined the Browning crew—just my pistol. Yet I was carrying it when I fell through the top of this miserable stinking bunker. Whenever *that* was. But was it before or after Dean was hit? It had to be after—just had to be.

It was much easier to close my eyes and visualize Bonnie McKenzie than to continue dwelling on my recent miserable history. But somehow it was important that I get things straight. After a while it dawned on me: I'd assumed that I made one trip back to the beach to reload, but there were two. I must have cadged a refill from one of the supply LVTs on one trek and maybe picked up a partial load from a casualty. Certainly there were lots of unused M1A1s on Betio Island. Losses among flame gunners were running about two out of every three.

It stood to reason, you know. If *you* were assigned to a last-stand bunker with a bunch of homicidal Marines headed toward you, which one would you shoot first? The one with the most terrifying weapon—right? Right. That was me: the Terror of Tarawa.

Where was I?

Oh. Yeah. How'd I get Dean's carbine again? He'd given it to me after he was wounded. Then I made those trips to the beach, but the first time I didn't have his piece because I think I refilled the bottles on my own pack. Next time I did have the carbine, apparently because I was looking for refills of fuel and propellant. After all, why lug the whole kit when a jerrican and a gas bottle will do? Okay, that makes sense. I could carry Dean's weapon and the refills at the same time.

But what did I do with the carbine in between? Give it to somebody else? Hardly makes sense—who'd want to carry two weapons?

Why in hell did it matter so much?

I remember wishing I had a pencil and some paper. Maybe I thought I'd write a Last Will and Testament or something—maybe just a note to my mom and sisters so they'd know I was thinking of them when I . . .

Belay that, boot! Sergeant Connelly was inside my head again, leaning close, bawling that rapid-fire stream of abuse that only Marine DIs seem able to deliver. *You don't frigging breathe unless I give you permission, yardbird! You people—it was always "you people"—live and die on my command! And I have not given you permission to die! Do you heeeear me?*

"SIR, YES SIR!"

Fifteen months later I still heard him.

I also heard other things, the oddest things. Like Sunday school. So help me, I started thinking of Sunday school. No damn reason whatsoever. Mainly I recalled the songs we practiced, and considering my appalling situation, the thought was either comforting or ironic. I remembered one in particular:

If you're happy and you know it, clap your hands (clap-clap).
If you're happy and you know it, clap your hands (clap-clap).
If your're happy and you know it, and you really want to show it, if you're happy and you know it, clap your hands (clap-clap).

I have no idea how long I thought, whispered, or gurgled those lyrics. Maybe for hours. But I was too weak and too damaged to clap my hands.

Another one was more appropriate:

Jesus loves me, this I know
for the Bible tells me so.
Little ones to him belong;
they are weak but He is strong.
Yes, Jesus loves me.
Yes, Jesus loves me.
Yes, Jesus loves me.
The Bible tells me so.

God's honest truth: I didn't know if Jesus loved me anymore, but I damn sure *hoped* that He did. The way it turned out, I guess that He really did, after all.

There was a story—it may be true—that the Marines found some Catholic nuns on an island where they'd hidden from the Japs for a couple of years. The sisters were French, and didn't speak much English. But within a matter of hours they'd learned basic American Marine English: "Can-dy ees dan-dy but liquor ees queek-er."

I hope it's true.

THIRTEEN

By evening of D plus one we had a damn good idea of what we were up against. Our combat veterans noticed a difference between the Tarawa Japs and the Guadalcanal variety. On the Canal we fought the Imperial Army almost exclusively, and it was a tough opponent. Its soldiers were extremely aggressive in an attack and tenacious in defense—very few surrendered. But according to some of our officers and senior NCOs, the Jap army was often sloppy and frequently overconfident. One of the elite units sent to Guadalcanal had cut its teeth in China, where it gained a fearsome reputation. But fighting half-trained, poorly led Chinese factions in no way prepared Colonel Ichiki's men for the U.S. Marine Corps. Basically, the battalion was destroyed in one night of combat; the survivors slowly starved to death.

However, the Japanese naval infantry was another breed of cat. That's what we encountered at Tarawa. Judging by their equipment and the handful of prisoners, they were neat, orderly, and efficient. In our terms, they were squared away.

Of course, it's probably not fair to compare a six-month meat grinder like Guadalcanal with a three-day fight like Betio. But unquestionably the land-fighting sailors were more flexible in combat. They had nearly identical weapons to the army—just less variety—but used them more skillfully. Their combat philosophy was more sophisticated than the army's, as proven by the layered defenses we found on Betio. Just because we took out one bunker or position didn't mean the next one folded up. Not a bit: The Sasebo Landing Force knew the value of infiltration and fluid defense.

We knew what was coming, and began making preparations. After a while I was detached from my impromptu machine-gun crew. Somebody figured that with the losses among flamethrower operators, I was semispecial and should be held in reserve for the next day. Consequently, I was pulled back to the second line, so I hefted the carbine with a fifteen-round magazine inserted and a couple of spares nearby. Later, there were thirty-round "banana clips," but I never heard of those until Korea. Anyway, we knew the Japs wouldn't attack until after dark, so I placed the mags within easy reach, where I could find them by feel. I even closed my eyes and practiced grabbing them a couple of times.

Foolish boy.

One thing I did sort of wonder about was whether Dean and I shot the same zero. The Corps was big on basic marksmanship, of course, and we learned in boot camp that when a rifle is sighted for one man, the next guy to pick it up may shoot high or low, left or right. Eyes are just different, and that didn't begin to account for variations in technique such as shoulder mount or cheek weld. As it turned out, such things didn't matter on Betio. The shooting that night was usually within pistol distance.

The one thing I did right was having that big Colt fully loaded: a seven-round magazine and one in the chamber. Against all regulations my .45 was cocked and locked in the holster. I had two extra mags for that, too, in my belt pouch.

They hit us at 2300, an hour before midnight.

I had heard that some *banzai* attacks were little more than drunken mobs of crazed Japs stewed on sake or even dope. They'd come howling out of the dark, tossing grenades and waving bayoneted rifles and bamboo spears. They'd scream "Maline you die!" (just like the movies) or curse Roosevelt (hell, some of us did that) and throw themselves on our lines, where the gunnery sergeants had laid overlapping fields of fire. Let me tell you: Whoever brings a spear to a machine gun fight is going to lose. Big-time.

But the *rikusentai* were a cut or two above that. They began with infiltrators sneaking up to our lines, and even through the lines in some places. There were scattered fights beginning that evening, with combat on both sides and even behind us, which made me *very* nervous. What was really spooky, but we didn't realize it just then, was that some of the fighting was with knives and bayonets. Good fire discipline in those platoons—shooting gave away our positions, which is what the Japs wanted. Eventually the infiltrators—somebody said a few dozen—were killed or driven off. The Japs were actually scouts, sent to probe our lines and find the seams of our unit boundaries. The survivors scurried back to their leaders with the information.

They didn't waste much time.

Shortly after the initial wave, the Japs sent out a larger group, trying to overrun some of our advanced positions. It was dark by then—dark as only the tropics can be, with that sudden loss of daylight—and visibility suffered. However, by that time we had artillery on Betio as well as Bairiki islet two miles east. The Tenth Marines had assembled enough 105mm pack howitzers to be really useful, and combined with naval gunfire, the first attack was blown to rags and tatters. Our artillery spotters were really good—they called fire within fifty yards of our MLR, and the Japs got little to show for their losses.

Around 2400 another attack developed, and this one more or less conformed to the movie script. Lots of yelling and indiscriminate shooting, but it didn't cause us any harm that I could determine. Other than to keep us wide-eyed alert.

While all the foregoing was under way, Hardy and I huddled with our new partners and realized nobody was likely to get any sleep that night. The usual drill was one man awake in each hole, but even without the shelling I don't think any of us would have slept. We were living on adrenaline, round the clock.

But a long, tense lull set in after that attack. Maybe four hours ticked away, and some of us actually did dope off for a while. I'm not sure if I did or not, but I sort of remember a twitch or nudge when the real deal exploded.

Somewhere around 0300 things really popped. A battalion or more of Jap marines launched themselves at our line, and these boys were dead-nuts serious. They began with machine-gun fire from concealed and exposed positions, obviously hoping to pin us down. Then the attack was fully developed: howling, shooting, throwing grenades, and hollering the full Hollywood script: "Japanese drink 'melican blood!" It would've been like kid stuff if it weren't so damned determined.

Nothing stopped those Japs—not even mortars or artillery. They were piled up by the score along the line but just kept coming. They simply did not care if they lived or died as long as they took some Marines with them. My hole was about fifty yards behind the MLR, and it was apparent pretty damn soon that they were coming straight for us.

I'm not going to say the scene was hellish—that's too trite. It was too complex, too violent, too beautiful for any one word. Star shells, orange-white explosions, red tracers, frenzied movements, screams, curses, and unrelenting gunfire.

A group of Japs surged past the MLR and came straight at us. Hardy emptied two clips from his Garand so fast that somebody said it didn't sound like he reloaded. Half-kneeling, I shouldered the carbine and opened fire. They were surprisingly difficult targets—bandy-legged little men racing through the dark, dodging and weaving. I probably shot five or six rounds without hitting anything before I told myself, *Front sight.* One Jap in particular seemed determined to skewer me with his bayonet. I put the front bead on his second button and triggered several more rounds. He just kept coming. I could not believe it; I *knew* I was hitting him, but he hardly slowed. He was within eight or ten feet of my hole when he sagged to his knees. I shot him in the face, and he pitched forward.

Another Jap emerged behind him. I shot him a

couple of times, then nothing. The bolt locked back on an empty mag. *Reload,* I screamed to myself. I groped in the dark for my carefully positioned magazines—and could not find them. Later I found one in the bottom of my hole. Apparently a Jap had kicked it in there while dying.

I was probably well into psychic trauma by then. My main weapon had failed to kill a determined enemy, and now I was empty. I reversed Dean's carbine, thinking to use it as a club, when I remembered the pistol. I dropped the damn carbine, pulled my Colt, and took solace in its weight.

I was aware of the physiological traits of distress: my elevated pulse, the pounding in my chest, the sudden leaden weight of my arms. My mouth was wide-open, sucking in the humid tropic air, eyes wide, but ears probably useless from all the shooting and shelling.

More Japs surged around us. Three came at us again, one shooting his bolt-action Arisaka from the hip—a waste of ammo. I pointed the Colt more than aimed it, one-handed as we were taught back then, and pulled the trigger. The .45 bucked in recoil, but I couldn't tell if I hit the Jap or not. He kept coming. I pulled the trigger again, this time aware that I had flinched badly—low and left like all right-handers. The Jap staggered, struck in the right leg. That big 230-grain bullet, propelled at eight hundred feet per second, took him down. I shot him again through the top of the head. Distance maybe eight feet. I shot at a couple more Japs. They went down. Maybe Hardy killed them.

Suddenly it was quiet. I was aware of something wet on my arm—blood. Not a lot but enough to notice. I didn't know what happened until I saw the greenish uniform of the dead Jap with his bayonet in our hole, partly on top of Hardy.

My trembling left hand fumbled its way to my mag pouch, found a reload, and seated it in the pistol. I looked at Hardy. He looked at me.

He was dead.

About daylight I went toward the beach, looking for a refill of fuel and more propellant. We'd be moving again, but without an A-gunner, and no refills, I was just another rifleman unless I got more napalm and hydrogen; maybe nitrogen, too, for the igniter. That was it! I remembered! I got permission from the squad leader—he was from another platoon—to go back to the grounded amtracks. They were meant as supply vehicles, anyway. One of our engineer "tracks" should have refills. *That's* what I was doing.

I picked my way back to Red Three, thinking I'd find somebody who could get me a refill. It wasn't far—maybe 150 yards—but tough going. The ground was incredibly tangled with palm fronds, tree trunks, shell holes, and debris. It was hard to make ten normal steps in a straight line.

Less than halfway along my route I detoured to the left to avoid a clump of splintered trees. The ground seemed to rise a couple of feet, but I went that way, seeking the easiest path. Abruptly I noticed a hollowed-out depression, obviously man-made, just to my left. It was an entrance of some sort. *Spider hole,* I thought, a position for a sniper or light Nambu. I flicked off the safety and turned almost 180 degrees, backing away from the possible threat.

Then I was falling.

I don't remember hitting bottom. Evidently I lost my helmet in the fall because I took a nasty thump on the back of my head. Poor discipline, leaving my chin straps unbuckled. I recalled feeling the footing giving way beneath me, a low crackling sound of something collapsing, and then falling backward. I tried to keep a grip on Dean's carbine.

When I came around, I was wet and smelly and mostly in darkness. *Carbine,* I thought. I felt with both hands but found nothing solid within reach. Just lots of water and spongy, filthy stuff. My head ached; I thought maybe my scalp was bleeding.

I remembered looking up. Jagged coconut logs and palm fronds silhouetted themselves against the brightening tropic sky.

The sky—I could see that and not much else.

Then I reasoned it out: I'd backed into the blasted opening of a dugout or bunker. Palm leaves from the ruined trees had fallen on top of the shell hole, looking like the rest of the vegetation I'd walked upon. *Wham.* I fell straight through, landing on my back and left shoulder, hitting my skull on something. My back and shoulder hurt in a persistent, throbbing sensation. I could move my extremities but didn't want to—normal motion caused too much pain. The one time I tried to sit up, a burning, stabbing sensation pierced my back. I passed out again.

FOURTEEN

They found me on D plus three, a couple of hours past daylight. Later the medic said I kept mumbling something nonsensical—"Clap your hands; clap your hands."

It was odd, you know? November was midsummer on Tarawa, and the equatorial heat built rapidly. I thought about that for a little while. Back home on 20 November there was probably snow on the ground. But that was clear across half the Pacific Ocean and most of the North American continent. There I guess it was only the nineteenth. Or was it the twenty-first? I never could keep things straight with the International Date Line. Hell, I don't know why I bothered—it didn't matter in my predicament. One day was just as awful as the next.

I don't remember a lot about the Marines discovering me; mainly American voices, distinct accents. There was somebody with a drawl, evidently the one in charge, and the inevitable New Yorker, all flippant and cynical. Odd thing about New Yorkers—

they have a deserved reputation for rudeness, but many of them naturally address a stranger as "buddy." It turned out to be the Navy corpsman. That explained it.

I couldn't see well by then; evidently some fuel in the bunker had got in my eyes. Additionally, my pupils reacted to the harsh sunlight after about fifteen hours in relative darkness.

Somebody coughed repeatedly, and it dawned on me that he was reacting to *me.* Actually, "coughed" is too polite a term. The Marine choked and gagged. Only then did I realize that I could no longer smell anything. My nose had shut down, almost permanently. The last thing I smelled in this life for about eleven years was the horrid stench of those rotting Jap corpses in that tight, confined space.

A couple of men lifted me out of the shattered bunker, and the corpsman went to work. He swabbed my eyes with something that burned, but after a while I could see form and color. I croaked something unrecognizable to me or to my saviors, but they knew intuitively. Someone poured water on a handkerchief and pressed it to my lips. They were caked with sand and filth, but I sucked every drop from the cloth and begged for more. "Don't give him too much yet," the corpsman said. "It might kill him."

Somebody came up beside me with a carbine. He said "I got your weapon, Mac. It looks okay."

I turned to look at the carbine, curious as to where it had been. Without quite knowing why, I raised a hand, and the Marine pushed it toward me, holding the foregrip. I ran my fingers along the stock and felt something odd. Peering closely, I saw two notches carved in the wood. They were pretty fresh.

It wasn't Dean's carbine. He hadn't shot anybody.

I fingered the kill marks a little more, and the Marine said, "I see you got a couple there."

So *that* was it! I was getting my memory back. When I left the MG crew to get more fuel, one of the ammo bearers had loaned me *his* carbine. I'd shucked my 782 gear including the web belt with the trusty Colt, figuring that I'd travel light and maybe carry more of a useful load. What became of Dean's weapon I couldn't recall.

The odd thing was why I took a carbine at all, since I'd been disappointed in its stopping power. I don't know—maybe I was getting rock happy by then. The failure of the carbine to stop a Jap with five or six center-of-mass hits at twenty feet or so really unnerved me. Later it was determined that the cartridge, though .30 caliber, was too anemic to knock down a determined adversary unless he was struck in the brain or spine. But the reliable old warhorse, the M1911 pistol, seemed to do the job. Believe me, I'm a huge fan of the late John Moses Browning. I guess I just didn't want to pack the web belt with the heavy pistol, ammo, canteens, knife, and whatnot. By that night I was tired, scared, and dopey—a bad combination when your life is at stake.

They placed me on a litter, and four men I never saw before or after took me to the aid station. Along the way I heard gagging, retching sounds that could only be the thick, liquid emptying of someone's stomach. Fervent curses, earnest blasphemy, followed. Then silence. They were reacting to *me.*

At the aid station a doctor, a navy lieutenant,

looked me over more thoroughly. He ordered someone to remove my dungarees; the orderly had to use scissors. I'd long since passed the point that I was aware of myself. The Japanese blood had clotted and stiffened my camouflage jacket and half the trousers. Some of it stuck to my skin. I didn't care.

Long story short, when I fell through the hole in that bunker I landed on something hard, resulting in a compression fracture of my spine. That's why I was partially paralyzed for all those miserable hours. The guys in sick bay said I was semidelirious the first couple of days, lapsing in and out of sleep or consciousness. I was disoriented, too: couldn't put things in order. I wondered if I'd spent one night or two in that stinking bunker, but it had to be one, the night of D plus two.

However, after several days I regained full sensation and partial mobility (though not all my short-term memory) so I wasn't sent Stateside. I recuperated in a couple of different hospitals, including one in Hawaii, which was tolerable. *Her* name was Helen, and she became my wife of fifty-one years.

Talk about silver linings . . .

FIFTEEN

I've had nearly sixty years to think about war and combat. People often confuse the two, but in modern war the "tooth to tail" ratio constantly gets less. Even in World War II, presumably the greatest of all time, for every trigger puller there were eight, ten, twenty other uniformed men and women stretching all the way back to the States. Clerks, bakers, instructors, doctors, truck drivers, mechanics; you name it. For the large majority, WWII was exasperating, inconvenient, and boring.

For others, of course, it was ugly, violent, and short.

There's only one way into this life, but there are so many ways to leave it. Wartime, of course, accelerates the process and adds an enormous variety of exits. You can be shot, bombed, shelled, stabbed, torpedoed, burned, or suffocated. You could as easily be killed by accident as by intention. I knew guys who drowned in training and in combat; I saw a man crippled by a crate that fell on him in New

Zealand. We camped near a heavy weapons company that lost a lieutenant a few days before embarking. He was checking a water-cooled Browning that had some sort of problem while the other gun in the section was being cleaned. Somehow, a round had been left in the chamber of the number two gun and it fired when a cleaning rod was pushed through the muzzle. The rod went clean through the lieutenant, and he bled to death before the ambulance arrived.

The thing that struck me was how capricious it all was. My pal Ben Youngblood was in the LVT next to me; it took a shell hit and started burning. The mortarman standing next to Ben was torn apart by the explosion, leaving brains and blood on Ben's fatigues. Ben sustained some hearing loss—that was all.

Dedicated riflemen felt that their skill with an M1 was the best life insurance possible, and for some it was. Others, who regularly shot Expert and treated their Garands like babies, never made it to the beach.

Rear Admiral Keiji Shibasaki knew that his island would be attacked, and reportedly he boasted that a million men could not take Betio in a hundred years. But 18,309 Marines and sailors did it in seventy-six hours. Every square meter of the place was preregistered by carefully sited artillery, grenade launchers, and automatic weapons. The same applied to the reef and the lagoon, with its viciously unpredictable tides.

In all, 1,009 Americans were killed on Betio plus 2,101 wounded. The Japanese fought almost literally to the last man: Seventeen naval infantry survived with 129 Korean laborers. The stench was appalling: about 5,000 rotting corpses over 291 acres.

Try to imagine how that smelled.

I've been asked many times if I was scared on Betio. The truth is, there was little time for fear. The worst periods were those two nights, waiting for the *banzai* charge that finally came early on D plus two. But while moving and shooting, making plans with squad leaders, most of us could function. That was due to our training and our leadership.

So was I scared? Well, I'll say this: For three days I was pretty damn *concerned.*

Sometimes people learn that I was a World War II Marine—a Tarawa Marine—and they ask how I feel about the Japanese. So I tell them.

They were Japs to me; they'll frigging *always* be Japs. But that was then; this is now. Far as I'm concerned, we didn't bomb them enough or hang nearly enough of them for their war crimes. MacArthur just plain let the emperor off the hook because of the postwar "big picture." Years ago I read that some bastard who had eaten the liver of an American POW was released from prison and elected to the Jap parliament. Well, that's way above my pay grade, but a Marine Reserve noncom has a right to his opinion, and you've just heard mine.

The *rikusentai*, the Jap marines, were doing pretty much what we were doing—serving our country. The fact that their side started the whole damned mess tended to get lost in the gut-level confrontations with rifles, satchel charges, and flamethrowers. Don't get me wrong: I don't admire the little bastards, but I still respect them as soldiers. They were incredibly tough, disciplined, and—contrary to what we expected—they could shoot.

I've met several Japanese people over the years, and in fact my Rotary Club has a sister organization in Yokosuka. We exchange visits once in a while. I've never been to Japan—don't ever plan to go there—but it's just not in me to hate anymore. I'm not sure that I ever did hate anybody, even on Tarawa.

Well, that's not strictly true. I hated Lyndon Baines Johnson and Robert Strange McNamara for the way they squandered my oldest boy's life in Vietnam, and *that's* a sentiment that will never die. The fact that Brian died in a stupid forklift accident at a place called Bien Hoa doesn't matter—the effect was the same as if a Viet Cong had shot him. He and fifty-eight thousand other Americans died for nothing. As the grunts said: He was "wasted."

But hate the Japs? No, not really. Not anymore. Hell, some of my VFW buddies won't even drive a Honda or a Subaru, but my daughter's Nissan was built in Tennessee. How can you hate anybody from Smyrna, Tennessee?

If I have any lasting regrets about the war, I suppose it's the fact that so little is known or remembered about the Pacific Theater. Kids today, if they know anything, talk about Pearl Harbor or Hiroshima—nothing in between. Tarawa was just about smack-dab in the middle, chronologically and geographically.

At some point I'm sure most of us on that miserable little island wondered if it was worth the death and suffering. After the war General "Howlin'

Mad" Smith, the V Corps commander, said flat out that Tarawa wasn't worth it. He said we should have bypassed it like we did so many other places. However, Major General Julian Smith, who led the Second Division, and most others, like Admiral Spruance, insisted it was worth the price, in lessons learned if nothing else. I guess that's true: Someplace had to be the first atoll, and Tarawa was small enough that we could make our mistakes there rather than in a much bigger operation, like Kwajalein or Saipan.

The strategists said we had to have the Gilberts in order to take the Marshalls. Again, maybe that's true—I just don't know. But one thing is certain. Nearing the end of my life, I've had plenty of time to think about what matters most: family, friends, and self-respect. We inherit our families and choose our friends, but we have to earn respect, including the way we see ourselves.

I'm eighty now, in declining health, but still able to enjoy life. I root for the Packers and sip some bourbon and spoil my grandchildren, which somebody said is the best revenge, even when they're college students. I still love my late wife; I cherish my family, and I value my friends, though I don't hear from many of my WWII buddies anymore—we're pretty thin on the ground these days.

But once in a while, I find myself thinking back to November of '43. It doesn't take much: a whiff of gasoline at the service station; a really hot, muggy day; a green uniform; even a bus driver's trousers. In those moments I relive horrific events on a miserable little island in a world that—amazingly—in some ways was better than now. Maybe there's even a little spring left in my step when I recall with a fierce, quiet pride: I was a seagoing Marine. More than that, I was a flame gunner at Tarawa.

Semper Fi, Mac.